Sinocide

Published by Dudley Court Press, LLC
P.O. Box 102
Sonoita, AZ 85637 USA
www.DudleyCourtPress.com

Also published by Dudley Court Press as a multi-format E-book through www.Smash-words.com; Kindle Edition at Amazon.com and as an iBook from Apple.com

Paperback ISBN: 978-0-9819291-6-3
Ebook ISBN: 978-0-9819291-7-0

Frederick Fisher

SINOCIDE

A FICTIONAL ACCOUNT OF THE BREAK-UP OF CHINA

Dudley Court Press
Sonoita, Arizona

To Eileen, my lifelong adventurous, spirited companion.

CAST OF CHARACTERS

GEOFFREY X. MARTINE	Lt. Commander (later promoted to Commander), U.S. Navy, Attaché to the Embassy of the United States, Beijing, China.
FAN RIQI	(Fahn Ree-chee) Vice Commissar of the Ministry of State Security.
OLIVER ABERNATHY	Personnel Officer of the Hong Kong Bank, and operative in the Royal Naval Intelligence, Hong Kong Branch.
HU BANYI	(Who Bahn-yee) Technical aide to Fan Riqi, Ministry of State Security
WU XIAN	(Woo She-ahn) Vice Premier, softliner, Minister of State Planning Commission.
YANG YUCIE	(Yahng You-chee) Vice Premier, Softliner.
MING QUAN QUAN	(Ming Shwan Shwan) Operative with R.N.I., One Legged Ming's daughter.
SOONG AIMEI	(Soo-ng I May) R.O.C. Ambassador, Taiwan.
LI QUOHUA	(Lee Kwo-who-wah), Elder States-man, R.O.C., Taiwan.
JAMES SHAN LEIGHT	Gem Dealer, Hong Kong.
ARTHUR FOWLER	U.S. Ambassador to China 1989-1990.
LENA LAO DUKE	U.S. Ambassador to China 1992.
PATRICK DUFFY	U.S. Embassy staff, Beijing.
EMILY FORBES	U.S. Embassy staff, Beijing.
TSAI AND XIU	(Tsigh and She-oo) Defectors.

TANG NAIWA	(Tah-ng Ny-wah) General of the 27th Army P.L.A., Commissar of the Central Military Commission.
LIU CHINAN	(Lee-oo Chee-nahn) General Secretary of the Chinese Communist Party.
CAI JIXI	(Tz-eye Gee-she) Minister of the Central Committee for Disciplinary Inspection.
CHOU SHI	(Joe She) Commissar of the Ministry of State Security.
FENG QIZI	(Fung Chee-zee), General of the Air Force, Republic of China.
MAO TZETUNG	(Mah-ow Tzee-dung), Great Helmsman.
DENG XIAOPING	Dung Chow-ping) New Helmsman.
WU MEILIE	(Woo May-lee) Daughter of Wu Xian.
CHEN LISHU	(Chun Lee-shoe) Student Leader of Chinese Academy of Social Sciences, (C.A.S.S.)
SUN QILI	(Soon Chee-lee) Student Leader of Beijing University, B.E.I.D.A.
LIANG PO	(Lee-ahng Poe) Communications labor leader.
WANG	(Wahng) Luxingshe Guide, Chengde.
WANG CHA CHA	(Wahng Cha Cha) Luxingshe Guide, Beidaihe.
FISHERMAN	Wang Cha Cha's Father.
FISHERMAN	Wang Cha Cha's Uncle.

Part One

ONE
BEIJING

3 JUNE 1989

Geoffrey Martine closed the door of the embassy and walked through the wrought iron pedestrian gate on his way out of the compound. He stopped momentarily outside the gate under the Great Seal of the United States; a marine guard greeted the tall, lanky cultural attaché. "Good morning, Commander Martine. Orders are to advise everyone to stay clear of the whole area from the Beijing Hotel down to Xidan Avenue including Tiananmen Square and the Forbidden City."

"I'll try to keep it in mind Jimmy," Martine said as he donned a bright-red bill cap and adjusted a cloth shoulder bag over his jeans and sweatshirt.

The marine logged "Lt. Cdr. Martine, exit 0805" and let him through. As the marine guard watched Martine turn down the corner from the Embassy at Guanghua and Ritan Roads toward the main avenue, Jianguomen, he noticed two men lounging near the corner who took a sudden interest. They split up to cover both sides of the street and openly followed Martine. The guard considered quickly getting a relief officer to cover the gate so he could run after the commander to warn him of the tails. Then he saw Martine turn his head slightly to see the followers. *That one doesn't miss much*, the guard mused to himself and turned away back to his duty.

The muscles in the back of Geoff Martine's neck tightened, signaling danger in an unpredictable situation. The men following him heightened his senses and increased the challenge. They had been on him since he arrived in Beijing three months ago. Wearing tourist-clone jeans, KSwiss tennies and a light gray poplin jacket, Geoff wore the red bill cap as a deliberate flaunt. He would be easy to follow until he didn't want to be followed anymore.

The eight-lane Jianguomen Avenue was teeming in spite of the scarcity of the usual cars, taxis, trucks and buses. People walked rapidly and overflowed the sidewalks into the adjacent bicycle paths. Bicycles, constantly overtaking each other, overflowed their reserved section of the avenue. The three-wheeled, human-powered trishaws enjoyed the luxury of the open motor vehicle lanes. An occasional truck or taxi made its way through the center, commanding a path with loud blasts of its horn.

Like vultures spotting carrion, several empty trishaws swerved onto the curb toward Geoff, jostling each other for the fare. One husky youth, exposing rockhard muscled legs in shorts, beat the others, braking to a stop inches from him.

"Tiananmen Square?" Geoff queried. The operator smiled and pointed to the empty seat, holding up a clenched fist. Geoff nodded an okay at the signed price of ten Yuan. It was twice what a taxi would have charged but there were no taxis on the street this morning.

Within seconds, the pedicab forged its way through the pedestrian and bicycle traffic to the middle of the avenue. They joined the throngs heading west to the Square. Emotion and noisy voices electrified the air, which was strangely clean without the vehicle emissions. Crowds were rushing, as if to get to an arena before a game started. Geoff turned his head slightly to watch another pedicab following with two black-jacketed men in it.

Approaching the Jiangomenwei traffic bridge, the youth barely slowed as he powered the pedicab up the incline and prepared to coast down the far side. A horde of angry people were in the middle of the bridge, surrounding a column of soldiers.

"Mahn mahn," Martine shouted at his driver to slow down. To himself he mused: *I can't afford to get mixed up with this right now. Mission comes first.*

The crowd was jostling the soldiers and shouting at them to turn back. The brigade officer waved his pistol in the air and screamed at his troops to proceed. The pedicab traffic hesitated, and then worked its way through the mass to move on.

Passing a street sign, Martine mentally noted the change of name. After the bridge it was Changan, the most important avenue in central Beijing. Martine and his muscle-powered chauffeur neared the famous shopping street of Wanfujing. The towering Beijing Hotel identified the corner long before they reached it. Concrete lane markers were askew. Stalled buses blocked the intersection. Debris and old tires burned noxiously. Lines of trucks, and other vehicles were stalled at the approaches to the center. Martine openly snapped pictures of the beleaguered area.

Martine shouted loudly to his driver, "Tiananmen Tiananmen." He urged his driver to go on with the other pedicabs, pedestrians and bicycles funneling through the breaks at the edges of the barriers. Pushing forward on the seat, he snapped off a dozen quick photos of the melee. Then he turned the camera toward the Beijing Hotel.

Shouting, "Bushir, bushir," the youth stopped pedaling abruptly, pointed to the camera and shook his head vehemently. Martine heard the youth rant angrily in the local patois. "Stupid barbarian, I should get my kuai before this donkey gets both of us in trouble."

The driver jumped out of the cab, grabbed Martine's arm, and motioned him to get out. Irritated, Martine forcibly shook off the grip, causing the driver to stumble and fall to the ground. He spoke to the young man in the patois with a wry grin twisting his lips. "Confucius once said that a stupid drover can be kicked in his genitals if he offends the ears of a barbarian donkey." Tossing a ten Yuan note, he left with a wave and a "tsai jian" for goodbye. From the corner of his eye he saw the two security agents arguing with their own cab driver. *Probably trying to pay with a travel voucher instead of cash*, Martine thought with amusement.

Martine surveyed the area in front of the Beijing Hotel. Locals intermixed with a few foreigners. The tourists were out early to join in the excitement. Trained and experienced, he easily spotted the government's security people. They watched for leaders of the rebellion and wrote in little red plastic notebooks.

Immersed in the crowd as he passed the next intersection, Geoff looked up to the roof of the Beijing Hotel. The foreign press had established themselves there to get telephoto views of Tiananmen Square and the throngs of people heading toward it. He mingled with the crowd, exchanging a few cordialities of "ni hao ma" in the excitement. The bridges leading into the Forbidden City came into view on the right side of the broad boulevard. Across the street spread Tiananmen, the largest public square in the world.

Martine took stock of the colossal sight: he remembered well the sheer immensity of the square. Now hundreds of makeshift tents were scattered in no particular pattern. Young men and women emerged from the tents, stretching in the morning sun. The sounds of voices gradually begin to roll over the area in an increasing hum. Plumes of smoke arose from small cooking carts. The greasy odor of the fried twisted bread would soon begin to permeate the air.

The area was so vast that Martine could barely make out clusters of the demonstrators around the base of the stark white Goddess of Freedom statue. He marked, for future orientation, the Martyr's column rising high over groups of people in the middle of the square. Glimpses of army uniforms indicated the military was on hand. Martine took note of the soldiers patrolling the area. They watched tourists and the local people alike, admonishing the few foreigners who dared to sneak pictures.

"Okay, Martine," he said to himself. "Mission time. Start a diversion; dump the black birds." He looked over his shoulder to make sure they were paying attention, flipped the small Konica out, extruded the lens and started to snap pictures. The two black birds immediately called out to one of the patrols, pointing at the provocation.

Martine saw the patrol take off at a trot headed his way. He tossed his red cap into a group of nearby students and took a dozen more duplicates from the shoulder bag. Smiling to himself, he spun in a circle, throwing them out to laughing recipients. Then he scrunched down and slipped into a dense group at the base of the Martyr's column.

Students exhorting the soldiers to go home saw what was happening to the tourist as the patrol chased over to where he had been. The din of voices became shouts of alarm. Clusters of students swarmed toward the area. A second patrol was seen heading to the melee. Martine caught a glimpse of his two black-jacketed pursuers, a moment ago gleeful over the trouble they had caused their quarry, now frantically trying to find him.

Free from pursuit for the moment, Geoff mused to himself, *Well that worked, hot shot. You got rid of the tails easy enough. Now you have to locate your contact before the goons catch up.* He threaded his way through the drab army tents, hunching over so he wouldn't stand out in the crowd. Each tent displayed a banner or sign identifying the resident's organization – a university, a technical school, or embryonic political group. After locating the sign he was looking for, he walked right by it. Circling around to make sure he had not been seen, he then ducked into the tent.

A man and a woman were sitting side by side on a cot, sipping tea from screw-capped jars. Surprised at the sudden appearance of the foreigner, the woman dropped hers, spilling the liquid on herself. Geoff looked at them, smiled and said, "Lt. Commander Geoffrey Martine from the US Embassy. I believe you sent me a message."

The couple stood up. "Fang Linxi," the man said, extending his hand to Martine. "My wife, Shen. We are honored by your presence, and surprised by your audacity. These are dangerous times. Were you followed?"

They shook hands and Geoff replied, "All the way from the embassy, but I know a few tricks from my espionage days. A number of your friends were good enough to spot my ploy and seem to have the black shirts and military patrols confused for the moment."

Fang peeked out of the tent opening. "There's a large crowd; some soldiers and our fellow students milling around the Martyr's monument. Strange, I see a few of my friends are wearing bright red caps."

Geoff noted that the man looked to be in his early thirties with a round cherubic face. A sweat-stained headband held in place a heavy shock of black hair. The character of Nankai University, Tianjin, marked the band, as on the banner outside the tent.

The woman appeared younger. She wore a similar headband, cleaner than her husband's. Fine black hair framed a gaunt face with high cheekbones. Her worried eyes continually shifted from the two men to the entrance of the tent.

"Please sit, Commander," the man said. "It is good of you to come."

"The name of Professor Fang Linxi is well known to us," Geoff replied. "You have been a friend of the United States for many years. Your work has enhanced the world's knowledge of astrophysics."

"Thank you. Our time is short, Commander. The PLA came to the outskirts of Beijing yesterday, rebuffed by the thousands of supporters of democracy."

Geoff nodded. "Our government has requested a meeting with your President, Liu Chinan. President Bush was liaison to China some years ago and has met personally many of the leaders, including Chinan. We have been given to understand one of your Generals, Tang, I believe, is the trouble maker."

Fang frowned. "The hard-liners are angry and have lost face in the world after the visit of Gorbachev. Our former president, who showed compassion, Zhao Ziyang, is missing. If the other softliner, Hu Yaobang, were still alive, they might have recognized our demonstration together. We have no more chance to settle peacefully with the Politburo."

"Yes, Professor, that is the information we received. What happens now?"

"Other students and leaders of the demonstration were already arrested off the Square where the foreign press cannot see and publicize it. A cousin came this morning to tell us the secret police have been to my house in Tianjin looking for me. The bottom-line, as I have heard Americans say, is I'm sure they'll use force to clear the square."

Fang looked over at his wife, who was trembling, and took her hand in his. "We plead for our lives. Will the United States give us sanctuary inside the embassy until sanity returns to our country?" He appraised the American and liked what he saw. Grey-toned red hair topped craggy, rough-hewn features. A wry half smile gave him a shy demeanor which Fang suspected was more disguise than reality.

Geoff looked down at the worried pair and fished a mutton-fat jadite rubbing stone from his pocket. The grey-toned, antique replica of a sea creature fit into the contour of his fingers. Unconsciously massaging the piece, he realized Fang and his wife were watching. He smiled and showed them what it was. "The fingers of Confucius. It helps me to think. An old antique dealer in Hong Kong sold it to me with instructions to commune with the ancient one when I needed to think."

"Confucius was known to be a great peacemaker as well as a teacher. China would be well to remember his philosophy and teachings today," Fang said ruefully.

Walking up and down in the narrow confines of the tent, Geoff worried the problem, mentally reviewing the protocol involving international situations like this. "How much time is there before General Tang Naiwa orders the square cleared?"

The professor replied sadly, "I don't know. My friends do not believe the army will shoot, but I know they will if ordered.

"And you two, as well as a thousand others in the square, will be directly in the line of fire." Geoff grimaced.

"As a matter of honor, my wife and I would lay down our lives if we thought it would mean something. Practically speaking, we know there must be some of us left to begin again when we free China from the iron grip of the Communists. As to the time, I would guess in the next forty-eight hours we will hear guns in Tiananmen and begin to count the bodies."

"According to international conventions, we can give you safe haven in the embassy, providing you get there under your own power. You must express a desire to enter because you fear for your life under political persecution."

"All too true, Commander. We are more than willing. Now we must conceive of a plan to get us from here to there. It won't be simple as I am known as a leader of the movement and under special observation."

His wife spoke up. "Let me check the area, Commander. I'm familiar with the MSS agents that have been watching us."

"Thanks, Shen. I'll firm up our plans with Fang in the meantime."

Shen returned a few minutes later and with a nod from her husband, advised, "As good a time as I can see, Commander. There's a considerable crowd near both memorials. The patrols appear to be grouping around the students with the red caps. I suggest you slip out the back of the tent and circle around to Changan."

"Thanks, Shen. I'd better get moving." Quickly shaking hands with Fang and with a pat on the shoulder for Shen, Geoff disappeared through the rear of the tent.

"Not to worry, dear wife," Fang said as the American left. "This Martine is a smart one, street smart I think they say. He would have to be just to respond to our note smuggled to the embassy and actually get here."

Ambassador George X. Fowler sat at a massive desk in front of draped windows. The high-ceiling baronial room was furnished in the diplomatic decor of formality. The newly elected President, George H. W. Bush, looked down at him from a photograph on the nearby wall. An American flag hung from a standard at his right shoulder.

"You see this flag, Martine? It's behind my chair. I'm the United States Ambassador to the People's Republic of China. Therefore, I decide, not subordinates. Give me one good reason that I already don't know for evacuation orders."

Geoff listened to the bluster, knowing the man was both drunk and nursed a serious grudge against his cultural aide. The appointment of a CIA station chief to an embassy was not the predilection of the State Department, or the Ambassadors. He reported directly to the Company and this rankled the man.

"All I'm suggesting, Mr. Ambassador, is that we make preparations to evacuate families and excess personnel. There's a distinct chance of explosive military action in the area around the Embassy and the housing compound. We could catch some stray gunfire."

"And who are these people you invited to take asylum at the embassy?"

Geoff patiently explained about the professor and his wife. "I merely advised them on international convention and the United States' policy in such instances. Surely you wouldn't turn away such an internationally known figure as Professor Fang Linxi and his wife if they appeared at the embassy gates?"

Geoff sat back in his chair as Arthur Fowler, Ambassador to the People's Republic of China for the United States of America, stood up to his total five-foot-seven height and exploded.

"What kind of crap is that, Martine? I've never heard of this Linxi guy you say is important. He wasn't at any of the functions I've been to since arriving. Do you know how many banquets I have had to sit through with nothing better to drink than that kerosene they call maotie and orange juice?"

"Mr. Ambassador, sir. The Linxis would not have been on the social circuit and it is unlikely you would have met them. The world situation is such that any embassy is subject to asylum requests for humanitarian reasons."

"Commander Martine, you are aware that I am a business executive, president of the Fowler Chevrolet Company of Muncie, Indiana. My friendship with the Republican Party has awarded me this post. I would have preferred Brunei but Mrs. Fowler, Florence, would have none of a small country she had never heard of. I am not the ignoramus you professionals seem to think I am. China is a major power in the world and I intend to serve here in the best interests of the United States. "

Fowler paused and Geoff took the opportunity to interrupt the tirade. "Mr. Ambassador, we professionals have the exact same purpose to assist you in that service. My two decades of experience in situations such as this is at your disposal. You have initialed and I assume read the current flood of dispatches. The students' democracy demonstration is and will be of international importance. In my experience we will be involved and perhaps in danger. I strongly suggest we take the prescribed measures of protection and probable evacuation."

"Commander, for your information, I have and do read all dispatches. In spite of our obvious negative opinions of each other, I do recognize your experience and professionalism. You are hereby assigned the evacuation procedure, if necessary. Prepare a note of whatever background you have on the Linxis for me and arrange a meeting here in my office on arrival."

"Yes, sir, Mr. Ambassador. I'll have Duffy in communications prepare the directive and have it on your desk within the hour."

Martine saluted by habit and exited quickly.

"'Patrick, we have work to do," Geoff said as he rushed into the communications secure room.

"Standing by," the genial Irishman said. "What's up, Geoff?"

"Start writing, Pat. Most of this you're aware of, but we need...." Geoff proceeded to explain the meeting with the Linxis and the agreement with the Ambassador. "We need this info to Washington ASAP."

An hour later Patrick reported to Geoff, "The Secretary of State in Washington and the Chief of Central Intelligence at Langley are reading the top secret, eyes-only messages now."

Geoff's coded dispatch was two short lines of information: "Fang Linxi and wife want out. Anticipate the axe will fall on Tiananmen within 48 hours." Fowler's separate cable to the Secretary was lengthy, complaining of CIA forbearance and was his third request for the recall of Martine. He inquired if there was a record of a Li Linxi, Professor of Astrophysics at Tianjin, and reported a rumor that the government may take action soon on the students demonstrating in Tiananmen Square.

BEIHAI PARK

A utility shed behind a small mountain of rock in the very center of the island park concealed the main entrance of the Ministry of State Security. Few officials and none of the populace of Beijing were aware that their beautiful Beihai Park concealed the covert operations of the feared Ministry. Diners feasting on the famous cuisine served in the Fan Shan restaurant never knew they sat directly above the secret facilities. The little known minister of the MSS would often dine and then disappear behind a concealed door to the office below.

In the subterranean office, an eight-foot high, twelve-panel coromandel screen concealed the often-used entrance.

Fan Riqi, Vice Commissar of the Ministry of State Security, thought of himself as the Chief of Espionage. He had trained with the KGB in Russia during the years of association of the two countries. He sat at a large, plain wooden desk. A life-size picture of

Chairman Mao was the only adornment hanging on the wall to his left. The bright eyes of the charismatic leader looked to the opposite wall, which was covered with an enlarged map of Beijing and its suburbs.

A computer screen, a keyboard, and a telephone console, complete with a taping device, filled a large part of the desk surface. Assorted brushes in an antique moss agate brush holder, a slate ink stone, a bronze frog-shaped water container, and a gold decorated ink stick contrasted with the modern electronics. The only other adornment on the desk was a striped malachite ashtray.

Two of his minions stood waiting nervously. Fan Riqi pulled a Great Wall cigar from the pocket of his jacket, peeled away the cellophane wrapper, removed the paper band, and scratched a match against the poorly made box to fire up. The first two matches broke. The third one took hold, starting a rain of ashes and sparks down Fan's shirt.

It was a deliberate ploy to heighten the tension of Captain Yao Lin and his agent, who were reporting on the Tiananmen Square demonstration. Fan's nature forced him to continue buying the poorly wrapped cigars and bad domestic matches. Imported cigars and fancy cigarette lighters were available to him as an important person in the bureaucracy, but they seldom found their way into the local shop he preferred to patronize.

Blowing a cloud of smoke, the Vice Commissar finally acknowledged the two men standing waiting for him. "Well, Captain. Have you something of value to report to justify the expense of our purchasing the new hand-held camcorders? If we don't show results soon, there is going to be a deluge of Ministers borrowing them for their personal use. I can guarantee, we will never see them again."

Fan ran his fingers through his unkempt hair, scratching the scalp. Dandruff flaked out, descending with the ashes spilling from the cigar, annoying the fastidious Captain Yao.

The Captain concealed his distaste at having to serve under this Shanghai pig. *The man's mind is cluttered with debris, like his clothes,* he thought to himself.

"Our agent reports a strange incident, sir. We followed the American we know as Martine, the CIA spy at the US Embassy, to

Tiananmen. After a blundering, obvious attempt to take pictures and lose himself amongst the students, we found him. He was leaving the Nankai University tents. Martine must have been there almost an hour cooking up something with the hooligans."

The Vice Commissar looked up at the gloating face of his captain. "That could be Fang Linxi. Put him on the top ten list, Yao. If either Linxi or his wife leaves the area, even to go home, pick them up for questioning. Make sure the questioning takes several days. As for Martine, print a blow-up of the shot you have and circulate it amongst our agents. I want him tracked wherever he goes outside the embassy. Channel that information directly to me as fast as it happens."

"Yes sir, Vice Commissar. I promise a web like that of the spider. He cannot evade our agents."

Fan scratched his scalp. "Yao, you're pretty thick with the military. What have you heard about Tang Naiwa, our illustrious general and his plans to clear Tiananmen?"

Yao looked at his superior. The pear-shaped head with eyes that pierced one's mind like a laser beam were impossible to lie to. In spite of his dislike for the man, he dared not evade the direct question. Yao's relationship with General Tang was supposed to be secret. Fan Riqi, true to his nickname, the Ferret, allowed very little to slip past his notice.

Feeling the sweat exuding from his armpits and beading on his forehead, Yao answered. "My compliments, Vice Commissar, there's little you miss. It's true. I happened to run into General Tang Naiwa yesterday. We compared notes about the rabble in Tiananmen and the urgency to disperse them. His manner suggested he was about to stop the mollycoddling and bring in the 27th battalion to clear the Square. He promised to coordinate any plans with our Ministry.

Fan rolled the cigar in his mouth, staring with no comment at the captain. He let a full minute pass before he spoke. "Thank you for the report, Yao. Please keep me informed. You may go now."

As the two men left, Fan Riqi swiveled his chair around to face the screen. Chou Shi, Minister of State Security, ranking member of the Politburo, stepped from behind the hinged tablets. "Interesting, isn't it, Fan? You're right about Yao. He's what the West calls a doubleagent. How soon will you replace him?"

Fan studied the round, smooth-skinned face, black hair streaked with the gray of age. The eyes were as devoid of expression as a metallic statue of Buddha. Short and rotund, Chou, known to be one of the powerful six insiders of the Politburo, spoke very little, preferring to stay in the background.

"It would be better not to replace the obvious fox with an unknown rabbit, honored Commissar. We'll take care to see that no important information is revealed to him. You sit with the bellicose General Tang Naiwa in the Zhongnanhai. How long can the softliners hold his tanks and guns in check?"

Chou Shi turned to disappear again behind the screen, leaving the answer hanging in the air. "As soon as Deng Xiaoping unsnaps the leash, the lion will spring."

Fan punched up the video channel on his monitor. He watched the Minister slide through the concealed door behind the screen and climb the steps into the restaurant. He leaned back in his chair, put his feet up on the desk, drew deeply on the cigar, expelled a series of smoke rings, and brushed the accumulated ashes off his shirt and lap. He mused to himself, "The 4th of June, 1989, will be a date to remember in Chinese history."

TWO
BEIJING

4 JUNE 1989

The rumble of heavy vehicles awoke Geoff at 4am, the noise loud enough to carry from Jianguomen a full block away. The faint sound of gunfire also came from the west.

"Patrick, are you on?" Geoff shouted into the intercom. "The army is rolling into Tiananmen. Code Red."

He slipped on his jogging outfit, buckled on the pre-loaded waist pack and ran down the stairs to the duty room on the ground floor. Patrick Duffy, Duty Officer for the night, almost knocked him down as they collided outside the room. "It's okay, Geoff. I've notified State. I'm on my way to wake up the Ambassador. He'll probably throw me out anyway and say I'm dreaming."

"Alert everyone to stay away from the windows in case we get some stray gunfire. Fowler's got to okay the evac plans. Get to work on the plane charter from here to Hong Kong. We'll need protected buses to pick everyone up for the airport as soon as you confirm the charter.

"What if the Ambassador balks and delays?"

"Send a follow-up report confirming the tanks and gunfire. The rules are we evacuate all families and excess personnel in a situation of this scope. State will know what you mean and they will climb all over Fowler if he doesn't act."

"Will do, Geoff. Where are you going? Certainly not out for your usual jog today!"

Geoff turned to the freckle-faced Irishman, who had already contributed ten of his thirty-two years to a diplomatic career. "Patrick, my friend, you have a suspicious look. I'm merely going jogging – for the record, that is. You wouldn't want me to give up my daily constitutional because a few tanks are on the street, would you? By the way, I'm leaving by the rear entrance. See if you can sweet-talk the Sarge into putting a guard there after I get out. If the State Security goons start chasing me, I may need someone to hold the door open on return."

"What are you up to, Geoff? This is no time to be running around outside. You know that door's always locked and barred. It's only used for deliveries and garbage removal."

"Yes, I know. Be a good Mick and take care of things for me, will you? I may have a delivery."

The red-head shook his head in resignation. "Wait until His Nibs hears you're out jogging with this going on. He could request your transfer again. This time they might listen to him."

Geoff emerged into the predawn. The sky was beginning to light up the summer morning, damp with humidity. Tanks, personnel armoured cars, and trucks packed with armed soldiers thundered by as he jogged behind the crowds of people lining Jianguomen. There was a notable absence of the usual rickshaws. A few brave souls made a surge out into the street to delay the military vehicles, but a burst of gunfire changed their minds.

After passing the Jianguomen Bridge onto Changan, Geoff saw a man step into the middle of the avenue in front of a tank, waving both arms high over his head. The watching crowd cheered at first and a foreign photographer took a memorable picture. One man intended to lay down his life in a vain attempt to stop the tanks. Only the swift action of another bystander, dashing out to pull him back on the curb, saved the bloodshed. The tank made no effort to slow down. Geoff could clearly hear the engines racing mercilessly to frighten the man even more. *This is going to be a bloody day at Tiananmen.*

Geoff approached the Wangfujing intersection, marked with burning rubber tires, smoke and flames. The Beijing Hotel looked forlorn in the early light. Throngs of people watched silently as the flames caught on to the buses stalled to block the intersection. Tanks were bearing down the center of the road, their hatches closing with loud clanks. He saw them barrel through the burning barriers. People watching from the curb, at first stupefied by the scene, began to scream and force each other back. Flaming debris scattered over them and around Geoff. Scanning the area, he saw press cameras pointing from the rooftop and faces watching from upper windows of the grand old hotel. *Good*, he mused with bitter optimism. *No way is the government going to keep this from the world.*

Scraping hot ashes from his shoulders and dodging debris, Geoff quickly took the inside road of the parkway behind the crowds. Hordes of people were running from Tiananmen, trying to escape what must be indiscriminate gunfire. The noise was louder as he approached the corner. Bodies lay in the street in front of the hotel entrance. Pools of blood stained the pavement

Streams of people fleeing up Wangfujing slowed Geoff as he merged with them. Screaming voices carried above the din.

Two young men, pulling open carts with still bodies on them, were resting as Geoff stopped to talk to them. "What's the situation at Tiananmen?"

Suspiciously, they looked at him and then at each other. "American? We don't know what you're doing here, but if you get out, tell the whole world what is going on here." First one then the other spat out the angry news.

"Machine guns from the tanks killed everybody around the Freedom Statue."

"A row of soldiers kneeled and fired like an execution squad at my group from Chnegtu. Murderers."

"I somehow survived and pretended to be dead, the only one left of my school."

"Eeyah! The tanks rolled right over the dead bodies."

"Hundreds dead; blood has painted Tiananmen forever."

"Terrible! Chinese soldiers killing Chinese citizens: China is committing suicide."

Choking with emotion, the men said no more as the headband harnesses tautened and the carts pulled off. Geoff noted one of his route markers. The Xinhua bookstore building near the corner on his right was shuttered and barricaded, as were most of the stores on the busiest shopping street in central Beijing.

At the next marker, not much wider than an alley, Geoff turned right, following the ambulance carts. They were heading toward his rendezvous point. He passed the barricaded Peking Duck Restaurant, the site of many enjoyable dinners. He remembered it being called the Sick Duck restaurant because of its proximity to Capitol Hospital.

Geoff jogged on through the crowds, watching to see if he had attracted any undue attention. "*So far so good, Geoffrey, no tails. It looks like the goons missed your rear exit from the embassy. Now cool your heels and keep your eyes open.*" Duffy often chided him about talking to himself, an old habit.

Geoff could see the Capitol Hospital at the end of the street. He remembered an American author describing it as a green-tiled roof with miniature guardians standing point on the ends. Patients wearing bandages and striped robes streamed out of the hospital to see what was going on. Bicycle-powered flat-bed wagons followed Geoff down the crowded street, injured bodies bouncing roughly on the hard wooden surfaces. Transportation of the sick and wounded hasn't changed in the past centuries.

Moans of pain and screams for help were overpowering as the hospital staff labored to take over first-aid requirements. Ambulatory hospital patients carried stretchers in and out of the hospital and then commiserated with anxious friends.

The non-conforming tall Westerner in jogging sweats stood at the side of the street, a blue knit cap with red and white stripes added to his attire. He waited impatiently as the tide of bloodied bodies flowed down the street into the hospital.

The wagons changed hands as soon as they emptied, with no regard for ownership. The tired pullers dropped in their tracks on arrival at the hospital and others quickly took up the makeshift ambulances to return to the scene of the carnage.

Geoff was almost ready to give up, fearing the worst had happened, when one flat bed came toward him, manned by a white-suited hospital orderly. He wore a white cap on his head and a sanitation mask across his face. The truck stopped momentarily. Geoff breathed a sigh of relief as he saw the orderly slip off the white mask and cap. The lettering on a sweat-stained headband was the Tainjin University symbol. The face, even from a distance across the road, was clear and recognizably Fang Linxi's. On the bed of the truck, a form wrapped in a blanket stirred, the head bandaged, oozing blood.

Stretcher bearers moved toward the make-shift ambulance, and the orderly waved them off, pedaling slowly through the crowd toward the easily recognizable tall figure in the blue knit cap.

"Put the mask and white hat back on, Professor," Geoff said. He removed his own blue cap and stored it in his waist pack. Beckoning the weary-looking Fang Linxi to follow him, he jogged into a side lane around the wall of the hospital.

As other carts piled in, the attendants just shrugged and took over the next victims.

BEIHAI PARK, MSS OFFICE

In the headquarters of the Ministry of State Security, Fan Riqi stood at the wall map of Beijing. He put small pin flags at various locations as Captain Yao Lin brought in the information. The red, white and blue flag with no name was in his hand.

"Where is Martine, Yao? When did they last see him?"

"Comrade Fan, we are doing the best we can. He thought he outsmarted us by leaving by the rear entrance of the embassy, but we caught up to him at Jianguomen. It was impossible to follow him in the dim light, once he got into the crowds at Wangfujing. There were thousands of people on the corner. I sent the two men assigned to him back to the usual jogging route he takes near the bridge to watch for his return. We have also lost Professor Fang Linxi and his wife."

"Lost them?" Fan erupted into red-faced anger. "Useless donkey's ass! With two agents assigned to their tent exclusively, how could they lose them?"

"Comrade Fan. Tiananmen is a disaster. Thousands of students milling around trying to escape certain death. Piles of dead bodies mowed down by the PLA. They must have had orders to clear the Square at any cost. Our agent on site reported a stray bullet hit the Linxi woman. Fang and his friends carried her back into the tent. The last glimpse we had of her was an ambulance cart taking her out of the Square and no sign of Fang Linxi."

"Fools, stupid fools," Fan raged. "First I have to put up with that mad dog General Tang, who plans on sweeping thousands of bodies away to cure a problem that will only get worse. Then I have to contend with your agents, Yao, who can't even keep track of their own bowel movements. If Linxi's wife is at the hospital, Fang will show up there."

Humbled and concerned for his own safety, Yao knew Fan might easily pull his pistol and shoot him on the spot. "Honored Commissar, we can still find them and as for the American spy, I'll backtrack him all the way to the American Embassy. Our red armband watchers may have seen him on the inside roads. He obviously didn't jog down Jianguomen with all this going on, especially if he is meeting the Professor."

Fan thought for a moment, dismissing Yao's comments.

"Get a car. Imbecile. I'm going to the embassy myself."

Geoff led the cart down a narrow lane, turning left and right at each narrow intersection, weaving through the ancient apartment-like Hutongs. The passageways angled, curved and often dead-ended, requiring him to turn around and go back. Only one familiar with the local rabbit warrens could find their way quickly to a destination. At each turn, they stopped to double check the direction. Sympathetic people gathered to help and fired questions at them as well.

"Is it true that hundreds of students were gunned down indiscriminately?"

"Are they just standing there letting themselves be killed?"

"Can the students fight back with anything?"

Linxi answered them, his voice choking with emotion: "Hundreds if not thousands have already been slaughtered like cattle. We may never know how many have been lost. There is nowhere to run as the army has posted killers at every corner. We have nothing to fight with except for the hope of Democracy one day."

A local breakfast queue crowded the next intersection, lined several deep to buy twisted fried bread and bowls of congee, the rice gruel. Geoff stopped the cart and whispered to Fang. "Let's catch our breath here and get you and your wife a bite to eat. We still have a half hour or more of traveling to get to the Embassy."

"Don't get up, Mrs. Linxi," he said, turning to the back of the cart. "We don't want anyone to see through our game. Your bloodied head wound disguise is very realistic."

Linxi, again his voice choking with emotion, blurted out, "Shen is not pretending, Commander. A bullet struck her outside the tent. She has lost a lot of blood with the head wound and has been in and out consciousness ever since. There was no use trying for emergency help at Capitol. No beds or cots would be available. Patients are lined up on the floor, I was told. I hurt with each tortured breath she takes. Will there be a doctor at the Embassy?"

Geoff groaned at the news of Shen's wound. "Yes, Professor, we share medical needs with a fine doctor at the Australian embassy." He gripped her hand for comfort and took a closer look at the wound. The flesh was torn badly along the side of her head above the ear, bruising spreading over the whole area. At least the blood had clotted, but the woman was obviously in shock and probably needed a transfusion as soon as possible.

Linxi bought twisted fried bread and a bowl of rice gruel from the cart. He tried to tip a few grains of the congee into Shen's lips. There was no response or movement from her.

"No, thanks," Geoff said when offered some, squeamish at the lack of hygiene that must go into the food preparation in this district.

The old woman tending the stall threw the empty bowl into a bucket of luke-warm wash water and asked Linxi, "Are you a student? Is it true they are shooting the demonstrators at Tiananmen?"

Linxi replied, haltingly, each word an effort of memory, fear and weariness. "It's terrible at Tiananmen... the soldiers... shot hundreds... wonderful young men... women... students... All they wanted was democracy... My wife was shot in the head. Now she may not even live until we get medical help."

Linxi quieted, trying to take control of himself, fearful of saying too much. The woman could be a watcher. "The hospital is too full, so I'm taking her to my parents' apartment for care. She must not die; we have our whole life to live together and our son in her belly is already five months old."

"Eeyah!" the woman said. "That's terrible. I hope she and your son survive. Who's the barbarian? Why is he with you?"

Linxi answered, "A tourist out exercising who got caught in the mess and is lost. He was good enough to help me get through the crowds. I'm taking him to his hotel by the back streets on the way to my parents' home. Changan is too dangerous for anyone right now."

As the three of them began moving again, Linxi pointed back down the street. "The busybody is calling over the old man with the red armband. He's a street watcher, traffic director and general spy for the government." As they turned the corner, they saw the man scurry down the street to a telephone booth.

Finally they reached the boulevard heading into Jianguomen Bridge and stopped to survey the area. Geoff said, "Crossing the boulevard is easy, not much traffic at this end now."

"We have been exposed," Fang said. "Surely the MSS will associate the missing professor with an American jogger. They will be expecting us to go to the American Embassy, and looking for us to exit these side streets to get there."

"You're right. There they are," Geoff said, spotting a brace of agents leaning over the top of a black car sweeping binoculars from side to side up and down the street. Pulling his head back into the alley, Geoff found himself surrounded by dozens of men, women and children. He understood some of the local patois well enough to follow what was being said between them and Linxi.

"MSS agents. Be careful," Linxi summarized.

"Neighbors passed the word about us and want to help. Our new friends spotted the official car and will do whatever they can to help us escape. The MSS agents aren't exactly friends of the people. What can we do, Commander?"

Geoff looked around. "Let's try a diversion, Professor. I'm going to make a run for it. They won't dare shoot me. I'm just a jogger out for a morning run, and I'm untouchable as diplomatic staff. You're going to switch clothes with the locals here, pile some bricks from that dump over there around your wife, and become a bricklayer going to work."

"Understood, Commander. With good fortune they will follow you and give us a chance to get across. I'll ask our friends here to fill the area with as many people as they can summon to confuse the black shirts out there."

"If we don't meet on the other side, Professor, circle back on Cha-oyangmena down to Ritan Park beyond the Embassy. You will find a side street leading into the alleyway behind the embassy building. The service door is self-evident, the only one there."

"Agreed, Commander. And if you're not there?"

"A Marine will be on duty and is expecting us. Once inside, you and Shen will be safe. I'll give you ten minutes to get covered up and then take off. Good fortune, my friends."

Geoff watched the neighbors form a crowd around the litter cart. Everyone pitched in to build a wall of bricks around the injured woman. Fang slipped out of the hospital coveralls, took the mask off, and dusted himself with debris. A few of the people scurried to nearby apartments to alert their neighbors to the action about to take place. In a few minutes, the boulevard had filled with people strolling up and down both sides of the street. Geoff nonchalantly walked out on the sidewalk and began to lope toward the bridge.

The agents picked him up at once and followed, one on foot, the other in the car.

"Follow me, boys. I'm like the Chattanooga Choo Choo," Geoff sang, as he led them far enough up the boulevard, then swung suddenly across the road. He saw them leap into action to follow, but the crowds surging around the men and car delayed them momentarily. He took off at a run and turned down a narrow alley on the other side.

Geoff slowed down to a distance-eating trot, taking every turn right or left. Daily joggings in the area around the embassy had made him intimately familiar with the side streets. On any normal morning, children giggled and waited to exchange "ni hao" with him. There was always a supply of lollypops or jellybeans in his waist pack.

Geoff came down the alley behind the embassy just as the cart came into sight. Linxi, who was hurrying to get to the doorway, stumbled under the heavy load of bricks. The cart spun against the wall with a loud crash. He grabbed Shen as the bricks tumbled off and a wheel collapsed.

Geoff raced to help. He called out to the marine guard who was waiting at the back entrance. "Johnny, grab the lady. Get her inside. Fang, walk to the door and follow them inside. We don't want anyone to say that we assisted or forced you into the premises of the United States."

The black Shanghai Special screeched to a stop at the curb just as the door closed behind the marine and his two charges. Geoff, nonchalantly leaning against a utility pole, watched a small man get out of the back seat and head toward him. His demeanor identified him as an official, though an unlit cigar and an unkempt jacket appeared incongruous.

"American, may I see your identification?"

"Nope. It's inside the Embassy," Geoff answered. "I don't carry any papers when I'm out running. Who are you?"

A hand extended politely. "I'm Fan Riqi, Vice Commissar of the Ministry of State Security. Are you attached to the embassy, sir? Please tell me your name and position."

Geoff straightened up to his full height and offered to shake hands with the man. "Lieutenant Commander Geoffrey Martine, Cultural Attaché of the United States Embassy."

"Thank you, Lieutenant Commander Martine. We are looking for two criminals, a man and a wounded woman on a hospital cart. Have you seen them?"

"Sorry, Mr. Fan, I can't help you."

Geoff watched the Vice Commissar look over to the cart, now askew on one wheel with bricks tumbled around it. He looked up and down the street, and then turned back to Geoff.

"Very interesting Commander Martine. It appears the criminal demonstrators have helped themselves into asylum with your assistance. Suggest to your new-found friends that it would be well for them to surrender. If you see them, that is."

"Vice Commissar, I have no idea what you are talking about. If I should happen to run into some strangers on my jogging route, I'll relate your request."

Geoff waved goodbye and started jogging around to the front of the Embassy. As he turned the corner, he saw Fan Riqi standing against the car, puffing on a cigar, scratching his scalp.

Fan watched the tall American jog off. *Yes, Commander Martine, we must meet again.*

THE EMBASSY

Fowler shouted at Geoff. "What'n hell do you mean, letting those people in here without my express permission? This is my territory. I warned you that I decide policy, not you, Martine."

Patrick Duffy was standing with Geoff in the Ambassador's office and interrupted quietly.

"Perhaps I should call a news conference, Mr. Ambassador. Dan Rather is still around and would be glad to get a story like this. I'm sure he would feature you in the interview for rendering aid to a wounded political refugee and her famous husband. Before you decide, this cable from the Secretary of State just came in. It seems State is very interested in Professor Fang Linxi."

Fowler's face was livid with anger. He stopped to read the cable. "All right, you two. Get out of here and get those people off the premises as soon as you can. Duffy, in the meantime you might set up that press conference so that I can tell the world about our famous guests."

Geoff winked at Pat as he addressed the Ambassador. "I've prepared an operative memo for your signature, sir. If you'll sign it, I can get on to the immediate problem of getting our guests safely out of the Embassy and out of China."

The Ambassador scribbled an unintelligible signature and threw the paper at Geoff without reading it.

"Thank you, sir. You look very stressed, Mr. Ambassador. Would you like me to send Dr. Hitikoshi in after he has finished attending to Mrs. Linxi?"

Geoff followed the Communications Officer without waiting for an answer from the fuming man. He overheard the secretary buzz the intercom. "The Chinese Minister of State Security, Mr. Chou Shi, is on the phone, Mr. Ambassador. He says it is something about one of our Embassy personnel helping criminals escape."

"Hey, Duffy, the Ambassador didn't mention the evacuation plans. Is everything in order?"

"He received direct orders from President Bush to be prepared for evac and to stand by for orders. A Cathay Pacific 737 is holding in Hong Kong. Buses are at the housing compound with gear all loaded awaiting the order to mount up and ride off. Minimum staff will stay, including you and I. State is assessing the situation and will advise, according to the last dispatch."

"Well done, Duffy. This outfit couldn't run without you. From what I've seen, the damage will have been done by nightfall. The surviving democracy demonstrators, if any, will disperse and the Politburo will have to handle the world clamor and disgust."

BEIHAI PARK, MSS OFFICE

At the Ministry of State Security, Commissar Chou Shi glowered at Fan Riqi while waiting for his call to go through. Captain Yao Lin cowered in the corner of the office, waited for the tirade and probable punishment that would soon be coming his way – a transfer to Urimiqi in Outer Mongolia, perhaps.

Fan Riqi, ignoring the Commissar's mood, reached for a Great Wall cigar. Unwrapping it, he bit off the end and lit up. Over the next five years, it would come to be a very familiar posture.

Part Two

THREE
BEIJING

10 APRIL 1994

"Commander Geoffrey Martine reporting for duty, Madame Ambassador."

Uniform cap tucked securely under his left arm, Geoff approached the desk framed by the window. The high-ceilinged room was comfortably familiar. The American flag still stood at attention behind it and now President William Clinton's image surveyed the premises.

Ambassador Duke sat in the same chair behind the same desk that Ambassodor Fowler had occupied the last time Geoff was in this office. Geoff studied the slight figure, almost swallowed by the big leather desk chair. Her hair, tied tightly in a bun, appeared to pull the smooth skin of her lovely face taut. A slight wrinkling at the eyes was the only sign of aging. He had read her books, including one written after the Tiananmen Massacre, which told horror stories of personal experiences. Close friends living in China had related their suffering under the Communist regime. It would be interesting to share the memories of Tiananmen with Lena Lao Duke, United States Ambassador to the People's Republic of China.

"Welcome back to Beijing, Commander Martine. I hope this tour of duty will be less eventful than the last. According to the reports I reviewed, your experiences in 1989 in the Tiananmen incident were extensive to say the least." The Ambassador arose, extended her hand, and smiled. "Shall we sit over here and have some tea? Tell me about yourself."

She took in the tall, athletic figure wearing regulation Navy whites with attaché gold cords looped around a shoulder. He returned the handshake, right side of his mouth twisted into a wry grin.

Grayish-red hair left a stray lock over his right eyebrow, adding to his boyish charm. In her mind, she visualized a casual Errol Flynn adventurer rather than the James Bond sophisticated spy she had expected.

"Thank you, Madame Ambassador," Geoff said.

The Ambassador motioned to a pair of lounge chairs pulled up to a low tea table. He followed her, watching from beneath lowered lashes. She wore a white silk skirt that clung to her hips and a matching silk shirt fell past her knees. The slight flaws in the shantung material only made her perfect skin more pronounced. An impressive belt hugged her narrow hips and the large mutton-fat jade buckle flashed wherever she moved, enhancing ever so subtly her aura of authority. Around her throat she wore a single strand of large freshwater pearls that accented the slimness of her neck.

On the tea table, a padded reed basket opened on a bright yellow decorated teapot and small matching cups. The pale green tea gave off a delicate aroma and was still hot from the cozy as he accepted it from her.

Geoff held the teacup up to the light and commented: "Eggshell porcelain, rare, from Jingdezhen in Jianxi Province. It allows the flavor of the tea to flow gently onto the tongue."

The Ambassador assessed him with a slight smile. "How interesting that you are aware of the rare arts of China."

"A friend and I were allowed to back-pack travel some years ago. We took advantage of the chance to visit many of the art centers of the country. Porcelain is fortunately one of the ancient arts that continues to exist."

"Indeed." The Ambassador seemed to be waiting for something more from him.

"I assume from the aroma that it is Hangzhou Dragon Well Tea, as well. My compliments. This is a change from my last visit to this office. I think this tour of duty will be more enjoyable. Now, what can I tell you about myself that isn't in the personnel file you have on the desk?"

Geoff caught her fleeting smile, somehow managed without parting her lips.

"You are observant, Geoffrey, but that's part of your training. Yes,

I have read about the famous agent Martine that succeeded in smuggling two good friends of mine, Shen and Professor Fang Linxi, out of the Square and somehow out of Beijing during the harrowing episode of Tiananmen. You must tell me how you managed that. Ambassador Fowler's report contained little detail except for his missing Cadillac. "

"It was a little tricky, Madame Ambassador. Whilst in Beijing, Mrs. Fowler had accumulated a considerable amount of antique furniture, porcelain artware, wood carvings, and assorted antique collectables. We managed to send the collection, loaded in two vans, escorted by Fowler's Yellow Cadillac, to the freighter port in Tianjin. Inadvertently, we claimed, the car got loaded into the container with the two vans being shipped to Hong Kong. The Professor and his wife were carefully tucked into the false trunk."

"Thank you, Commander. The full tale is perhaps material for a book one day. I note that you are a full Commander now," she said with a knowing smile. "You were born in Australia, I see. How did you get from there to here in forty-six years?"

"My father was in the diplomatic service after the second world war, stationed at a consulate in Hobart, Tasmania, at the time," Geoff answered.

Seemingly genuinely curious, the Ambassador leaned forward. "And your mother? "

"Mother's an Aussie. Dad died when I was nine years old, and we moved up north to Queensland. When I was college age, Mom decided she should get me out of my SCUBA gear and away from the boats of the Great Barrier Reef." He shrugged with the ghost of a wry smile.

She murmured, "That must have been an enjoyable life for a young man. What made you decide to leave it behind?"

Geoff shrugged. "Mother's practical insistence. And I realized there had to be a better future for me than teaching the tourists how to avoid sharks and stay alive twenty meters under water. "

"Entering Annapolis needs influence. How did you manage that?"

"My father's connections. I wound up there and managed to graduate, albeit near the bottom of the class four years later. The

Company recruited me, I think, because I had more demerits than any other cadet. There was a certain clash between the strict rules of the Academy and the unstructured life I had known before. My accent didn't go over too well with the WASPS that buzzed around me; that created a few of the memorable incidents."

Lena Lao Duke watched her new attaché as he related the parts of his background he cared to tell. The deep-set blue eyes had outdoor weather wrinkles at the corners that smiled with the right side of his mouth from time to time.

"You didn't mention how you learned Mandarin, Geoffrey. Your file says you are linguistically comfortable with it and Russian."

"Yes, ma'am. I learned Russian at the Academy and the Company had me brush up on it during their training period. A Chinese friend from Cairns taught me some of the Cantonese and Hokkien-style street lingo. We spent my year of grace before beginning duty touring the Mainland and got to know a few of the young people in this country. My friend's family came from Fujian Province. They immigrated to Australia after the Communists took over." A fractured smile became a pause.

The Ambassador filled the silence by reaching over to refill his cup. He took a ragged sip, feeling the conversation was starting to trespass on fragile territory. He wasn't sure he should keep going, but something about the woman's serene encouragement made him want to go on.

"I don't mean to pry, Geoffrey, but I have the feeling you are leaving out the end of the story."

Geoff gently sipped his tea and studied the few grains of leaves that had settled in the bottom.

"My friend was killed, Mrs. Duke." Weathered wrinkles tightened; the deep blue eyes welled with tears. "We were both young and I suppose too naïve with no fear of traveling alone in China of the sixties."

The Ambassador placed her hand over his. "Tragedy leaves an imprint on the soul and memory, Geoff. I apologize for my intrusion. You need not continue."

Martine continued as if he had not heard her. His voice now filled with anger and resentment. Duke saw a fist tighten whitely on an arm of the chair. "Mao's Red Guards were active at the time, left over from the Cultural Revolution. They resented our freedom, our Australian passports, our fancy camera and our relationship. A group of them went wild one night in Shanghai, raped and beat her to death in the park next to the Bund. They tied me to a tree and made me watch while they took their vengeance against the intellectuals and capitalists."

The Ambassador sat back, deeply sorry she had dredged up such pain. His fist relaxed now as the anger abated. The other hand held the delicate cup, which she feared would be crushed into angry shards. He curled his hand around it instead, moving a finger around the edge, caressing the fragile porcelain. A tear leaked from the corner of his right eye, ignored until others followed it. He was forced to wipe them away, angrily.

"Sorry, Mrs. Duke, I hadn't meant to tell that story. Please do me a favor and keep it quiet. It's not in my dossier at the Company and I would prefer they didn't know. Anyway, the police refused to do anything about it. Life was so cheap in China then. The Australian Ambassador listed it as an unfortunate tourist incident, and had me shipped out early the next morning."

"You must have loved her very much, Geoffrey."

"Yes, Mrs. Duke. A scar remains. The stories in your books are all too real. Social circles of our society do not readily accept mixed cultural love affairs."

The Ambassador paused for a moment, allowing time for both of their emotions to settle, and then pressed on in a formal business tone.

"There are things to do now that you are here. We must become current on the rumblings all over China. Please read over the reports on my desk. Compile a synopsis and your opinion of what might happen in the immediate future.

"By the way, an old friend of yours, Patrick Duffy, is now my assistant. A marine Master Sergeant by the name of John Johnson is also here on his last tour before retiring. Both appear to know you well."

"Yes ma'am. We're three musketeers with five years of gap to catch up on. We're meeting in the secure room tonight after chow with a couple of six-packs of beer to loosen up our memories."

The Ambassador laughed. "Using the secure room for secrets? Three bachelors catching each other up on their adventures? I'm not invited, I presume, because there might be some deeds that I and the service do not need to know."

"Very perceptive, Mrs. Duke. My duty, not in the standard personnel file, of course, was Israel, working with my counterparts the Mossad. Duffy spent his in Washington D.C. amongst the bureaucrats to earn his Ambassador certificate. Johnny is always in the middle of a firefight of some kind. We'll have to find out which ones he got into this time."

Mrs. Duke laughed again, smiling, and gave him leave to go.

COMMUNICATIONS SECURE ROOM, BEIJING EMBASSY

Beer cans popped and Geoff raised his toast to friendship. "Good to see you two again. Patrick, congratulations on your advancement in the Diplomatic world. Assistant Ambassador now?"

"You'll be full Ambassador soon," Johnny put in. "We do remember Fowler, the Muncie Indiana Chevy dealer, don't we? Boy, did I get a kick out of shipping out his Cadillac with the precious cargo inside."

"How about you, Geoffrey?" Duffy asked. "I haven't heard where you went from here after Fowler got you transferred out."

"No harm done by Fowler. We didn't get along, as you know. I spent about a month in Hong Kong, Singapore, Malaysia and then got reassigned to Israel. The Company wanted me to get some experience working with the Mossad. And Johnny, I heard you turned down a commission in order to keep the Master Sergeant's stripes."

Johnny chuckled. "No gold braid for me. Not my style. This is my last gig. I'm out after this hitch. This overseas pay makes my retirement a little sweeter. Besides, Hong Kong is about the greatest R&R a marine can get."

"Johnny, you're a real nookie lookie. I hope you're being careful with all the exposure to AIDS around the world," Patrick said. "Where've you been the past five years?"

"Marine instructor and sometimes drill sergeant at Quantico. Good duty, spent time with my family who live there."

"How about you, ace?" Patrick tossed the ball back to Geoff. "Would you care to tell us why you've been reassigned to bouncing Beijing? After the Tiananmen affair five years ago, I'm surprised you have the nerve to show up again. The elephants at the MSS have long memories."

"We place our bets and take our chances, you redheaded mick," Geoff answered. "What happened to that Qantas stewardess you were so hot after the last time we were here? I thought you were about to settle down on the beaches in Queensland and let her support you for the rest of your life."

"Old sods," Patrick said. "'Twas like this. Alice had a friend in every port, as I found out later. I just happened to be her Beijing connection when they lit here once a week. I found her out when I arrived in Hong Kong one weekend. She was shacked up at the Shangri La with a dude from Germany. Going with her is like that book Evan Green wrote, Alice to Nowhere."

After two hours of upmanship, Johnny said good night and departed for the marine's quarters. Geoff cleaned up the beer cans and poured black coffee for himself and Patrick. They settled back with steaming mugs, legs draped over the arms of the deep cushioned chairs. "Patrick, you've been here for a year now with Madame Duke. Bring me up to date with the facts and the rumors."

"Tit for tat, Geoffrey, me boy. The Company isn't assigning you here just to practice your Mandarin. Want to cough up?"

"Never try to outfox an Irishman," Geoff said wryly. "What have you heard of Hong Kong going independent even before the handover to China? That's the brunt of what I'm supposed to dig up. Who's behind it and how far advanced are their plans?"

"We haven't got much on that, Geoff, though the rumors are flying. When you get to Hong Kong next week, look up your old friend Oliver Abernathy, the banker type with Hong Kong Shanghai Bank. He should clue you. As for Beijing, it looks like there'll be another worrisome demonstration on the anniversary of the Tiananmen Massacre."

"Damn, I wish we could sit in on a meeting at the Zhongnanhai

Complex. The break up of the USSR brought down so many walls of Communistic ideology. The Politburo must be watching and listening. It would be interesting to hear what they say, what they react to and implement. Let's jog down Changan tomorrow and check out the complex. We can't get in but maybe we can catch some of the aura by walking around and observing the street and the people."

"Okay, Geoff. I need the conditioning anyway. As for our take on China: the Politburo is paying attention to Gorby's survival and gradually pulling the Ruskies out of the economic mire. Japan has automobile factories over there and would love to get their chopsticks into China in a big way. China's joint venture with Boeing is working out, and Archer Daniels Midland has revolutionized the production of edible grains and vegetables here. The world is ready to help China get free, but they have to clean up their act first. What say the undercover world?"

"President Clinton is worried. Republicans in Congress are stirring the pot, trying to get re-elected at the next go-around with Reagan as president. The Company is trying to verify the rumors here and sent me back to work on it. With the Ambassador's permission and your help, I'll prowl around here for a few days and then skip into Hong Kong to see our friend."

The two tall, athletic Americans in navy blue sweats set an easy pace as they turned on to Jianguomen heading for the bridge.

"After the bridge, the street name changes to Changan, and all the memories of eighty-nine," Geoff said, and then added. "You did notice that we have company?"

"Can't miss a black Shanghai Special moving a jogging pace right behind us. You arrived yesterday, and they're on you this morning. How does it feel to be so popular?"

"Fame has its drawbacks, Pat. When we get back to the embassy, let's try to find out if the same guy, Fan Riqi, is still the Vice Commissar of the MSS."

They jogged up to the crown of the Jianguomen Bridge and down the other side, both breathing harder. "Uh oh, Geoff. Look who's here." The black Shanghai Special had pulled up almost alongside them, two heads peering through an open window. "We must have dropped out of their sight when we came down off the bridge."

"Thought they lost us, I bet. Just wave, smile and continue on our way. Ni hao," he shouted with a smile and a hand salute at the nearest head only a few feet away. The car quickly dropped back, the two heads jabbering at each other.

As they came into the central area of Changan, Geoff said, "Okay, Pat, now we walk and I talk for a while. I'll do the guide bit to help me get my bearings again. We just passed the Forbidden City. Not hard to recognize with that 50-foot-high picture of Chairman Mao. Tiananmen Square, of course, is that huge open area on the other side of Changan. Now we're approaching the Zhongnanhai Complex, infamous heart and soul of China, political capitol of the Republic. There are residences and large meeting rooms inside those big grey walls, did you know that?"

"The stone lions I'm looking at now are almost elephant size. Symbolic guardians, I suppose. Do you know just how large this complex is?" Patrick asked.

"If I remember correctly, the complex is at least a mile square. You're right about the symbolic lions, but don't miss the real guards with the AK47s on either side of those giant red doors."

"Uniforms are different from the army and local police, Geoff. Who are they?"

"An elite guard unit, not affiliated with the Army. They run security for the whole complex. They're from a tribe of ancient warriors, Mongols, Kublai Khan descendants, guards for the elite of the Party. Many of the Politburo reside here with their families. They also make political mischief, I'm told, in a large ornate central room. The meetings are said to last for days sometimes."

"I would imagine they don't have time limits and floor rules like our Senate and House of Representatives. You're right – it would be very interesting to get a video tape of one of their sessions. But, enough, Guide Martine, enough for this tour. Shall we head back? Thanks for a very informative view of the heart of Beijing. I'll do well to get back while I still have the energy to run. Just a lope please, Geoffrey."

BEIHAI PARK MSS OFFICE

"The Shaolin teams are launched, Comrade Commissar," Fan Riqi addressed his superior in the Covert Office of the Ministry of State Security. He thought of himself as an espionage chief at this moment rather than a policeman.

"There are eighteen teams of two agents trained and assigned to specific tasks. The monks of the Shaolin Temple have taught them well. They carry only a thin wire garrote for a weapon and fight with a hand chop or foot kick. I have met each team and assigned them a special password. They report to Yao Lin, but I will be their final authority."

Commissar Chou steepled his hands. One of the most powerful five or six men in the country, he exuded danger. "And does your illustrious Captain Yao Lin still maintain a relationship with General Tang Naiwa?"

After a long intentional pause, Fan smiled. "Yes, the fifth team reports Yao's activities while pretending to be his favorite agents. Tang and Yao have a weekly meeting that we monitor. The information we are allowed to receive is that the General is training a special corps of civil control troops in case the student situation should arise again."

When Chou had gone, Fan Riqi watched on his new video cameras as his superior left the office and passed through the restaurant overhead. In the six years Fan Riqi had worked with Chou Shi, there had never been a point of mutual trust.

The Minister never used an extra word, expressed a personal confidence, or had a close friend that Fan knew of. His quarters in the Zhongnanhai Complex, like those of the other leaders, were austere. Nevertheless, whenever he was summoned to call at his superior's home, Fan saw samples of every modern electronic device. Japanese manufacturers needed his approval to sell their products to the massive local market.

"Samples," they said. "Try this new VCR, Mr. Minister. Please test the latest facsimile machine, Mr. Minister. We need your opinion of the Z6000 compact disc, Mr. Minister. This hand-held camcorder will be a great asset to your Ministry, Mr. Chou." All this was done to oil the bureaucratic channels for importing such goods into China.

Fan ruminated. Now there was this new video coverage of the meetings, unauthorized and unknown to the Politburo members. The concealed cameras would augment his files, which were already bulging with history of the leaders. Conspiracy, corruption, nepotism, all would have video backup. Conversations in corners could now be recorded without the participants knowing. Something was cooking in the quiet brain of Chou, but no data was leaking out to give Fan a hint.

Relaxing in the chair, he put his feet up on the scarred desk, rumpled his hair and scratched his scalp with less enthusiasm than usual.

After a while, the Vice Commissar pulled a Great Wall cigar from the pocket of his open jacket. He went through the self-imposed ritual of biting the small point off, lighting it, spilling ashes down the front of his shirt to mingle with the scalp residue already there. Now to enjoy his other vice. He turned on the player and inserted a tape. He visualized himself as a famous chief of police detectives and he collected forbidden video tapes of such programs. Agents returning from the outside world brought him dubbed recordings of the American detective show Colombo and the non-violent MacGyver. He knew them all.

Later, Fan buzzed Hu Banyi, his administrative assistant and a computer genius. Hu created the software programs Fan required. One contained a list of more than 200,000 dissidents, providing instant details of who, where, and what they had done to earn the disapproval of the State. Cross-referenced with the names of family and friends, it provided control for the inevitable crackdowns required by the Politburo.

Fan used another program to keep track of aliens and foreign spies who pretended to be someone else. One name had popped up on the morning checklist of foreign arrivals. Geoffrey X. Martine, assigned as attaché to Ambassador Duke. He noted that the rank was now a full Commander in the US Navy, status with the CIA not known.

"Now this Martine," Fan said to Hu. "We have no record of him for the past five years. In 1989, he was identified as the CIA. Chief of Station. I met him outside the embassy when Professor Fang Linxi and his wife took refuge. He engineered their escape. Now he has suddenly reappeared on the scene. There has to be a reason when the CIA sends its top agent into Beijing."

"Comrade Fan. The bishop on the chess board is elusive, moving obliquely behind the lines of the battle. Martine is like the bishop and requires special attention."

"Well put, Comrade Hu. I'll have Yao put a team on Martine. Set up a red-alert file on him."

Pointing to the outer office and his ear, Fan inserted a tape of a high-pitched opera performance. He motioned Hu over to the exit screen and spoke into his ear.

"This afternoon we'll go over to the Zhongnanhai and check the installations of the new equipment in the general meeting room. Later this month, we need to take a trip to a couple of vacation spots. The Politburo will be visiting Chengde and Beidaihe for their summer meetings."

Hu nodded at the information. He valued his special relationship with his superior and keenly felt the thrill of planning matters of political intrigue under the guise of social intimacy.

Aloud, he said, "Whenever you call, Comrade Vice Commissar. The new equipment has arrived. NEC included an electronic chess board that moves figures around the board on direction. It operates either with a mouse or telephone modem for long distance competition. I'll bring it over to your apartment tonight and we'll try it out."

FOUR
ZHONGNANHAI, BEIJING

15 APRIL 1994

The eighteen-member Politburo, ruling committee of China, met in the central building. A three-day session had been called prior to the two official Spring Plenums. One was to be held at the ancient city of Chengde, where the empirial court of the dynasties traditionally went to escape the fierce heat of Beijing's summer. The other would take place at Beidaihe, a resort city on the shores of the Bohai Sea, north of Beijing.

Wu Xian, the eighty-one year old Elder Statesman, Vice Premier, Minister of the State Planning Commission and one of the six members of the Standing Committee of the Politburo nodded drowsily. The Vice Premier sat in one of eighteen overstuffed armchairs arranged in an oval grouping. Next to him sat Yang Yucie, an outspoken softliner, like himself. Low tables in the center held tea cups, assorted packages of cigarettes, ashtrays, and matches.

The old one listened to the babble of voices teasing his perception. The rattle of porcelain teacup lids and the flick of lighters marked pauses in the speeches. First drags created new clouds of smoke that filled the upper levels of the high ceiling. Noisy air-conditioning units attempted to clear the tepid air.

From this room, the forces of the Chinese Communist Party flowed through the Politburo, the eighteen most powerful men in China. They ruled over one billion people, 25% of the world's population, the largest citizenry of any country in the world.

Wu Xian pretended senility, babbling uncoordinated speech from time to time. He concentrated when the others thought he was drowsing. The ruse enabled him to catch snatches of undercurrent thoughts and the actual mood of the Politburo.

The Minister of the Central Commission for Disciplinary Inspection was speaking loudly enough to quiet the rest of the group momentarily. Cai Jixi was a hardliner, used to enforcing the four principles of Deng Xiaoping. Wu Xian knew them well: Upholding the Socialist Road; The People's Democratic Leadership; Leadership of the Communist Party; Marxism-Leninism-Mao Tsetung Thought...

Cai Jixi commanded attention with his loud voice and Szechuan accent. "The students are restless again, fomented by their overseas counterparts. I condemn them as traitorous young people who attend universities in the Western countries and refuse to return and fulfill their obligation to China and the Party.

"Those ungrateful wretches are urging our students to push again for immediate democracy. Fools that they are, they don't even know the meaning of the word and forget the lesson of past demonstrations. They talk of freedom of the press, individualism, even a right to select their education courses and careers. There is no patience for the slow emergence of the New Society. We must devise a plan to stop them once and for all.

"The Central Commission for Disciplinary Inspection has thousands of names and will control the dissidents. Remember," he said, looking around the room, "There are sons and daughters, nieces and nephews of members in this room on those lists."

A wave of angry muttering rolled over the room. The bald threat of blackmail did not sit well. Picking up a file folder, Cai Jixi removed a yellowed newspaper page, waving it at the group. "Comrades, I will read this article from the People's Daily:

"Under the leadership of the Central Committee, the heroic people of the Capital crushed with one stroke the counter-revolutionary incident in Tiananmen Square. The whole Nation warmly supports the two resolutions of the Party, vehemently denouncing the counter-revolutionary activities of a handful of class enemies and indignantly criticizes the crimes of a certain Comrade in attempting to subvert the Dictatorship of the Proletariat and restore Capitalism."

Wu Xian leaned over to his friend, whispering: "Written for the party, by the party, about the party. Will they ever learn the openness of truth?"

Cai Jixi continued, speaking loudly over the general murmurs of the bored audience. "Please note the date, Comrades, the 17th day of April, 1976, six months before Chairman Mao's death, and three years before we let Deng Xiaoping subvert us with the Dengist decade of reforms. Again, in 1989, we had to put down the counter-revolutionary activities and remove Zhao Ziyang, the weakling, from the Secretariat and his other commissions. Each time these events happen, we will have another Winter of Reaction to quiet them."

General Secretary Liu Chinan stood up, interrupting Cai Jixi. He pounded on the table for attention, his shrill voice almost screaming, demanding attention. "As Mayor of Shanghai during the June 1989 affair, I quelled all the disturbances in greater Shanghai without the interference of the People's Liberation Army or the killing of many innocent bystanders. We caught and quickly executed the three hooligans who set fire to the train and caused the death of many harmless spectators." After a sideways look at General Tang, his voice calmed to an inspirational tone. "There are other ways to quell demonstrations."

Wu Xian mentally noted the possible swing of an important vote. He concentrated as another voice spoke above the others in the guttural tones of the Inner Mongolian Province. Wu Xian reminded himself that it was from this direction that the Mongol hordes had conquered and laid waste to China in another era. Subsequent generations retained the genes of violence.

The voice of Tang Naiwa, General of the 27th Army, rose over the continuous murmur. Wu Xian likened him to the ancient warrior Kublai Khan. Tang had been elevated to the Politburo after the deadly elimination of the unarmed student demonstration at Tiananmen Square on the 4th of June five years ago. Now he was the self-appointed leader of the hardliners, arrogant and militaristic.

The harsh voice of Tang Naiwa boomed through the room like a cannon. "The White Browed Clique, elders of the Party, is becoming dull with toothless mouthing and spongy brains. Have you forgotten the dedication of The Long March led by the Great Helmsman, Chairman Mao, and the thousands of lives it cost? Have you forgotten how my Glorious 27th Army dealt with the 1989 student demonstrations and saved Beijing?"

Wu Xian listened for a time to the voice droning on about the soldiers' lives lost, no civilian casualties and the lying foreign press. "The fool will bring China down, as he nearly did five years ago," he whispered to Yang Yucie.

The harangue went on for an hour until the General Secretary called a recess for lunch. The garrulous General faced Wu Xian and his neighbor Yang, shaking his finger at the pair. "You old ones with toothless gums and arching spines should retire to Beidaihe or Hainan before you become a dead martyr like Hu Yaobang or a missing person like Zhao Ziyang." He laughed. "Some of those traitors to our party are reported to have died of cancer or are just not here anymore. At least we don't shoot those fools in public, like the Americans and their Kennedys."

Wu Xian noticed ears perking up at the mention of Hu and Zhao. Both leaders had once been respected members and friends of this group. Wu Xian mused to himself that Mao Tsetung was never accused of humanitarianism when it came to getting rid of a rival or dissenter.

Wu Xian, along with his friend Yang Yucie and the MSS Minister Chou Shi, caucused before leaving for lunch. Chou, at fifty-five, was the youngest member of the Politburo, Wu and Yang the oldest. Chou seldom made a speech. Yang often spoke for the softliners.

"You will speak after lunch, my old friend," Wu Xian addressed Yang. "The Politburo must hear a rebuttal, no matter how quiet the voice. Perhaps Minister Chou would care to comment on the General's call for outright war against the people."

Chou said quietly, "Tempt the snakes out of their holes, so we can cut their heads off."

Yang Yucie spoke up. "Chairman Mao said: 'Let the hundred flowers blossom and a hundred schools of thought contend.' Modern history does not record an execution of this plan, only the destruction of the flowers as they blossomed. The Tiananmen tragedy ploughed thousands of the tender sprouts into oblivion. Yes, I will speak this afternoon, but to a deaf audience."

"Comrade Chou," Wu Xian asked. "Do you foresee another uprising soon?"

"Aged and revered Comrades, I will inform the Politburo this afternoon of the dangers already clear. Another student uprising is probable. The hardliners in Taiwan are again rattling the drums. They believe our economic problems leave us vulnerable now. Hong Kong is considering seceding from the Mainland to become an independent country before the 1997 takeover. Rumors abound of a similar movement in Hainan. They would like to be economically free and allied with Hong Kong. The Dalai Lama is considering returning to Lhassa and demanding that the United Nations expel all Han Chinese from Tibet. There are rumblings, Comrades, from every perimeter of our country."

Wu Xian pretended to doze through most of the afternoon, as the General continued his harangue for permission to save China with tanks, guns and planes. Yang Yucie began the rebuttal, looking to gain support for the softliners.

Chou Shi proffered his warnings in a very short speech. Secure in their cocoons woven by General Tang, few paid any attention.

After the meeting, Wu and Yang retired to their apartments in the complex. Chou Shi watched General Tang enter a long black car that waited for him outside the Zhongnanhai on Changan Avenue. He caught a glimpse of a passenger inside the car, Captain Yao Lin.

BEIHAI PARK, MSS OFFICE

"The first full run of our new video system worked fine," Fan Riqi said to the three men in the office. "Good work on setting it up, Comrade Hu. A job well done, Team Wu, for infiltrating the meeting as service people. Now we have to reprocess the thirty hours of tape into the essence of that session. Prepare for a long night, Comrades."

Voluminous spume was culled over the course of the night, leaving the essence of plans revealed by the General. The weakness of the softliner's rebuttal underscored the mood of the Politburo. The Beidaihe and Chengde meetings would be their last chance to sway the leaders away from military crackdown on any dissidents. Private caucuses held during lunch and recesses revealed important information about possible splits and reactions.

Fan Riqi fell asleep on the leather couch in his office, an expired cigar drooping from his fingertips. Hu gave final instructions to Team Five. "Leave the finished document in my safe. Destroy all residue. Forget everything you saw and heard."

The Shaolin team created one copy and then followed their instructions.

FIVE
HONG KONG

20 APRIL 1994

The red light of the Star Ferry gate changed to green. A bell rang announcing the boarding. Waiting crowds surged forward, down the ramp, and across the draw gate onto the upper tier of the boat. Geoff wore a plain white t-shirt, faded jeans, a light poplin jacket, and a camera around his neck. He edged through the crowd to the forward compartment, reversed the back of the seat to face forward on the last bench, and sidled over to the window.

A pretty young Chinese woman, not much more than five feet tall, he judged, dressed in a tight blue denim mini-skirt and eggshell silk blouse, took the seat next to him.

"How long does it take to get across?" he said, in an evident ruse to strike up a conversation.

She clenched her shoulder bag tighter, moved slightly away from him, and without even looking at his face, replied, "Seven and a half minutes."

"That's strange. Another person told me it was ten minutes and I don't even know where this scow lands." Geoff looked squarely into her face. Dark brown eyes flickered beneath purplish eye shadow. Tiny red lips spoke, almost without movement.

"Sometimes we have to wait for the opposite ferry to clear, which would take a couple more minutes. The scheduled time is seven and a half minutes. We land to the left of the building over there, called Wing On House. You can see the sign on the top of it from here. Enjoy your visit, tourist," she said with a smile.

The woman stood up, her head about even with Geoff's while he was sitting. A small piece of cardboard fell off her lap as she arose and moved away. He bent to pick it up. It was a weight tab from the scale in the ferry waiting area. The fortune on one side read: "Fear the East Wind. Welcome the West Wind." On the other side, the weight was 45.5 kilos, the number 1506 penciled in underneath it. The tiny doll-like figure disappeared into the mid-ship crowd waiting to disembark.

Geoff looked for her again when the ferry docked. The crowd surged, merging with the other passengers, all rushing to their trams and taxis on the Hong Kong side. The mini-skirted figure had melted into the scene. He took the overhead walkway around the General Post Office and down the long elevated open passageway over the street traffic. There was no hurry, still forty-five minutes. Seven-thirty she had said, room 1506 Wing On House noted on the weight ticket. Continuing on the overhead ramp, he crossed over Des Vouex Road, down the stairs to the street level and over to the opposite corner.

Geoff stopped to buy a Herald American from the street kiosk, looking casually around to spot anyone trying to follow him. There could be one or a dozen – no way to tell on these crowded streets. With a half hour yet to kill, he tucked the paper under his arm and merged with the crowds. The wealth of jade, pearls, diamonds, and gold ornaments in the jewelry windows continually amazed him. The glass reflected the people traffic around him. *Watch it, hotshot. There's someone out there. Melt into the crossover traffic when the street light changes and keep your head down. You stand out like a flag pole on this street.*

Geoff took another look around, joined the next traffic mass crossing back, and entered the Wing On House. It was time. He took the elevator to the eighteenth floor and walked down three flights to the fifteenth. The office numbered 1506 had a plaque beside the door that read "Trans-Pacific Publishing"; it was closed except for a desk light visible in the reception area. His watch read exactly 7:30. An unmarked door down the hallway opened. Dark brown eyes flashed at him and a tiny dark head of black silk hair beckoned. Quickly, he slipped in, the door closing behind him.

Three men were standing in the room. Two Chinese half-crouched on either side of the inner office door, and a tall graying Englishman relaxed at a desk on the side of the room. The woman he had met on the ferry smiled and extended her hand. "Welcome, Mr. Tourist. Quan Quan, deliverer of secret messages."

Geoff bent down to the child-like figure, completely covering the tiny hand with his. "Nice to meet you, Quan Quan, all ninety-nine pounds of you, allowing a half kilo for the clothes, of course," Geoff said with a wink and a grin.

Quan Quan smiled back, and then turned to introduce him to the others. "You know Mr. Abernathy, I assume. Mr. Tsai and Mr. Xiu, this is the American, Geoffrey Martine."

Abernathy spoke first. "Glad to see you again, Geoff. It's been quite a while since we worked together. Five years since you pulled that hat trick getting the professor and his wife out of the Embassy and onto the container ship. All we knew was to meet the ship when it arrived and take off container number 1376787 as quickly as we could. That was a surprise. We opened it and found the Ambassador's limousine with the two of them sitting in it, right as rain."

Geoff's eyes crinkled, the half-smile emerging from the side of his mouth. "Good to see you, Ollie. Sorry we didn't get a chance to talk about it then. My boss offloaded me on the first plane leaving Beijing, which just happened to be going to Singapore."

He went over to the other two men, dressed in black jeans and dark shirts, and extended his hand. "Geoffrey Martine, gentleman. Ni hao mah," he said. "I understand you have a message for my government."

"Hao mah, sheh sheh," one answered. "I'm Tsai and my companion is Xiu. The immortal, who watches over us, has indeed brought good fortune, Commander Martine. We too have heard of your exploits."

Geoff looked at them both without commenting on the title they used with his name. This was no chance meeting. These men were well-informed operatives who knew him and the fact that he was in Hong Kong.

Abernathy absorbed the scene without comment, then turned to the woman. "Quan Quan, would you be good enough to man the security desk in the outer office? The screen at the desk monitors the hallway and fire exits. In case of a disturbance, just punch number three on the keyboard. It will flash a red light in here."

"I'm familiar with the system, sir. We have coverage in and around the building by Hong Kong Police plain clothes units. It would be very hard to penetrate."

All eyes followed as the mini-skirted figure walked out.

"Your assistant appears very efficient, Oliver," Geoff commented.

"Hong Kong born and bred, Geoff. Survival and efficiency is their creed."

Tsai spoke, regaining Geoff's attention. "We too have heard of the great escape you engineered, though up to now we did not know how it was accomplished. Our congratulations, Commander Martine; you may be called upon to do another evacuation soon."

The office was decorated for consultations: comfortable chairs, coffee table, service bar in one corner and published books mounted like pictures on the walls. The desk Abernathy stood behind was off to one side, equipped with a communications system, black onyx twin pen set and business cards.

"Please sit, gentlemen," Abernathy said, standing to face both the inner and outer doors. "Martine, as you appear to know, is the United States Naval Attaché to the Embassy in Beijing. I understand he has the authority, if the occasion warrants, to report directly to his President. In this instance, I have secured permission to report directly to our Prime Minister. Anything you tell us here will be relayed directly to the top of our governments."

Geoff studied the two agents as Abernathy spoke, assessing the various possibilities of their visit. They remained inscrutable while listening to Abernathy, no facial expression or exchange of looks between them.

Abernathy continued. "You requested direct contact with our leaders. It's not possible under the existing circumstances without exposing them or you to unnecessary risk. You can speak freely to Commander Martine and me. This is a safe office, quite often used by Her Majesty's Royal Naval Intelligence."

Tsai spoke up. "You mentioned a code name in our discussion earlier today, Mr. Abernathy: SINO-CIDE. How did it come about?"

"Our countries, with the Australians, Germans, and Canadians, have been watching events about China. We have combined our various information sources and data under that name. The American President suggested it because of the deep concern he has for China's regression into doctrine instead of democracy. In short, we believe you blokes are committing suicide, as a nation. The past five years since the Tiananmen Massacre have had horrendous ripple effects in our countries. We have been monitoring the internal upheaval. Believe me, speaking for England, Her Majesty's Government will do anything in its power to help alleviate China's problems, as we see them."

Geoff added, "Our President has taken much political abuse for his continued friendship. Maybe you didn't hear at the time, but right after the Tiananmen Affair, he sent our Secretary of State, James Baker, to China secretly. His mission was to try to bash some sense into your leaders' heads. Instead, the President got bashed by the media and Congress for even trying.

"Ex-President Nixon was then invited to go over and put his two fen into the affair. Your guys jerked him around, smiled for the cameras, treated him to a banquet, and told us to mind our own business. Gentlemen, please tell us who you are and what group you represent before we go any further."

Tsai and Xiu looked at each other, shrugged, and Tsai nodded an okay for his friend to speak first. "We are special agents of the Ministry of State Security, of which you have limited information. Officially, our designation is Shaolin Wu, the fifth team of specially trained operatives."

"How many teams are there? Where are they stationed? How do you know about Abernathy and me? What's your specific assignment here? Does your leader suspect you have information? Is it possible you were followed by another team?" Geoff fired the barrage of questions at them, and was about to continue with a few more.

Tsai let his lips form a slight smile. "Mahn mahn, Commander, slowly slowly. We are defectors from the Communist system, not traitors to China. There is some information we are willing to divulge, but we look forward to returning to our homes and families some day with respect. The teams we speak of are all graduates of the

Shaolin Temple Martial Arts School and carry no weapons, except our physical training in defense and offense. This is equivalent to, but far more intense, than what you call Karate. Other than our bodies, our one offensive weapon is a wire we carry, in your language a garrote, for extreme emergencies." Tsai, without appearing to move, suddenly had a thin wire in his hand drawn from a hidden recess. Leather hand loops would allow him to pull the garrote tight without cutting the fingers.

Geoff and Abernathy instinctively reacted by stepping back and crouching to fend off whatever might come next. Tsai smiled thinly and shook his head. "No, I'm not attacking, gentlemen."

Tsai coiled the wire and returned it to a side pocket at his thigh. "As for the other teams, we suspect there are about eighteen, but have little knowledge of their disposition. We're all completely autonomous and report to no one outside the borders of the Mainland."

"Geoff," Abernathy said. "There's little we can verify of their story. They walked into the Bank this morning and filled out flawless employee applications. Quan Quan brought them into my office for interview and they dropped the story on me that they have special information to impart to our leaders. When I asked why they were talking to a personnel officer, Tsai here just smiled and asked to have you included. I didn't even know you were in Hong Kong, but they did.

"The whole incident was bizarre enough to arrange this meeting. Orders are that if anything happens to either one of us, they're not to leave here alive and they know it. We know of their organization, the Ministry of State Security, but not of these special teams. It must be a very select force that Chou Shi has built up, that is, if he is still head of the organization."

"You are right, Mr. Abernathy," Tsai said. "Chou Shi is our Commissar and has reorganized the entire force in the past five years, a direct result of the Tiananmen affair. Outside Beijing, we contact our company, Shaolin Branch of the MSS, through the business offices of the China National Arts and Crafts Corp. We communicate under the pretext of being merchants with a code based on trading goods and paying contracts."

Geoff watched the two carefully during the discussion. Both appeared extremely bright, well but commonly dressed, spoke English with only a slight accent, and would melt into any Hong Kong crowd easily. "All right then, why are you here? If you are claiming political asylum, why go to Abernathy? Please tell us how you singled the two of us out."

Tsai released a thin, knowing smile. "Commander Martine, you are the CIA Station Chief for China, well documented in our files. The escape you engineered five years ago has been a classic example in our orientation program. We heard three days ago that you were headed to Hong Kong. Fan Riqi, our leader, thought you might be up to something and sent us in to watch you. Your normal base in Hong Kong is the Shangri La, so it was not difficult to pick up your trail. Mr. Abernathy's designation as Chief of Royal Naval Intelligence, Hong Kong, under his cover as a bank personnel officer, is also well known."

Tsai continued, bolstering Geoff's suspicions even more. "May I suggest that whatever you think of the MSS, do not underestimate them. Under the guidance of Chou Shi and the dedication of our Vice Commissar, Fan Riqi, we have gathered a good deal of information on the outside world as it relates to China. Xiu and I lost close friends during the Tiananmen Massacre and have waited these five years for a chance to further the cause of Democracy."

The young man was ardent. He stared unflinching into first Abernathy's eyes and then Martine's as he spoke. Each word was expressed slowly, sometimes with difficulty, as he sought the correct English word or phrase. "A few days ago we were assigned to cover meetings of the Politburo in the Zhongnanhai. Yes, we spy on our own leaders. On the orders of Chou Shi, we taped the entire three days of the pre-plenum meeting with new camcorder devices. Tapes were edited and condensed for the Commissar. We have brought a copy of that footage to you to take to your leaders. It will make them aware of the evil still lurking within the Politburo and the struggle by the softliners to change the situation. There are dangerous men in command in our country. With this new information, it's possible that friendly countries can save China's remaining good leaders and thousands of lives."

Oliver and Geoff exchanged glances, not willing to interrupt the emotional discourse of the young agent. Geoff shrugged his shoulders at Oliver with eyebrows raised in an "I don't know" attitude.

Tsai was breathing hard, each word emphasized, the tone increasing, obviously emotional. Xiu laid a hand on his arm and took over the story. "When the students demonstrate this year, on the fifth anniversary of the Tiananmen Disaster, it's possible they will be annihilated. Somehow you must help us prevent that, or China will become a great danger to world peace in the next century."

Geoff paced the room, stopping in front of each agent to look him in the eye, and then went over to the desk facing Abernathy. "This is a bunch of crap, Ollie. These two may be what they say, agents for the MSS, but to think someone is going to let them copy the tapes, get out of the country, and throw a pitch at us is nuts. They're leading us down the country lane. The only part I can't figure out is why." He pursed his lips. "Tell you what, fellows. Leave the tape on the desk here and take off. We'll get a real kick out of seeing the inside of the Zhongnanhai or wherever your movie director staged this stunt. The next thing you know, someone will attempt to kill them to impress us. Is that how you see it, Ollie?"

Before Abernathy could answer, a red light over the inner door flashed. There was a loud noise in the outer office. Abernathy swore under his breath, reached for the phone, pressed three and whispered, "Trouble, activate Prince Andrew, activate Prince Andrew."

Running feet sounded outside in the hallway. Geoff was at the side of the outer door in a moment, waiting for it to burst open. Tsai and Xiu took positions on either side of the inner door, crouching, hands at either side poised as weapons. With a gun suddenly in his hand, Oliver nodded. Geoff pulled his door open and then stepped back behind it, flattened against the wall. Oliver crouched behind the desk, gun ready. Tsai and Xiu at the same moment pulled open their door and in a well-rehearsed action somersaulted into the outer office.

Abernathy, gun extended, was trying to cover Geoff's action and that of the two agents airborne in the adjoining room. He moaned at what he saw through the open door: Quan Quan slumped over the monitor in the outer office, her silky black hair spread over the keyboard.

Flashes of black cloth moved faster than the eye could comprehend. The crack of feet and hands against bone and flesh resounded as blows were traded. In the jumble of flying bodies, the attackers were recognizable in black turtlenecks, heads covered with a black cloth, slotted for eyes, nose and mouth.

A similar form flew through the open doorway from the hall. Oliver tried to target the fast-moving figure. At the instant of entry, he saw Geoff slam the door hard trying to catch the figure as it entered. The attacker was too fast, catapulting across the room. There was no chance to get off a shot. Geoff was in the line of fire. The human missile landed. Abernathy felt the gun tearing out of his hand, flying through the air. The last thing he remembered was trying to fend off a blow aimed at his head.

Geoff saw the gun fly through the air and Ollie go down from a hand chop. There would be no time to get the gun before the figure reached him. His mind generated reactions, body tensing for the battle to come. This guy is good, hot shot. Set yourself for a flying body. In a continuing motion, the masked figure swirled off the incapacitated Abernathy and somersaulted through the air. Geoff recoiled at the impending danger. The body hit him full on, forcing him to crash against the wall. Geoff had just a moment of reflex action to lift a knee against the attacker's groin. The momentum did the damage as the two bodies met. The masked figure screamed in agony as he curled in a ball on top of Geoff.

Stunned and breathless, unable to gain enough strength to strike back until his lungs recaptured vital air, Geoff finally rolled the groaning body off him. Reflexively, the attacker began to uncoil, trying to get his feet under him to spring back. Geoff was the first to rise and quickly kicked the attacker behind the ear with one foot and then spun around and stomped on the injured groin full force with the other. The psychological effect of severe pain plus stunning action was part of the jungle-fighting technique Geoff had learned the hard way. In his youth he had had to defend himself in the wild brawls in North Queensland against unruly white and aborigine adversaries.

Abernathy dragged himself up off the floor, holding onto the desk for support. "What happened?"

"Get the gun, Ollie. It's in the corner. I'm going to see how the rest of the team made out."

Tsai and Xiu were standing over the other attacker, who was slumped on the floor between them. Feet were pounding down the hall. The staccato of automatic weapons blasted their fury. Screams of pain and shouted commands filled the air, indistinguishable from the surrounding noise.

Geoff rushed over to Quan Quan, fear of what he might find tensing his face. He slipped his hand under the chin and lifted the lovely head toward him, feeling for a pulse in the neck vein. The eyes were glazed over, but his fingers felt the slow throbbing beat of life. He breathed a sigh of relief.

"She's alive, Oliver, probably a neck chop. Better get an ambulance. This lady is going to have one enormous headache."

Drawn guns appeared at both doors of the office as agents cautiously entered. "You all right, sir?" the OIC addressed Abernathy whilst checking out the room.

"Alive, Peter. What's the damage out there?" Abernathy was leaning against the door jamb for support.

"The two outside took out four of my men before we could get them. Two are dead and the other two look in pretty bad shape. Our lads were hit in the knee cap and head. The attack was so fierce there was no choice but to cut the bloody bastards to bits. I would have liked to keep one alive to see if we could get anything out of him. What's the score in here?"

Geoff answered. "It looks like our Shaolin team took care of this one." He pointed to a crumpled figure on the floor. "With luck we can get something out of the one in the other room. He did irritate me, and I lost my temper somewhat. Damaged, but alive."

In the hallway, the two surviving security police were stretched out on the floor, waiting for medical attention and moaning with pain. The dead officers in the hall were gruesome. A telltale ribbon of blood oozed out of their necks from the garroting. The other two forms were clad in black pants, turtleneck jerseys and head masks. One still held a round loop of wire in his hand, dripping blood. The whole hallway was crimson with blood spattered on the walls, ceiling and floor.

"We had to empty our autos, sir, to stop them. Our men were down almost the moment we sighted them. They looked like monstrous bats attacking."

Abernathy looked at Tsai. "You did warn us. These are your Shaolin Teams?"

"Yes," Tsai answered, pulling the mask off the man he had taken down with the aid of Xiu. "I know this one. He and his partner are, or I should say were, the cream of the group. They trained at the Temple when we were there and often competed against us. He headed right for me, and could have taken out everybody had we allowed him."

Geoff beckoned to Abernathy, Tsai and Xiu. While Peter's team took care of the clean-up, they talked quietly in a corner of the back room. "My apologies for doubting you," Geoff said. "It looks like your teams play for keeps and Comrade Fan is on his toes. They must have missed the tape or suspected you. Do you agree, Ollie?"

"Most assuredly. Let's make some copies immediately with English translations and get them off to our principals at once. Mr. Tsai, Mr. Xiu, will you be good enough to assist us? Both Martine and I are proficient in Mandarin but we don't want to miss any nuances or innuendos. Then we have a further problem. You certainly can't return to China, and it won't be safe in Hong Kong as soon as word seeps back what has happened."

Tsai answered quietly. "Proceed, gentlemen. We have a maximum of twenty-four hours until they send follow-up teams. Xiu and I will take care of ourselves. It will be better if you don't know where we are."

SIX
WASHINGTON, D.C.

21 APRIL 1994

The Air Force jet with a single passenger landed smoothly at Andrews Air Force Base, appearing out of the early morning fog on the deserted runway. Geoff thought the scene was eerie. He saw a car waiting in the swirling mist, a trench-coated figure standing beside it. "Thanks for the lift," he said to the pilot. "Not bad time, considering the seven-minute stops at Honolulu and Luke. You going back to Guam right away?"

"After some shut-eye and Jacuzzi time to loosen up the muscles at the BOQ here at Andrews," the pilot replied, stretching his arms. "Don't forget to put in for your frequent flyer mileage."

"Do you think they'll include the helicopter sector from Hong Kong to the flattop and the rocket jock that shot me from the ship to Guam?" Geoff asked with a grin.

"No problem, Commander. The Company will give you double mileage for that segment – hazardous duty, you know."

The trench-coated figure waited at the ramp with an extra coat over his arm. Geoff hoisted himself out of the seat and climbed down the side of the aircraft. He stretched arms and legs and jogged in place to get the cocoon seat kinks out of his muscles.

"Commander Martine? Shadron from the White House Secret Service detail. It's a little chilly at two in the morning," he said, holding the coat open. "The President is expecting us."

The deserted streets of the capital further emphasized the eeriness of the past eighteen hours. Agent Shadron asked no questions and the driver of the black Lincoln stayed mute. At the gates to the White House, he automatically rolled down all the windows. Shadron flipped open his badge, Martine his passport, while guards on both sides flashed lights around the interior. Waved in, they drove around to the rear. "Please come with me, Commander Martine," the close-mouthed agent said.

Geoff followed his guide through the labyrinth of hallways and up the elevator. Shadron knocked lightly on the door as they reached the Oval Office and opened it without waiting for a reply.

"Commander Geoffrey Martine, sir." Geoff walked in and the agent closed the door behind him.

The President, who was sitting at the desk drumming his fingers, arose as Geoff was announced. Secretary of State Christopher and CIA Director Twetten sat at either end of the leather sofa, coffee cups on a table in front of them. Geoff walked across the deep plush carpet, which was emblazoned with the United States Coat of Arms, and came to attention. He saluted his Commander in Chief, President Clinton, who returned the salute before coming around the desk to shake hands with Geoff.

"Welcome home, Commander. You know the Secretary, of course."

Both Christopher and Twetten got up and shook hands with Geoff.

"You've raised our antennae, Commander. Is there a story that goes with this earthshaking tape? Can we save China from herself?"

"Yes, sir, there is a story. As for saving China, I'm just a gopher. You people are the experts." He opened his shirt to reveal the cartridge taped to his chest. "Let's get this masterpiece off me and plug it in. Then you can see for yourself. The translation was done hurriedly by the Britisher, me and two Chinese agents. Want to put this in the VCR, Chief?" Geoff addressed Twetten. "We'll see what goes on in the Red House of China."

The lights were dimmed so they could see the screen better. They sat for the next two hours watching excerpts of the stellar performance of the Politburo of the People's Republic of China in secret session at the Zhongnanhai in Beijing.

LONDON

Oliver Abernathy greeted the Prime Minister, the M15 Chief, and the Secretary for Foreign Affairs at Number Ten Downing Street. They all sat in the drawing room to view a duplicate of the tape being run in Washington. Just as it finished, the phone rang. The Foreign Secretary answered. "Prime Minister, it is the President of the United States."

"Bill? Yes, this is the PM. I was about to ring you up. I assume you've seen the tape. They're a confused bloody lot, wouldn't you say?" He paused to listen, and then replied. "I agree, we have to talk. It looks like the play is on the side of the good guys. I'll show this to Bonn and Canberra, and you contact Toronto? They're vitally interested also." He paused to listen to the affirmation from Washington. "Thank you, Bill. Please give my regards to Hillary."

The Prime Minister addressed Abernathy. "Oliver, we've known each other for almost a quarter of a century since you were first posted to China. I respect your knowledge and love of the Far East. Please give me your worst and best scenario of the events now emerging in that complicated part of the world."

M15 brought over a cup of tea for the exhausted messenger. Unlike his CIA counterpart, Oliver did not have the capacity to sleep through a problem. The Hong Kong and Shanghai Bank had appointed him as Branch Manager in Shanghai during the Cultural Revolution to endure the mindless humiliation of foreigners. Marriage to a Korean wife did not improve his chances for promotion within the staid parameters of the Bank's moral views. Working under cover with Naval Intelligence provided the opportunity to actively assuage the constant abrasion of his feelings for the Communist leadership of China.

"Prime Minister, Foreign Minister, M15, we could evaluate for weeks and months, as we already have since the 1997 accord. My personal opinions, in disagreement with the contract, are well known to you in this room. Briefly, if the hardliners led by General Tang Naiwa succeed in brushing aside or burying the few sane heads in the Politburo, there will be pure dictatorial anarchy. The students will erupt. That is an event you may count on, possibly by the 4th of June on the anniversary of the Tiananmen Massacre. Unlike the European

Eastern Block changes, it will be a bloody, bloody affair. There will be suppression on the scale of Cambodia, Viet Nam, Stalin's Russia, and Hitler's Germany. Not only will the mainlanders suffer horribly, but Hong Kong will be devastated."

Oliver took a sip of tea while the PM sighed in response. "Hong Kong, created by Great Britain to be the Pearl of the Pacific. It is our greatest economic and humanitarian adventure, and if things go badly in China, our current success will become a limp nameless bead in the vast Pacific."

"Yes, Prime Minister," Abernathy agreed. "Hong Kong, I predict, will not accept Communist domination in any form. All financial activities will leave, accompanied by all, I repeat all, brain power of any kind. The hundred years of Great Britain's extraordinary effort to make an economic wonderland of a mere island in the South China Sea will be lost like Atlantis. And then there is the domino effect on the weak links in Southeast Asia."

"Pray tell us the other side of the coin. What if we would and could help the softliners?" The Prime Minister's face was lined with worry. Wrinkled brows and pursed mouth showed his deep concern.

Oliver sipped his tea and looked over to the Department Chief. "Twining's Orange Pekoe, M15? Very good, sir, thank you." Marshaling the last of his strength, Abernathy sat up straight in his chair and continued. "The other side of the coin is that I feel there's a chance. Martine and I had a long talk with the two Chinese agents after the bloody episode. They have probably given their lives to bring out this tape. We expect them to be hunted down by the MSS. There is no deviation allowed from one hundred percent loyalty."

Abernathy paused to formulate a thought, his physical weariness now becoming more evident in slurred speech and eyes straining to stay open. M15 spoke up. "Oliver, you're past exhausted and need to rest. Give us a concise summary and we'll meet again tomorrow to flesh out a plan."

"Yes, sir, I'll try. Wu Xian is the principal softliner, supported completely by Yang Yucie. According to Tsai, the agent, Wu pretends senility, but they have noted he misses nothing and is probably the sanest member of the Politburo. Wu Xian is in imminent personal danger and may disappear like his predecessors who dared to oppose

Deng Xiao Ping and Mao Tsetung. If he can be freed, it's possible that he can initiate a survival plan."

Struggling to keep his thoughts straight, Abernathy said, "Let me leave you with this. Tsai has a female friend who is close with Wu Xian's daughter – both are university students in Beijing. Her estimation of the situation is that if Wu Xian cannot sway the Politburo in the upcoming plenums, he would like to defect and work from the outside."

"I assume Geoffrey Martine has given the same information to President Clinton?"

Seeming to have gained a second wind, Abernathy brightened in the summation. "Yes, Prime Minister. I'm sure Geoff will have given the same story to his superiors, but that's not the whole tale. There is much talk in Hong Kong of seceding and initiating a new country. Border provinces of the mainland that are familiar with and enjoy economic autonomy could possibly join them. Then there is the wild card, Taiwan. Old followers of Chiang Kai Shek still dream of taking over the mainland."

"So, Oliver, you and this Martine have thought of a plan to save the whole of Southeast Asia?"

Oliver's conservative lips allowed only the ghost of a smile to show his answer. "Yes, Prime Minister. We should help Hong Kong organize and arrange a political miracle. Martine will attempt to contact Wu Xian to defect and escape. Otherwise, the United Kingdom may have five million Hong Kong residents camping on its doorstep. We would have to contend with a boat-people emigration of twenty percent of China's mainland population. Two hundred million people."

BEIHAI PARK, OFFICE OF THE MSS

Vice Commissar Fan Riqi slumped at his desk. Half-glasses sat on the cluttered surface next to the ashtray containing his partially smoked cigar. Both of his hands massaged his scalp to stimulate the brain, and his eyes narrowed to a murderous glint. Captain Yao Lin was standing at attention in front of the desk, lips trembling, sweating in the air-conditioned room.

"What do you mean they got away? It's your job to see that the teams remain on a leash, assigned to do exactly what we instruct them to do, no more, no less. Tell me exactly what happened and don't leave out or embellish anything. If I detect one nuance of falsehood, you will never leave this room alive. Do you understand, Yao?"

Chou Shi, listening from behind the screen, eyes closed in concentration, compressed his lips in anger. The round face, prematurely bald, behind small, square, gold-rimmed glasses, gave him the look of a Buddhist scholar. News of Shaolin Wu's defection had surprised and frustrated him. He did not like surprises.

His computer-like brain scanned over the details. He needed to have control over the loose ends. What was Tang's part to play? How much did Fan Riqi know of the overall general plan? Had the Politburo's plans been exposed by Shaolin Wu's defection? He needed to compartmentalize, then act. First, eliminate Wu Team. Then find out Wu Xian's plans. Control the students, Hong Kong, Hainan and Taiwan. He had come too far to fail now. China had to have one leader, a new Great Helmsman.

Captain Yao Lin spoke slowly, thinking each word, knowing his life depended on an answer that Fan would accept. "Teams Ar-shir and San-shir-san were sent into Hong Kong to pick up defectors and spies. Shaolin Wu was directed to follow the American spy when we discovered he was leaving Beijing. If you remember, we were concerned at his sudden departure so soon after arriving. By sheer good fortune, Team Wu was seen by San-shir-san going into the Hong Kong Bank at 1300 yesterday. San-shir-san happened to be riding by the entrance on a tram and recognized them. They had trained at the same time at Shaolin. As is required, they reported the incident. Wu Team didn't convey the same information when they checked in.

I was alerted and directed Ar-shir team to pick up their trail. It led to the office in the Wing On House that we know to be a rendezvous for the British Intelligence. We were in trouble. Obviously they wanted to earn money selling secrets to the British."

Fan put his glasses back on and tilted back in his chair to see the nervous underling better. "I know that, fool. You are severely criticized for not knowing the team could be susceptible to treason. It's necessary that we re-evaluate all the teams for a possible re-occurrence. Run their histories through the profile program and see if we can pinpoint any future problems."

"Unfortunately, there is more, sir. A fight of some consequence ensued. The two follow-up teams appear to have been eliminated and Wu Team is missing. Our agent in the Hong Kong Police Department called in. Two of the officers have been killed, another two severely wounded. Six body bags were removed from the building. Ambulances took four more officers to the hospital. Our operative is trying to get more exact information."

"Damage control, Comrade Fan, damage control," Chou Shi announced after the underling had left the room. "This Democracy idea is a virus creeping throughout the country. We must regain the initiative. There has to be some plot going on with the American spy reassigned here. You and the brain Hu Banyi get your heads together and give me a situation update. The country is rumbling from one border to the next. The next Plenum of the Politburo is in one month. We must have a complete report by then. We can decide counteraction. Don't disappoint me, Comrade."

Fan watched him disappear behind the screens and then followed him on the monitor into the restaurant. Relaxed now with Chou gone and the minions dispatched to various assignments, he propped his feet up on the desk, fumbled through the ashtray to find a stub long enough to relight, and punched a button on the console.

"Comrade Hu," Fan addressed the man when he responded to the summons. "Tonight we have a meeting, my apartment, six o'clock. I'll prepare dinner for us. We have much to discuss over the chess board."

SEVEN
UNIVERSITY OF HEBEI

25 APRIL 1994

At the University of Space Technology in Hebei, small groups of male and female students laughed and talked in the fresh air, crisp with leftover winter. The sun warmed them from the constant chill of poorly heated dormitories. They tipped their faces to the sun and discussed forbidden subjects. Signs posted around the campus read:

ALL INFORMAL MEETINGS OF STUDENTS OUTSIDE THE LECTURE HALLS ARE LIMITED TO TEN PERSONS UNTIL FURTHER NOTICE. VIOLATION OF THIS RULE WILL BRING IMMEDIATE DISMISSAL FROM THE UNIVERSITY. Signed, the Central Committee for Disciplinary Inspection

"Remember when Professor Fang Linxi and his wife escaped?" asked one student from a group lounging under a banyan tree. "A brother at Berkley in America got word to me, if you remember, how the Americans acted to help them break out. Can you imagine what would have happened to them if they had remained in China after the great demonstration?"

"And then we got the three gooks called Administrative Coordinators taking over our campus," sneered another member of the group, pointing to the sign. "It used to be fun getting a gang together for a discussion on how we would change the country or have a beer bust. Now we have to sneak around just to pass the word about our plans."

"I'm a third-year astrophysics student," a woman spoke up. "They are threatening to withhold my graduation certificate if I miss those stupid meetings the three of them give. The very title of the lecture, Teaching Students Proper Respect for the Party, makes the bile rise in my throat. Can you imagine, they actually think we would listen to that prattle! It's disgusting."

"Sister, I hear you. If we skip class, they have the authority to throw us out or to prevent us graduating and securing jobs in the space program."

Gaining bravado from the conversation, the students' voices became a clamor more in line with their private thoughts.

"Hebei has become a police state, centered around our campus. They are afraid of us."

"What you say about being a police state is true. Our leaders intend to keep us knuckled down forever. What will they do when we demonstrate again? Shoot down more of us until only robots remain?"

"The government claimed only a few students were hurt and none killed in '89. We counted 1289 empty seats at UST alone. Will we ever know what happened to everyone?"

"Yes, Brother," another young man replied. "Our fellow students at the University of California, Berkeley, are gathering the data. The 159 Universities involved in the Tiananmen Massacre in 1989 reported their Empty Seats. The latest total is 22,689 students classified as dead, missing, or escaped. Berkeley organizers call their group the Chinese Students' Council."

"Do you really think they can make their voices heard?"

The young man replied boldly, "My contact with the West said donations from friends and overseas Chinese around the world fund it. They are following the same system used by the Jews after the Holocaust to maintain a permanent data bank including every one of the unfortunates."

"So many," murmured one of the students who had been quiet so far. "My cousin, who was there in Shanghai at the time, said the train plowed into the crowd, killing and injuring dozens of people."

Another voice added, "Seventeen people executed in Jinan, their crimes never published."

"It seems like all of us know of one incident or another," said a young man with long hair and a guitar on his lap. "I climbed Mount Huangshan this spring. Three students from Hefei University that I met there told me the total list was more than 150,000."

The woman astrophysicist broke in. "I have heard that almost all forty thousand of our fellow students in the United States have officially joined the Council. Branches are in universities all over America." Her voice dropped to a whisper as two more students joined the group. "The Council gets most of our information to us through the Voice of America broadcasts. They maintain contact with each other covering every province of China. Maybe this time we'll succeed."

"Yes, Sisters and Brothers, we have a better communication system now, but we must keep tight to the rules. Pass the word. We have forty days to wait. Never use names when we talk or communicate. Sister, Brother, Teacher, Professor, Aunt or Uncle is sufficient."

The speaker dropped his voice, speaking with intensity. "The State Security people are all over our campuses, but we can usually spot them. If a video camera shows up anywhere, turn your back on it. Our joggers will jostle them and dump the cameras on the ground. We want them to see pictures of the backs of our heads only."

The guitar player broke in with the voice of a leader with experience. "Plan your vacations well in the next two weeks. Go to the major mountains: Emeishan in Szechuan, Huangshan and Moganshan near Hangzhou. Lushan is important, and Taishan in Shangdong Province near Tsingtao. Mount Wu Yi in Fujian Province is hard to get to, but if someone can visit relatives there and make the climb, there should be many students to meet with. This is the critical period to exchange information by word of mouth."

"What about the few students that refuse to participate, Brother? Are they safe to be around?"

"There are always a few who fear to participate. Dissent is a privilege. However, to prevent the leakage of information, it's best to just ignore non-participants. If you detect government spies, pass the word around, so we will all know who they are."

The woman spoke again. "The big question is, will the government use their guns and tanks again? They have in every other demonstration, What's to prevent them just killing or imprisoning us, as they did the others?"

"The world has changed, Sister. Poland, Czechoslovakia, East Germany have become openly democratic. Russia is groaning with changes. Gorbachev is trying desperately to lead them out of the mire of revolting provinces. Our leaders are forced to see the future."

The guitar player strummed his guitar lightly before putting it aside. "Communism and Dictatorships are anachronisms. We were idealists in 1989, anxious to let our leaders know how we felt and how much support we had from the people. Deng and others led us to believe they had changed. Now we are pragmatists and our plan is completely different."

"Is it true that the PLA knows the true story of the '89 Massacre and will not shoot, even if ordered?"

"You are a fool if you believe that, Sister. Soldiers that don't follow orders are shot. I served two years in the 38th Army. Let me tell you, it was survival all the way. You have no idea how many military executions happen in peace time. I knew one young officer who questioned his superiors about an order to take his men on a training mission into a swamp during a storm. We went anyway and three of our men drowned during the overnight exercise. The officer was court-martialed the very next morning and executed that afternoon. His crime was questioning an order. The loss of his men in the swamp was of no consequence."

Another student was nodding. "When ordered, the Army will shoot to kill. We must confront the leaders, not the military."

"What of the plan that we have been working on for many years to disable the PLA from within, through our families who have soldiers? Are the reports true that the soldiers will just melt into the countryside and go home? The military vehicles will suddenly have sugar or sand in their gas tanks. Fuel depots will mysteriously catch fire? Is all this possible?"

"There is truth to that, Brother, but we do not know which units. There are rumors of Air Force pilots who will defect with their planes to foreign airports. The Voice of America reported last week that Taiwan and Hong Kong are standing by to receive them."

"The military used helicopters during the 1989 demonstration. They could do immense damage to our demonstrations if we gathered in one place like Tiananmen Square. In my estimation, the Army doesn't need its tanks, armoured carriers or platoons of soldiers. One copter with napalm or poison gas could do as much damage as a whole army to a congregated group."

The woman asked. "Will we stick to our original plan then, Brother?"

A new voice popped up, belonging to a male student recently enrolled in the Astronaut Department.

"Exactly what is our plan, Sister?" He leaned over to the senior student who had done most of the talking.

Suddenly, the gathering under the tree disappeared with a flurry of "got to go." The astronaut student was now a solitary figure left on the ground, estranged. Angrily, he mumbled to himself. "I spoke too quickly. Two weeks training is not enough. Now I have a problem. What can I report?"

Later that night, he met his partner outside the campus and recited gleefully. "Comrade, I have been very fortunate to break into one of their cells. They have a plan to commandeer a helicopter and drop poison or napalm on our beloved PLA. We should take precautions to prevent any of our aircraft from being stolen."

"Well done, Comrade. Keep up the good work. We will meet again in three nights. Keep your ears open and try to be a good student, so they won't suspect you."

BEIHAI PARK, BEIJING

At the headquarters of the MSS, the reports filtered in, reviewed by Yao Lin. Summaries prepared by Hu Banyi became the weekly Ministry report. Fan Riqi then reviewed the data with Chou Shi for presentation to the Politburo.

"We are hearing wild rumors from the campuses. One tells of a possible helicopter hijacking to bomb our troops. Another says our troops probably will turn and shoot all their officers if ordered to shoot on civilians. Chengtu says there is a plot to let all the animals out of the zoo, creating havoc." Scratching his head, Fan smiled at his superior. "Our soldiers may shoot a civilian, but will they execute a panda wandering the streets looking for bamboo?"

Chou Shi did not smile and Fan Riqi moved on to the next stage of his report.

"Comrade Commissar, look at this report from Jimei University, Xiamen, Fujian Province. The students had a secret meeting at

Gulang Yu, the Island offshore. An American couple joined them as they climbed the scenic mountain. They left the next day on the passenger ship to Hong Kong. Our agent was sure they carried a message out to the students in Hong Kong. Each of our campus agents reports accelerated activity, group discussions and an intense addiction to the Voice of America broadcasts."

"Comrades," Chou Shi said addressing Fan and Hu. "What is your summary analysis?"

Fan tilted his chair back, propped his feet up on an open desk drawer, and meshed his fingers against his chest. "Having learned the lessons of 1989, I project there will be a demonstration of some kind on the fifth anniversary of the Tiananmen Affair. Public squares in the major cities will be empty except for token groups. The people will show some other measure of support. One report stated that workers will join the demonstration by striking. The general information we are getting from the campuses is drivel, deliberate disinformation. We assume our reporting teams have blown their covers, outsmarted by the students. The students will not repeat the 1989 mistakes. Their information travels by uncontrollable lines of communication, domestic and international."

Fan looked questioningly at Hu Banyi. Chou Shi had gathered up the report, put it into a brief case and left through his usual exit behind the screen.

"He didn't even say thank you, or goodbye," Hu said.

ZHONGNANHAI, BEIJING

The Standing Committee of the Politburo met to receive Minister Chou Shi's report. Six men, the most important in China, directed the Politburo. The Politburo headed the National Congress. The National Congress represented the Chinese Communist Party. The Chinese Communist Party directed the destinies of over one billion people.

Wu Xian, senior member of the Standing Committee, assessed the others mentally as they entered the room. General Secretary Liu Chinan, the Chairman, stood on the mountain and leaned whichever way the wind blew. Tang Naiwa, General of the 27th Army, spoke for the hardliners. Cai Jixi, Minister of the Central Committee for Disciplinary Action, constantly pressed Tang to become even more aggressive. Yang Yucie, Vice Premier, was a solid softliner.

Chou Shi entered the room last. The sixth member of the committee was the epitome of inscrutable. He stood clear of opinions, seldom speaking at length. The head of the State Security, the dreaded MSS, retained his position by fear, trained in the art by the Russian K.G.B. A small person with a round balding head and gold-rimmed glasses, he had a habit of appearing or disappearing unobtrusively. Tang, jokingly, once accused him of walking through walls to exit a room, ghost-like.

After Chou Shi had given the weekly report on subversiveness in the Nation, Tang burst out laughing. "Dolts. Do they think we are donkeys, easily fooled by false trails? I think the students will fill the People's Squares again all over the country, as they have done time and time again. They will brush their posters, beg for conferences to attain democracy, and copy the stupid Western slogans."

Silently, against the insulting tone of Tang's interruption, Chou Shi thought, That laugh will cost you your life, Tang.

"I have heard one rumor that you didn't report, Comrade Commissar. At Xidan, they are building another Goddess of Democracy to parade again. Whatever they do, we will have them in a box this time. My army is deployed properly. The poison gas idea isn't too bad, if we can control it. I'll have our meteorologists do some programming to predict the weather in each expected trouble area, especially the direction of winds. My Chemical Warfare Division is researching a nerve gas that was invented but never used by the Americans and discarded by their soft-headed Congress. It would be perfect to take out a whole group."

Chou spoke softly. "General, may I respectfully point out that the gas you talk of could kill millions in our crowded cities. This would include your vaunted army and their families."

"Did the Great Khans worry about a city's population? If they refused to capitulate, he simply exterminated the whole town, men, women and children, and burned their buildings to the ground. New cities will emerge from the wreckage, and the western world may even help to rebuild them. We plead a horrible accident and request help from the International Red Cross. They will rush to aid us."

An anxious rustle of papers could be heard suddenly around the table, but the General seemed not to notice. He continued on, warming to his theme.

"Remember how the Russians pulled the wool over the world's eyes when their nuclear plant at Chernobyl blew up. The United States sent doctors to help the victims and technical men to help them correct other plants so it wouldn't happen again. The Red Cross donated millions of dollars of relief funds to aid the unfortunate. A million people are like a single feather on a duck. It will grow another quickly."

A slow smile spread across his face, his eyes distant, as if he looked at a scene already occurring in his mind's eye.

"Yes, when we invoke our plan, every province will kowtow. The students and intellectuals will knock their foreheads on the floor three times in front of us and we will control the country as we see fit."

Wu Xian and his old friend Yang Yucie looked at each other in dismay. The General was a raving lunatic and they hadn't recognized the depth of it. Cai Jixi applauded loudly. Liu Chinan sat back in his chair with his mouth open in amazement. He wished himself transposed to his quiet retreat in Beidaihe and wondered how he was going to get out of this inevitable horror.

Chou Shi mentally recorded all the words, the nuances, the facial expressions of the short speech. Chou loved power and intended to get it for himself. Tang would have to be eliminated quickly.

EIGHT
TAIPEI, TAIWAN

30 APRIL 1994

The Grand Hotel, sitting high on a hill overlooking the widespread city of Taipei, still breathed of yesteryear's opulence. Cars swung up to the red-pillared entrance. The huge lobby, with a high ceiling, bespoke of palace ambience rather than a hotel. Built in 1950 on the arrival of Chiang Kaishek and his Nationalist entourage, it was now middle-aged, almost a half-century old. The glitzy demeanor of the downtown hotels with their international names captured most of the tourist and business travelers. The Grand catered to foreign dignitaries, formal weddings, and meetings of the Old Guard.

Madame Chiang Kaishek, the former Meiling Soong, was named the Dragon Lady by the foreign press. She had designed the Grand Hotel, which was eventually called the Grand Lady, to replace her palatial residence in Nanking, which had been so hurriedly vacated when the Nationalists evacuated to Taiwan after being defeated by Mao Tsetung.

The Chiang Kaishek era passed with his death. The recognition of the People's Republic of China as the official Chinese government suspended the Taiwan Republic of China in mid-air. Some of the Old Guard of the Nationalist's Kuomintang still dreamed of overthrowing the Communists and retaking control of the mainland.

The meeting room in the Grand Hotel, designed exclusively for the General's paranoia of secrecy, was windowless, properly filtered, air-conditioned and swept for bugs. The wealth of the government supplied state-of-the-art equipment, unlike its counterpart across the straits.

The Central Advisory Committee of Taiwan, twenty men and one woman, sat around a long carved rosewood table inlaid with slabs of scenic marble. The table was an antique from the Qing Dynasty, taken, along with thousands of articles of furniture, jade, cloisonné, carved lacquer, porcelains, and other artware, when the Kuomintang made their exodus from the mainland in 1949.

Members of the Council sipped tea from rare eggshell porcelain cups and comforted themselves in idle moments with the decor, symbolic of their homeland. A series of twelve panel screens partitioned one long wall into small alcoves for private discussions and caucus. On the north wall were scroll paintings depicting the Imperial Palace, gardens, and characters from the Red Mansions epic. The soft hills of Kwelin with the River Li in the background decorated the side wall.

The Central Advisory Committee had originally consisted of the Old Guard, who had come across the channel with Chiang. Nepotism appointments had replaced the old ones as they died off.

This committee met to advise the government during moments of severe trauma. Once had been when the mainland People's Republic of China was recognized internationally and replaced the Taiwan Republic of China at the United Nations. The Committee convened again when Chiang Kaishek died and a successor had to be named, stirring a great controversy as to whether young Chiang could handle the job of dictator.

They met when corruption and partisanship created ugly repercussions within the American-educated younger generation.

In 1989, the enormous trade and gold surpluses threatened to drown the country in success. Irate trading partners needed pacifying. Changes were necessary. Democracy was tentatively and gingerly tried, the strings loosened and then tightened until no one knew what the policy was.

The impact of Mainland China's leadership and political deterioration was the impetus for the current meeting. The chance had emerged for a forty-five-year-old dream to come true.

"The fools in Beijing have finally defeated themselves," one member was saying. "What we couldn't accomplish by force, they are doing for us. The Chinese Communist Party has shot itself in the foot, and may well point the gun to its head very soon. Now is the time for us to act."

Another speaker, decorated in the uniform of a General of the Air Force, said, "They still have over four million men under arms and another twelve to fourteen million in reserve. Our reports show they have thirty-five full strength armies. The control lies in the hands of General Tang Naiwa, Commissar of the Military Commission. I knew him. We were both lieutenants during the Japanese occupancy. It was Tang Naiwa that surrendered his whole unit to Mao outside Nanking. He sought to save his skin when it looked like he was going to lose the battle. Tang was a bully with a warlord temperament. It was Tang's 27th Army that fired on the students in Tiananmen Square five years ago. The strategy of committing an entire army to an unarmed opponent is typical of his military ability. A brace of water hoses would have flushed the whole uprising down the drain."

"General Feng, I understand you have a plan to subvert the Communists and retake the mainland. There are many of us who would laugh at such a grotesque suggestion. Would you mind explaining exactly what you have in mind?" The speaker was Li Quohua, by seniority the leader of the group, addressed simply as Chairman. He was of the Old Guard.

General Feng Qizi of the Republic of China's Air Force, Commissar of the military forces, thought carefully before replying to the old one. The words of the Elder Statesman angered him. There should be only enough of the plan revealed to assure they would not block him.

Many in the group, like Li, had long ago given up the dream of invading the mainland. They were wealthy, owned fine homes, and were free to travel as they wished. Their children were educated in the finest schools of the Western World. Desires of their youth to revenge themselves against the Communists had faded as their bellies and their pockets filled.

General Feng, seventy-eight years old, bald, beardless, skin blotched with age, bridled his anger and frustration. He slipped a nitro pill under his tongue to ease the stress restrictions forming in his chest. "Yes, we have a plan. The Yellow Dragon, as some of you know.

"On the 4th of June this year, the students of the mainland universities will demonstrate to memorialize the Tiananmen Massacre and their brooding desire for democracy. The government leaders and the military will be involved with the shooting of their children; they will have little thought of us. The mooncalves have long ago forgotten our threat to their existence. They pass us off as another nodule of China that will eventually return to the fold, like Hong Kong. Because of security leaks within our own group here, I cannot reveal the details of Yellow Dragon. You have my assurance that by this time next month, the Kuomintang will again be the leaders of China. The people exposed to capitalism will welcome us from every corner of the country as their saviors. Hong Kong will rush to amalgamate their wealth of commerce with ours, as many of our business people have already done. The Communist Party will collapse. Their leaders, like rats leaving a sinking ship, will race each other to join us."

"Eeyah! Madness! What is he saying?" A chorus of voices interrupted Feng, as the surprised members listened to the unbelievable words.

Li Guohua rose up from his chair at the head of the table, pounding the gavel for attention. "This is a formal meeting of the Central Advisory Committee. All who desire will have the chance to speak, even if we have to stay all night. All decisions concerning the direction of this government will be taken by a majority vote. No one of us, including General Feng, can act without our approval. General, you will reveal the plan in all its detail to this committee, security notwithstanding. We will then call for a vote."

The General flushed, eyes narrowing in anger, as he tried to control himself. "Gentlemen, I meant no usurpation of power from the Committee. I am your servant. You have seen to my appointment as Supreme Commander of the Armed Forces and I am executing my duty in that regard. Our National Security is obviously involved. If we don't assert ourselves, the military junta of China will eventually absorb us. Their leaders have turned their back on democracy and reform, reverting to the armed might they need to retain power.

"Allow me to meet with the Standing Committee of this group, just the six revered leaders who have given us the wisdom of their judgment and experience these many years. If they decide to inform you all, and allow the world and our enemies to know our plans, then so be it. I can reveal that we have been in contact with many elements on the mainland. They desire to join us in a coup. There should be very little bloodshed, only those who refuse to accept the inevitable."

"Very well, General," Li answered. "We will discuss the aspects of your proposal here, and advise our acceptance or denial, subject to an in-depth review by our Standing Committee."

"What of the Americans, General?" another voice questioned. "Most of our military strength is supplied by them. Our economy is so dependent on exports to the United States that their manufacturers rail against us constantly. Dare we do this without their approval?"

"With the mainland in our hands, the Americans will turn cartwheels to do business with us. To the capitalists, China is a market place with a potential of a billion customers."

Li turned to the only woman at the table. "Madame Soong, you have a comment for us?"

The men all turned to the middle of the long table where the woman sat fingering a delicate jade carving hanging at her throat. Soong Aimei, simply groomed in an embroidered pale gold cheongsam, black hair tiered in coils atop her head, was the embodiment of the ageless beautiful women depicted in the scrolls on the north wall.

Li addressed her again, sensing her reluctance to speak out. "Certainly none amongst us knows the Americans as you do. Your father, may he rest easy with the Immortals, served us well. We remember the difficult years after the debacle created by Kissinger and Nixon. You were with him during those years and must have gained an intimate knowledge of their thinking."

Soong Aimei arose so gracefully that the motion itself was imperceptible. "Gentleman, I'm honored to be a member of this committee. It was difficult for my father to be an ambassador, literally without a country, after our Republic was repudiated by the United Nations. Father fought the diplomatic battles with the United States Department of Commerce over trade differences, tariffs, and the deceptive practices of our own manufacturers. The American Congress wanted to use us as a military base for their Pacific protection.

Nevertheless, their president realized the need to recognize a country with 25% of the world's population as a nation."

Soong looked around at the faces, trying to perceive their mood. She could imagine the Politburo in Beijing sitting in a similar session. Some would not like to hear the truth, preferring an ideological answer. There were members of this group who could easily return to China with the dictatorship tactics of Generalissimo Chiang if they could take over. Warlord mentality was in the genes of their ancestors and in theirs. Lust for power would overcome common sense.

Aimei was proud of her ancestry. The Soongs were a diverse old family in China with many branches. Madame Chiang Kaishek and Madame Sun Yat Sen were Soongs. Aimei's father came from a little-known branch in Yunan Province, the name causing more trouble than the approbation it brought.

Aimei decided firmly and unequivocally. She was a Soong and would speak as her heart dictated. She left her chair in the manner her Radcliff public-speaking course had taught her, and began walking around the table. The tactic made the audience follow her with their eyes.

"Gentlemen of the Council. It's my fate to be a messenger – interpretive, opinionated, but still a messenger. History relates that such a courier is often killed. I realize the danger and can sense the animosities of some members in the room. There are those of you, imbued with your desires and opinions, who will ignore the message.

"First, you must believe that the world has changed, past tense. It has indeed changed, whether you like it or not. That is a simple fact. The Mainland Chinese hierarchy refuses to accept that fact and that is the principal reason they are in the deep trouble they find themselves in today. From that analysis emerges a probable event. The Chinese Revolution, for it is a revolution, will be successful in my opinion. The power unleashed since the Dengist Era cannot be reversed, guns and tanks notwithstanding. The people know those aligned with the Western World have material comforts. Education, adequate living quarters, cars to drive that we own, and a right to come and go freely that can't be denied. For example, try to stop one of this group from sending his daughter or son to Radcliff or Harvard. Would you give up a second home in Hawaii and a bank account the government knows nothing about?"

Soong Aimei paused and looked around her at the faces, some smiling. Others displayed guilt-formed masks hiding their feelings. She stopped at her seat, took a sip of tea, let the words sink in, and listened to the murmurs around her. She let the buzz keep up for a few minutes before resuming. "You ask me if the Americans will support an invasion effort. My answer is no, not the slightest possibility. The leadership of Congress, the President of the United States, and Secretary of State Albright, will not support you. In fact, they will condemn you and seek economic sanctions against you as they did with South Africa. You need only turn back a few pages of history to the Cuban Invasion for your answer. Never again will the United States allow itself to be led by military advisors who look at peace through the barrel of a gun."

She turned to the General. "Various United States' high military officers have met with you, General Feng. Please don't humiliate yourself by denying it. Their promises are hollow. They would like you to test their new missiles, invasion craft, and stealth aircraft. We must be strong and not provide the proving ground and resultant cemetery caused by such weapons."

When Soong paused for a moment, the quiet voice of Li spoke up. "What if they don't support us? Without their aid, can you see any success of the plan the General proposes?"

Madame Soong returned to her place at the table and turned to Chairman Li. "You and the other calm voices at this table know the answer to that. It will be another defeat, costing many lives, an embarrassment to the world, and a setback to our international position far greater than the disenfranchisement of the last decade."

"Thank you, Madame Ambassador. We value your opinion as highly as we did your esteemed father's."

The General pounded the table. "This Ambassador talks with the softness of a woman. She is completely disarmed by the Americans. We have waited almost half a century for the time to take back our nation. If we don't act now, with or without American support, we will never have another chance. The Communists have failed economically and politically. They will fail militarily. It's our turn to rule China."

Chairman Li Quohua looked around the table with a wry smile. He knew every person intimately, their families, their backgrounds. There had been extreme suffering when they or their fathers were uprooted from homes on the mainland and forced to reestablish in Taiwan. He remembered the vehemence, the bitterness of those years, the vows for revenge against the Communists.

Li was also aware of General Feng's security service using the power of blackmail on members of this group. Ruthlessness was part of the heritage of Chiang Kaishek, including the willingness to kill enemies and those who disagreed with him.

The elder statesman spoke. "Members of this council, I think we should take a wider view of our future and the mainland. It is not a narrow lane, but a wide boulevard with many access streets and tantalizing dark alleys filled with danger to all. The ability to shed blood is inherent in our genes. The eminent writer of China, Harrison Salisbury, has described us as un-humanitarian. The killers at the Tiananmen Massacre ordered the spilling of blood with no compassion or regret, in fact gloating over the bloody solution to the demonstration. These were the same military leaders who sent hundreds of thousands of their soldiers to their deaths at the Yalu River in Korea against the Americans. The idealistic American President Truman could have annihilated both North Korea and a million of the Chinese troops gathered at the border. He chose to lose the war instead and relieved one of their greatest generals, MacArthur, in the disagreement over humanitarianism."

Pausing to see how many nods of agreement he might get, Li thought of his counterpart in Beijing. Would his old friend Wu Xian be pleading the same saneness to the Politburo in the Zhongnanhai? Enough bloodletting, enough, he would think. They shared the love of China, Li in exile, and Wu imprisoned by his hardliners.

Chairman Li continued. "We must be careful of the wisdom and advice of our generals. They are hired and trained to serve the people, not control them or lead us into unnecessary wars. There are those amongst us" – he looked directly at Feng – "who would do just that. It behooves calmer heads to take charge. Have you considered the probability of success of the expected demonstrations in China, as Madame Soong has so wisely expressed? Power outside China's borders will help them. If there happen to be heroic changes in China in the next generation, we may see a democratic government emerge similar to what we are planning."

The Chairman paused, taking a deliberate break to refill his tea cup and sipping it while looking around the table. He saw Feng's malevolent eye deliberately marching around the table trying to affix each member with a dire warning. The eye stopped for extra moments on Soong Aimei, unnoticed by her, as she was caucusing with her neighbor.

Li shuddered with the thought of what Feng would do if denied his Golden Dragon plan.

"If China is ever to be united with all of its factions, we must have a modern government. What would be wrong with a formula based on the United States Constitution? It initiated a unique society that after two hundred years now leads the world. With our various systems over the past five thousand years, China remains a nation just emerging from its cocoon. Taiwan, Hong Kong, Hainan and all the provinces could be independent states sending their duly elected representatives to Beijing to provide a peaceful government. Far fetched? What if it is possible? Do you still want to be an invader of a sovereign nation, your own nation?"

Li Quohua rapped the gavel on the table before anyone else could speak. "We will allow a half hour for caucus, and then take a vote. Please do not leave the room."

The twenty men and one woman assembled thirty minutes later, wrote their votes on ballots and gave them to the leader and his secretariat to count.

"Members of the Central Advisory Commission, on the motion to subject the invasion plan to the Standing Committee for review, the count is ten votes for and ten votes against the proposal. Therefore, I cast my vote nay. It's the decision of this committee that there will be no form of interference with the mainland demonstrations or government. General Tang, you are ordered to scrap the Yellow Dragon and destroy all the details. The meeting is adjourned."

NINE
TAIPEI, TAIWAN

30 APRIL 1994

It was nine in the evening. The lights of Taipei made a giant multi-colored panorama of the city. On the surface, the streets were alive with ribbons of moving vehicles creating a kaleidoscope of colors. Neon advertising signs rudely plastered the towers of construction crane booms that dominated the steel frameworks of the buildings.

Three old friends, part of the old guard of the Central Advisory Committee, looked over their domain from the Presidential Suite of the Sheraton Hotel.

They occupied the central room of the suite, which was designed for entertaining and greeting dignitaries. Two bedrooms with private baths were off to one side, a butler's pantry and dining room on the other. Furnishings were elegant. Silk brocade upholstery covered the sofas and chairs. A curio cabinet displayed antique porcelain figures. A fat blanc d'chine Ho Ti, the Laughing Buddha, gleefully sat on the concert grand piano.

The old ones sipped their cocktails and snacked on dim sum from the silver chafing dish on the buffet while they waited. The conversation had been light, none of them willing to speak openly until the whole Standing Committee had arrived.

"We have created a magnificent city from a bare framework in the past forty-five years," one member observed wistfully from his place by the window. "The lights extend as far as the eye can see, and our commercial enterprises extend around the world from our shores."

His companion sighed as he paced the outskirts of the suite. "When are the others coming?"

The third, seated in a chair on the other side of the room, did not seem concerned. "Soong Aimei and Chairman Li Guohua told me they will arrive together. There was a family wedding to attend."

"What about the General? Certainly Feng wouldn't miss a special meeting?"

"There was a message at reception when I arrived. The General is delayed, but suggests we start without him."

The impatient one rubbed his hands together, though it was not cold, and peered over his colleague's shoulder at the bright lights below. "The street traffic is heavy tonight. It will take them extra time to drive here."

At nine-thirty, the chimes of the doorbell played their musical tune. One elder got up to open it. A uniformed waiter was there with a food wagon sprouting several silver chafing dishes. "Your dinner, sirs," the waiter announced.

"We requested service at ten. You're too early."

"Sorry, sir, we must have the order confused. Let me set it up on the buffet and light the warmers. I'll return when you ring to serve you."

With hardly a pause, the three old friends returned to their nostalgic conversation. "It would be wonderful to visit Fuzhou."

"Walking on the Bund in the cool of evening, seeing the anchored ships of commerce, was one of my greatest pleasures."

"I assume the summer meetings of the P.R.C. are still held at the Central Beach Hotel in Beidaihe? I remember so clearly the fresh early morning air and the fishing boats just coming in with their catches."

"Can you recall how cold the winters were and how hot the summers in Beijing?"

"Yes, a recent article reported Beijing to be so smog-filled in the summers that one can hardly breathe."

As they spoke of days long gone by, oblivious to their imminent danger, the waiter had re-entered the room silently and now faced them with a machine gun at his hip. He crouched, apparently undecided whether to fire or to wait until the other dignitaries appeared.

"Eeyah!" The old one by the buffet screamed to alert his friends.

Realizing it was too late to save himself, he started toward the assassin, hoping to wrench the weapon out of his hands before he could fire. His foot caught in a small rug and he fell forward, arms reaching out to cushion the fall.

With events dictating a decision, the waiter triggered his weapon, missing the falling body. The stream of bullets hit the back of the elder statesman facing the window instead, some missing his body and shattering the pane of glass in front of him. Blood spattered in all directions; the dark red liquid sprayed out, shining grotesquely in the reflection of the outside building lights, staining the shards that remained in the window frame.

Turning to the figure now trying to get up and lunge toward him, the gunman released a second flurry of bullets into the head and upper chest. Because of the shooting angle and the short range, bullets sprayed through the body, spurting blood toward the assassin.

The gunman turned toward the third victim. The old one had dropped from the chair to the floor to shield himself. The assassin walked carefully around the couch and chairs to find his quarry curled into a fetal ball. A hail of bullets raked his body, leaving not even a moment of life in which to cry out.

Tossing the gun to the floor, the hitman quickly removed the blood-spattered white gloves, waiter's jacket, shirt, and pants. He reached down to wipe some blood spots off his shoes with the shirt and donned a light grey sweatsuit that had been concealed in the food wagon. He took a last look around, walked nonchalantly out the door and over to the passenger elevator. Emerging on the ground floor, he passed the Hotel Security people rushing to get on the elevator.

Madame Soong and Chairman Li arrived at the hotel at nine-fifty in time to see police cars pulling in, followed by a media truck. An aggressive media team, recognizing the well-known leaders, rushed over, rudely shoving a microphone into the car. "Chairman Li, please comment on the brutal slayings of our elder statesmen a few minutes ago."

The cameraman caught the expression of shock on the two faces as they started to get out of the vehicle. Soong pulled the Chairman back into the car without a word to the reporter and shouted to the driver, "Move, and get out of here." Cleared by alert police, the vehicle fled from the scene. Soong Aimei picked up the car telephone, made two short calls, and ordered the driver to go as fast as possible to the private plane entrance of Chiang Kai Shek Airport.

Quietly, she spoke. "With your permission, respected Chairman, we are leaving Taiwan immediately."

The face of her friend and mentor grew pale as the blood flow slowed, and he looked eerie in the dim light of the car. Splashes from street lights and the unending strings of neon signs entered brightly through the windshield, subdued through the dark glass of the side windows. Soong reached for his hand. She saw the tears rolling in slow motion down the smooth, round, ancient cheeks. He was mute with shock, his mind for the moment beyond reception.

Li Guohua had recovered somewhat by the time they landed at Kai Tak Airport, Hong Kong. "It has begun, Little Jade. The General has fired the first shots and our old friends are the victims. Why them instead of me?"

"Dear friend, you haven't called me Little Jade since I was a child. Fate determines our fortunes. We take comfort because we live, to avenge our friends and give cause to their deaths. Have faith, honored uncle. Kwan Yin, the Goddess of Mercy, will see to our safety." Soong fingered the jade carving at her throat. Kwan Yin's strength would be sorely needed to pull them both through the next few days and the future.

"With you by my side, Little Jade, and in the many arms of Kwan Yin, I take strength. We must live for the day of emergence from this day of horror. Please see to security and then a meeting with our Hong Kong supporters to discuss the future."

"We are in an era of technology, Honoured Uncle. Security is already in force as we speak, if you'll note the car following us. There will be the news media to deal with, for we are embedded in happenings that are resounding around the world. For the moment, however, my apartment here at Harbour Village will be sufficient to live and work from. Rest assured we do have many friends in Hong Kong."

The shocking news of the assassinations in Taipei exploded the next morning around the world. American television networks received the relay just in time for the evening news programs of the previous day. In Sydney, the morning Today Show informed Australia. The appalled faces of Soong Aimei and Li Guohua captured in that moment of horror filled the screens. The media related unconfirmed reports, wild and rampant rumors about China, Hong Kong, and all Asia with its possible effects on the world. The various networks interviewed their standby notables, Bush, Clinton, Kissinger, and Brehzinski.

BEIHAI PARK, BEJING

In the Beijing headquarters of the MSS, Fan Riqi and Hu Banyi sifted the meager amount of information from Taipei. The rumblings of Formosa, now known as Taiwan, always reverberated to the Mainland MSS.

"Surprisingly, there was no previous information or rumors from our contacts in Taipei that there might be a coup," Hu mentioned.

"The problem here, Comrade Hu, is a possible connection with our own military." Fan blew a circle of smoke toward the ceiling, put his feet up on the desk and lifted his hand to rake his scalp. Controlling the addictive urge, he grabbed a pad and paper and instead doodled a man in a military uniform.

Hu Banyi summarized. "The coup is fresh news, but we have suspected a connection, even the possible persons. So far we do not have firm evidence. Feng Qizi and Tang Naiwa did know each other in their youth. Therefore we must consider a possible collusion. Is it possible to have Tang followed by the Shaolin teams without Yao knowing?"

"It is difficult to operate with a known spy inside our tent, Comrade Hu, but an excellent idea. Let me work on that angle. There are two teams that have no love for Yao and I'm sure will cooperate."

US EMBASSY, BEIJING

Patrick Duffy conferred with the Ambassador. "Mrs. Duke, do you know the Soong woman personally? Geoff called from Hong Kong and said she arrived safely with Li Guohua. They are in seclusion but he would like to arrange a meeting."

"Aimei and I are old friends, though sometimes we disagree about the politics of Chiang Kaishek. Her father, the former Ambassador to the United States, used to bring her with him. We spent many happy weekends at my husband's estate in Virginia. Later, I'll try to make a personal call and set up an introduction for Geoff. Send a message to him to stay in Hong Kong until we can find out how this will affect China. He'll get more information there than we can get here."

"Yes, Madame Ambassador, I'll get right on it."

MILITARY HEADQUARTERS OF GENERAL FENG QIZI

TAIPEI, TAIWAN

The General paced back and forth, livid with anger. The unfortunate brunt of his vehemence stood at attention, perspiring with fear. "Fool, yak dung, witless camel, is there no one I can trust to carry out a mission? Captain, the assignment was a simple maneuver using non-uniform troops. Why couldn't he wait and take out the other two as well?"

"General, I don't know. There was no way I could tell. The agent came out of the hotel, jumped into the car I had waiting, claimed the mission accomplished, took the envelope with the 25,000 US dollars, and skipped out the other door as I was starting up. I would have gone after him, but the police sirens were closing in. It wouldn't have been a good idea for me to be seen there. We have all available security men out looking for him with orders to shoot on sight. He won't get away."

TAIPEI, 1 MAY 1994

Military Headquarters called a news conference for twelve noon. The reporters crowded into the pressroom to see the podium flanked with military brass. Chairs had been removed to allow for the additional media and journalists milling around nervously. Television cameras operated by military photographers focused on the representatives of the press.

The press notice informed them that press cameras and tape recorders were barred. Official video and printed releases would be available shortly after the meeting.

The room quieted as the General entered from a back room, marched to the platform, and stationed himself between his subordinate commanders.

"I am General Feng Qizi, Commanding General of the Republic of China, Armed Forces. Taiwan is in chaos with the assassination of the three members of the Central Advisory Committee and the sudden disappearance of Chairman Li Guohua and Madame Soong. As of twelve noon today, I hereby declare Martial law. All elected government agencies of Taiwan, including the People's Congress, and media communication of any kind are suspended. The Central Advisory Committee is also suspended until further notice. After this meeting, all foreign media have twenty-four hours to leave the country. Our Communications Director will supervise all subsequent news distribution."

"General Feng, does this mean you are declaring yourself the Dictator of Taiwan and re-establishing the KMT Republic of China party, thus eliminating the Democracy movement of the past years?"

The young red-headed reporter from CBS had done the unthinkable. The others around him, who had seen coups before, shuddered at what might happen. They moved around him, trying to conceal who had actually spoken out. The red shock of hair refused to be daunted. "Follow up, General. Do you have any connection with the Generals on the Mainland, who are rumored to be trying a similar coup?"

Motioning to a pair of nearby airmen stationed as guards around the room, the General spoke angrily. "Place that man under arrest. You are declared persona-non-grata. You will be escorted under guard directly to the airport and placed on the first available commercial plane leaving the country. There will be no questions. You have your statement. Press releases are waiting for you at the door. That is your story. I remind you that you have until noon tomorrow to leave the country. Any of our citizens caught talking to you will be placed under arrest as a spy and held for trial by a military tribunal."

The airmen hustled the young reporter out of the room. One of his team tried to snap a picture of it with a small camera. A guard saw the flash, promptly seized the camera, split open the back to expose the film and threw the camera to the floor, pounding it with the heel of his boot.

Voices rumbled amongst the crowd as the journalists were escorted to waiting buses.

"Here we go again, another coup."

"Better stick together in case one of us is picked up."

"Let's all run in different directions. They don't dare shoot."

"Don't believe it, buddy. Those guns are loaded."

"I wonder what Art had on the General that made him so mad? I bet he had a lead to that Mainland tie-in."

"Maybe. All I hope for right now is that he doesn't shoot his mouth off and gets on a plane and out."

The world's television stations broadcast the interview and announced the coup in Taipei. The newspapers and the magazines ran in-depth background stories for the next two weeks to fill the pages, hoping for a complete story. There was nothing else to report from Taiwan, now a closed country.

Kissinger made a statement for CNN and Australia's ABC. Secretary of State Albright refused to be interviewed on Meet the Press or Face the Nation. The Prime Minister of England, the Prime Minister of Australia, the President of the combined German Republic, and the President of the United States all refused to make statements to the media through their respective press secretaries.

The ever-contentious US House of Representatives met in emergency session and put up a bill to sanction Taiwan for all incoming and outgoing commerce, financial or material, until press communications opened.

The few countries that retained consulates in Taiwan sent all dependents and excess personnel out on the first planes available. The streets of downtown Taipei were suddenly clear of traffic jams, the amount of vehicular traffic reduced by two thirds. At the National Museum, Taiwan's major tourist attraction, registers showed thirty-two people visiting the next day.

Taiwan and the Republic of China stood down, waiting breathlessly for the other shoe to drop.

TEN
HONG KONG

3 MAY 1994

The fire-red Ferrari swooped into the driveway entrance of the Shangri La Hotel, Hong Kong, arresting the startled eyes of the doorman and the dozens of guests standing by.

Fire-red lipstick adorned the smile on the pert young woman driver's face, which barely rose above the dashboard. "Taxi, sir?" the driver said to the tall man with the slightly grayish red hair standing wide-eyed at the curb.

"Why yes, ma'am, if you're heading my way," he answered, reaching for the door handle.

Geoff folded himself into the seat and leaned over to give the pretty lady a kiss on the cheek. A few of the onlooking guests raised cameras to capture the scene of two beautiful people in the extraordinary car as the doorman closed the door.

"How does a secretary rate a half-million Hong Kong dollar car?" Geoff said, trying to keep his face away from the cameras.

"Easy when you have an old Chinese pirate for a father," Quan Quan replied with perfect aplomb as she whipped the car out of the Shangri La driveway onto Mody Road, tires squealing. "When I was a child, he had a fleet of junques transporting goods he never revealed. Now he has as many towers and high rises as he had junques. He also has a few properties in Singapore, Kuala Lumpur, and Bangkok."

"Another Hong Kong success stories. What will happen to your father's Hong Kong holdings when the Chinese take over in 1997?"

"In the talks now going on between Great Britain and China, they promise self-government, as they now have with other autonomous provinces."

"And Poppa Pirate has faith in their promises? That's hard to believe."

"Poppa's opinion is very simple. China needs Hong Kong for its great port and access to the world for both import and export of goods they desperately need. Primarily, it's tech, tech, tech. Poppa still lives on the junque, improved with a few modern conveniences. He's delighted when people call him a pirate."

"Are you the family heir or are there other pirates in the family?" Geoff asked curiously.

"My two brothers manage the family property, live in penthouses here and there, and call themselves financiers. That's the whole bit. Now you know everything about me." She turned her head for a moment toward Geoff and gave him a pixie's wink.

Geoff smiled, not having the slightest idea what that endearing wink meant. Tonight's invitation to the Abernathy home for an informal dinner covered a secret meeting arranged by Ambassador Duke and Oliver's friend, Soong Aimei. Quan Quan had offered to pick him up at the hotel. Geoff, expecting the usual taxi or company car, had shaken his head in disbelief at the sight of the fire-red Ferrari swooping in to the hotel entrance.

Excitement generated by the ride and the noise created by the wind whistling through the open car windows limited the conversation. The Ferrari cleared the congested streets of Kowloon and turned up the hill road to the Custom House Compound.

A small, red toenailed bare foot down-shifted the Ferrari Daytona, and Geoff felt the manual five-speed's powerful V-12 engine take hold on the hairpin curved road as they began climbing the steep hills above Kowloon.

Geoffrey Martine, ex-Thai Boxer, Black Belt Karate veteran of untold physically demanding adventures, was white-knuckled on the handgrip of the passenger seat. Only a guardrail separated him from the precipice a few feet away. The KPH needle fluttered between 100 and 120 as the ninety-nine-pound woman calmly accelerated. They came out of the curve fishtailing onto the straight. He reached into his pocket and pulled out the jade finger charm. Quan Quan smiled as she caught a glimpse of it.

Geoff began to relax, settling into the seat. *This woman must be a*

Gemini. One month ago, she was a quiet unassuming assistant for Abernathy, delivering a message to me on the ferry, almost getting killed in the following melee. Now she's a racecar driver competently enjoying the thrill of speed and danger.

Enjoying the scenery, he remembered Oliver explaining that the Bank owned the property as residences for its overseas executives. Brits and Scots who did not earn enough salary to afford the five-to-seven thousand dollars a month for apartment rentals elsewhere were kept in a modicum of decent habitation here.

The car turned into the compound, coming to a gentle stop near the row house marked fourteen. "Smooth flight, Mon Capitaine. I think you just broke the Concord record." Geoff exaggerated a deep exhalation. "Do you always fly with the throttles all out?"

"My brothers enjoy fancy cars, and give me their old last year's models when they buy a new one. We also have a family yacht, but this 1992 Ferrari and a rocket boat from New Zealand are my thrill fun."

"Golly gee," Geoff said. "These modern children sure have fancy toys. What else do you have in the toy room for sport and entertainment?"

Again with that pixie wink of conspiratorial mischief, Quan Quan answered, "Well, against my father's wishes, I also fly the company jet, a Lear 25 Turbo. I'm licensed for private and commercial flying."

The petite woman raised her nose and eyebrows and mimed tossing a pilot's scarf around her neck.

"Oh yeah?" Geoff responded. "I bet he secretly loves the idea as much as I do."

She smiled wickedly. "If you need a pilot sometime on one of those adventures I've heard tell of, let me know."

After opening the car door, she slipped her tiny bare feet into a pair of open-toed pumps. Opening the glove compartment, she removed a long rope of pearls. Double draped around her neck, they became an elegant waterfall cascading down to accent the apparent cleavage.

Grinning, she said, "Getting dressed for the formal party inside."

Geoff straightened his tie and jacket, and cuffed his shirt sleeves. Then he walked around and kissed Quan Quan lightly on the lips. "You look a lot better than the last time I saw you. Are there any repercussions from the blow you received during the office affair last month?"

"Three days of severe headaches, and a month of physio for my neck. I'm fine now."

Slowly and deliberately, Geoff looked her up and down. "I would have to say better than fine. You Chinese have a word for it, tsui hao, very best."

"Commander Martine, please retain your decorum this evening. Leering is frowned upon in distinguished company." Reaching up, she pulled his head down from his six-four to her five-two, and gave him a quick, light kiss.

Geoff paused for a moment to smile before taking her hand to walk up to the open door at number fourteen.

A man walked out of the shadows alongside the house. Geoff released her hand and instinctively went into a crouch at the sudden appearance of the agent.

"Easy, sir. Hong Kong P.D. May I see your identification please? Good evening, Ms. Ming."

Geoff straightened up, slipped his wallet out, flipped it open and asked, "Amex or Naval I.D., officer?"

"The Naval card will be sufficient, sir. Sorry for the inconvenience."

The officer disappeared back into the night. Geoff belatedly noticed a car parked across the road with two more men sitting in it. *Careful Martine,* he said to himself. *You're in dangerous waters. If you can see three, the rule of thumb is, there are at least six out there somewhere plus the opposition hiding under some rock nearby. You left your gun back in the hotel safe, stupid ass.*

"Geoffrey!" Suzette Abernathy called exuberantly from the open door. The young man next to her came running down the steps and path ahead of his mother. Stopping in front of Geoff, he stood at attention and saluted. Geoff returned the salute formally and ruffled his hair. "Quan Quan, this is Alexander Abernathy. I used to bring him toys in Shanghai years ago, and now I've brought ... whoops, left it in the car. Back in a minute." Loping to the car, he took a bag from the back seat.

Walking back to the house, he checked the perimeters of the area, just in case. The lightly guarded compound entrance gate was down the road, maybe three hundred yards. A row of occupied houses dimly lit the compound area. Trees and shrubbery provided shadows enough to conceal anything.

At the doorway, Suzette was looking up and down at Quan Quan, making no effort to introduce herself. Geoff could see Quan Quan's chin jut out, affronted at the obvious snub. "Excuse me, Suzette, I forgot to introduce my companion. Ms. Ming, this is our hostess Suzette Abernathy. Suzette, my driver and friend Quan Quan Ming."

"You're the Miss Ming that works with Ollie? Why haven't we met before?"

"It's nice to meet Mr. Abernathy's family, Mrs. Abernathy. He talks about you all the time."

"Please go in and make yourself comfortable, Ms. Ming. Alexander and I would like a few moments with our old friend."

With a swirl of her full skirt, Quan Quan turned and sailed into the house without another word. Geoff, ignoring the obvious discomfort of both women, turned to the young man and presented a wrapped gift from the bag.

Alexander gleefully accepted the gift. "Thank you very much, sir. Swindon's wrapping. It must be a book. An American spy story, I hope?"

Geoff ruffled his hair again. "Right on, Alexander. Ludlum's latest, *The Seoul Transgression*. Enjoy it. The background will be familiar to your mother."

"Now my turn, Geoff." Suzette claimed a hug.

Geoff wrapped her tightly with his arms and leaned down to receive a kiss on each cheek. "And how is the lovely Korean doll that I'm so jealous of Oliver for?"

"Aging, dear Geoffrey, aging, and none of your nonsense about not looking any older. Ten years is it since we were all in Shanghai? You don't look the worse for the recent battle I heard you had in Oliver's office."

"You wouldn't want to see the blacks and blues of my current body colors. Still aching here and there, but my handsome good looks and cheery disposition keep the girls chasing after me. You, my Korean doll, look as beautiful as ever, regardless of your own opinion."

Oliver had joined them at the door and they all laughed at Alexander's excitement. Suzette watched her son dash off to his room, tearing the gift wrapping off, and then said, "Thank you, Geoffrey. That was very kind of you to remember him that way. Now tell me, Oliver, how come I've never met that woman Geoff brought up with him? I had no idea you had such an assistant in your office."

"Suzette, don't tell me you're jealous. That's not like you. You're embarrassing our guest."

"Sorry, Oliver, but you know I am a very jealous wife." She reached up to kiss him.

Geoff offered another gift from the bag, this one to Suzette. "For our hostess. The lady at the Peninsula shop told me they're the finest Belgian chocolates."

"Why thank you, kind sir. You remembered my affinity for chocolate. Rest assured I will share them with no one." Suzette reached up and gave Geoff a kiss on both cheeks.

"I thank you too, Geoff," Oliver interrupted. "However, it's time to get on with our mission. Please come in and meet our guests."

A man and a woman sat at a cocktail table near the window of the living room. Their intense conversation gave Geoff a moment to study them before social necessity interfered.

A perfectly shaped nose and chin emphasized the high cheekbones of the woman. Unfettered black hair streamed down her back to the waist. She was dressed in a gold-threaded cheongsam, split to the thigh, and matching slippers. A chain of carved jade links hung from each ear. A jade bangle circled her wrist. As the woman turned to face him, he noticed a carved jade figure swinging on a gold chain at her throat.

"Soong, this is Commander Geoffrey Martine of the United States Navy. Geoffrey, please meet Soong Aimei, an estranged diplomat of the Republic of China."

"Excuse me for staring, Ms. Soong. You remind me of the ladies painted on the classic porcelain urns I have seen."

Soong held out a hand devoid of any rings. On impulse, with

a sudden burst of continental savoir-faire, Geoff raised her hand to his lips.

Soong smiled like an Empress receiving homage. "Thank you, Commander. It's a pleasure meeting the famous adventurer Geoffrey Martine." The perfectly modulated Boston-English accent caused Geoff to raise his eyebrows.

"My accent, Commander? I was born in Shanghai just before the Communist takeover. Raised and educated in the Eastern United States, my father called me a diplomatic brat. I acquired the Boston flavor of English at the source."

"James Shan Leight," Oliver said as Geoff politely turned to greet the distinguished looking man who had stood up when they approached him. "Purveyor of rare jewels, Managing Director of Qing Gems, Cricketer, Rotarian, a long list of civic commissions, and considered the most eligible bachelor in Hong Kong."

Leight smiled, shaking his head at the introduction. "My publicity agent. It is a pleasure to meet you, Commander."

Geoff returned the firm handshake, instantly taken with the courtly manner of the man. He had fine black hair, a pencil-line mustache, and a slightly graying small goatee. "Impressive credentials, Mr. Leight. The pleasure is mine."

Leight pulled up a chair for Quan Quan, who was apparently well known to the guests. She had greeted each demurely with a light kiss on both cheeks. Oliver played host by serving cocktails.

Geoff said, "Excuse me for staring again, Ms. Soong, but I have never seen jade of that transparency and intense color before."

"The Kwan Yin that Madame Soong wears on this chain has twelve arms, each presenting a different token of love and goodness," Oliver noted.

"From Mr. Leight's firm?" Geoff asked. "You told me he was the prince of the Hong Kong Jewel Thieves."

Everyone laughed, including Leight, who just shook his head. "We take no credit for those treasures. They are heirlooms of her family."

"And what about your family? How did you get to be such an influential man?" Geoff asked.

"My father was a diplomat serving in India and the neighboring states most of his life. My mother is a Nepalese from Darjeeling. Like Aimei, I was a diplomatic brat, raised in the English Colonies of India, Nepal, Bhutan, Pakistan, Afghanistan, Ceylon and many others. These places are still an excellent source for me to purloin rare jewels."

"Prince of Thieves indeed," Geoff commented.

Leight smiled. "I take pride in Oliver's thief jibe, for rare gems have been the means of transferring wealth for many centuries. With their great beauty, wealth, and easy transportability, jewels are desired by everyone, including pirates and beautiful women. I am merely a conduit. And you, Commander? From Oliver's tales of the great Martine, it would seem you must be the hero of all of the James Bond stories of mystery and intrigue."

"This group is unique," Geoff answered. "I was a diplomatic brat too, following my father around Australia."

Then Suzette called them to dinner, interrupting the conversation. The aroma of the food steaming on the buffet elicited murmurs of anticipation and appreciation from the guests.

Afterwards, coffee and brandy in the living room relaxed everyone, keyed up from the wine and dinner. Oliver went around the room, looked out the windows, and opened the front door to talk briefly to the agents watching outside. "All right, my friends, all seems clear. What can you tell us of your plans, Jimmy? What can we do to help?"

"We appreciate the interest of your respective countries, gentlemen. For the moment, we do not choose to scatter any chaff to the wind, nor show where we store the rice. We will advise you of the implementation at the proper time."

"Wow, that's cutting us off," Geoff said. "How about the UK, Ollie? How does the PM feel about Hong Kong seceding from the mainland and thus nullifying this century-old agreement?"

"As you say in your country, old man, I plead the fifth amendment. No comment."

"Nothing like an open heart-to-heart conversation, is there? Oh well. Madame Soong, am I also to report a big nothing to your friend, Ambassador Duke, about your plans?"

"Please give Lena my fondest regards. Tell her I still remember fondly the summers with her and Warren at the estate. Both she and Oliver urged me to meet with you, guaranteeing your confidentiality. We have waited for the old hardliners to die so the hatreds could die with them. Now instead of dying, they are rearing their ugly heads again in a final spasm of evil. Li Guohua and I dare not return to Taipei. Except for the merest chance of good fortune, our families would be offering paper dragon boats for our souls."

"Excuse me for interrupting, Madame Soong," Geoff said. "Feng is virtual dictator of Taiwan. This is the same plan that put Stalin into control of Russia for so many years. It also included death, millions of people killed, the exact number unknown to this day. You are two people defending what was a democratic republic only a few days ago. Good Lord, Madame, what will you do?"

"We have to remove Feng and elect a government that will not let this happen again," Soong said passionately. "General Feng has issued orders for our arrest for leaving Taiwan without permission. That is a death sentence that we must avoid."

"You are brave people fighting against tremendous odds, Madame Soong." Geoff said. "What word do you wish us to pass on to our governments?"

"Your governments must consider Li and myself as the Government of China in Taiwan as a government in exile. Our intention is to free Taiwan from Feng's grip and join Hong Kong as part of the new nation our friend Jimmy here has been reluctant to talk about. Chiang Kaishek's obsession of returning to the mainland is a curse that we must exorcise. Those plans are still in abeyance, waiting until sanity again returns to the South China Sea."

Geoff stood up to stretch, facing the window. He saw a tiny spark of flame just before the crack of the gun reached them. In a single motion, he threw himself across the cocktail table, right arm encircling the slim form of Aimei, carrying her with him to the floor. The window shattered a moment later. Above them, a bullet carried across the room where her head had been and buried itself in the bookshelf.

At Geoff's shout of "Down everybody!" Quan Quan dropped to the floor. Voices shouted outside as the security unit reacted. Two of the guards entered the house, defending against a diversion by the attackers. Security took up positions in the front and back of the house, Stens and pistols at the ready.

"Everybody stays down," Geoff hollered.

Suzette rushed in from the kitchen and Alex from the bedroom. Both were pushed to the floor as Oliver took a flying tackle at them. A fusillade of shots came through the broken window, spraying the room with bullets. The sound of returning gunfire echoed from outside as the guards retaliated. Geoff eased himself off Madame Soong and pushed her toward the sofa where Leight had taken cover. Jimmy reached out and pulled her over. Oliver had an arm around Suzette, pulling her off to the side of the room and pushing Alex ahead of him.

Quan Quan crawled over to where the guards crouched outside on either side of the big window. An agent threw a spare pistol to her. She sat on her knees facing the door, holding the gun with both hands in case the attack force tried to crash in.

Ten minutes later, the head of the guard unit came in as Oliver and Geoff got up to check with him.

"We caught one. The other got away. We don't know if they had backup or not. It sounded like two vehicles escaping down the road. There'll be a team waiting for them at the foot of the hill. Hong Kong hooligans, hired by someone they never met, our captive said. He said there is a one hundred thousand US dollar price on Madame Soong's head. Anyone that can prove they killed her by turning in the Jade Kwan Yin gets the money."

"What about the other diplomat who escaped with her?" Ollie asked.

"We checked with the detail around Chairman Li downtown. He is still secure and we doubled the guard around him. Would you like us to escort Madame Soong back to her apartment?"

"No, I have a better idea," Quan Quan said. "Geoff and I will drive her and Jimmy. You can follow, if you like. Have one of your demolition men go over my car to make sure the goons haven't planted a bomb in her."

The guards left to check out the car and to send one of their vehicles ahead to make sure the road was clear. Geoff looked over at Soong and Jimmy Leight. "You two all right?"

Aimei answered in a lighthearted tone to relieve the tension in the room. "A few nicks and bruises from that tackle. I suppose you played football at Annapolis? Thank you very much, Geoff. One or more of us would surely have been wounded or killed without your warning. Please finish what you came to tell us about your plans."

"Happy to be of service, Madame Soong. What I was going to say is that my orders are to help a high official of the Politburo defect and escape the mainland. His identity is a secret, even to me. His intention is to request asylum in the United States. My job is to get him out of there and into a safe place. We have only rudimentary plans, which you have no need to know. I'll wing it when I see the lay of the land. That's it. Wish me luck."

His lopsided grin eased out as he straightened his clothes and gave the high sign of a thumb up, then pointed to the door at Quan Quan.

Suzette gave Geoff a shaky hug and a kiss on both cheeks. Alexander gravely shook hands. Oliver put his arm around Geoff's shoulders with a parting word. "Have a good show, old man; you know where to reach me."

Aimei and Jimmy tucked themselves into the tiny back seat of the Ferrari. Geoff, with a borrowed Sten in his lap, buckled the seatbelt. Quan Quan revved the engine with bare toes curled on the pedals to have full freedom pumping the car.

The lead car left ahead of them, and another followed. Two more cars would pick them up at the foot of the hill and provide an escort to the Canton Road Apartments.

"How fast do you go downhill?" Geoff asked. "If you go any faster than we did coming up, we could just engage the wings and fly down."

Quan Quan, subdued by the near death of Soong and the danger to the rest of them, smiled weakly at Geoff. "Don't alarm the passengers, Commander. This red bird may just fly through the air if we need to get away from trouble." Turning around to reassure the two passengers, she saw it wasn't necessary. Both looked serene and confident. Danger had touched their lives before and they had confidence in this wisp of a woman, knowing her reputation.

With a spray of flying gravel, the red car spun its wheels out of the compound and down the hilly road like a racehorse released from the starting gate. Less than halfway down, the four occupants simultaneously saw the advance police car. It was smashed sideways, straddling the road, crushed against a large truck that blocked the center of the road.

As they bore down on the scene, the headlights caught bodies slumped in the wreckage. Four men were facing them in the dark with heavy automatic weapons pointed directly at the car. The vertical wall of the hill was to the left, with less than five feet of clearance. On the right-hand side, two feet of the flat roadway was open, edged by a 30-degree embankment and a guardrail on the rim of the hill. The total opening was less than eight feet between the wreckage and the rail. Geoff pointed his weapon out the window and braced his left arm on the sill.

The four attackers spread across the highway, one on the embankment, another standing next to the crashed police car, his hand raised palm out, signaling them to stop. "Kidnapping," Geoff shouted, "Let's go for it, kid."

Quan Quan, without a moment's hesitation, hollered to her passengers in the back seat to get down. The tiny foot pressed forward and down to the floor and the car swerved across the highway to the slanted narrow opening. The Ferrari catapulted forward with all the power of twelve cylinders. Geoff braced himself as if he were leaving the flight deck of a carrier in a Navy fighter.

Geoff sprayed bullets to the left side of the road, hitting two of the attackers before they could fire. The bright light of the headlights revealed the men buckling over, weapons flying through the air. Their confederates on the other side, directly in the line of the speeding car, desperately tried to dodge out of the way. The car tilted as it hit the embankment and struck the two men at the knees.

The man on the left pitched up on the cowling, smashed against the windscreen, and slid up and over the car. Geoff shuddered as he saw the terrified face hit the glass inches away. Nose and face disintegrated with the force of the crash. Blood splattered. The body disappeared, thumping as it hit the roof and fell to the road behind them.

The right edge of the Ferrari's bumper caught the man on the embankment. The force of the impact tossed him in the air and over the railing. He screamed as he disappeared. He was still holding his weapon, finger locked to the trigger, bullets spraying harmlessly overhead.

Angling gracefully, as if on a graded racetrack, the speeding car turned back onto the road. Now unstable, the wheels spat the dirt of the embankment. Quan Quan downshifted and pulled the hand brake, locking the four steel discs. The next hairpin curve rushed at them. The wall of the hill loomed, ready to do what the gunman had failed to do. Inches from the wall, the car spun in a 360-degree turn. Quan Quan released the hand brake and engaged the foot brake and accelerator with a heel-and-toe action.

"Think she hit one-fifty, Mon Capitaine?" the half-smiling Geoffrey spoke.

Glancing sideways at Geoff, Quan Quan pouted. "Maybe two-hundred? At least one-seventy-five."

"Must have been good, because I think my blood pressure hit two-hundred on that one."

"Good on you, darlin', nice shootin'. Glad you enjoyed it."

Geoff turned around to see Jimmy helping Aimei to an upright position against the swaying of the car. He had thrown himself on top of her at the beginning of the episode.

"Everybody all right back there?"

"We're okay," Aimei replied. "A little crushed in body and spirit, at the moment. Being shot at twice in one night is too much. Now we owe our lives to you again. What happened? All we could see was the roadblock with guns pointing at us. Then we ducked."

"Not too much," Geoff said laconically. "The banditos apparently trapped the police car ahead of us, the one that was supposed to take you down to the city."

"Two more good policemen killed," Leight added. "This has got to stop. There are too many rogue elements here attracted by the enormous wealth passing through Hong Kong. Murder, kidnapping, theft and now hired mercenaries."

"I'm thinking of entering Quan Quan in a few of the world class races when this is all over. We can't lose if we get some wheels like this Ferrari under her," Geoff said.

The red sports car pulled up on Canton Road in front of the exclusive Harbour Village Apartment Complex. A cordon of police formed around them to take charge of the passengers.

Geoff took his leave, lifting the delicate hand of Aimei Soong to kiss. The handshake with James Shan Leight was even firmer than before, with the man's eyes boring into his, exuding confidence in the future. Both Aimei and Jimmy hugged and kissed Quan Quan, promising to see her soon.

Quan Quan shifted into second, eased out the clutch, and revved the engine. They headed toward the fly-over at the end of Canton Road. Braking suddenly, she pulled over to the curb. "Geoff, I've been through a lot of heavy trauma since meeting you and so far survived. May I be so bold as to say you attract me as a port in a storm. We have until noon tomorrow until your plane leaves."

ELEVEN
BEIJING

5 MAY 1994

"Mornin' Geoff. How was the R&R in Hong Kong? I heard you got back yesterday." Patrick sat next to a sleepy-eyed Geoff having breakfast in the embassy dining room.

"Tiring and interesting, Pat. The Cathay Pacific flight arrived late. I turned in and slept around the clock. How's the Good Lady holding up with all the fluff in the air?"

"We'll find out this morning. Staff meeting called for ten, in the big office. You, me, and the Ambassador."

"Hmm. Is that so? I'll put together something so the Madame won't think I've been goofing off. What has the China Daily been saying about the coup in Taiwan?"

"Geoff. You know those birds. The official attitude is: what coup? That's the second item on the agenda this morning. You are the first and third."

An hour later, dressed and groomed, the two men were waiting for the meeting to start. "Good morning, Madame Ambassador," Duffy and Martine echoed in unison as Lena Lao Duke entered.

"Good morning, gentlemen. Welcome back, Geoffrey. I hope your visit was fruitful and you have news of my friend Soong Aimei. Patrick, will you close the door, turn up the music and pull the chairs close together." At Geoff's questioning look, she added, "There's a new report out that the Chinese have bought Russian listening devices. We are being careful."

She took a tablet from her desk, pulled her chair close to the two men and continued. "Care to give us the benefit of your recent adventures? You sure do get around: the White House one day and the Shangri La in Hong Kong the next. I wasn't aware you were in Washington until I saw a commendation come across my desk for review. Apparently, I act in the capacity of a commanding officer for military personnel under my roof. How are all the good folks in the Oval Office?"

Geoff rubbed the side of his cheek with a finger and drawled, "Top secret has a habit of seeping out through the bottom of bureaucratic officialdom. So much for security, Mrs. Duke. We had somewhat of a melee in Hong Kong with the MSS's new Secret Service teams. Fortunately, I survived and had the good fortune to take a message to home base. Sorry. You'll have to get the details through State the next time you see the Secretary." Geoff looked up, brushed the cowlick out of his eye, and used his most sheepish look to get past the irritated look on the Ambassador's face. "I can tell you that I may have to take a couple of tourist trips around China in a week or two."

"Another secret mission, I suppose. Blast the regulations. This is my turf and I'm the last to know. How is Soong? You were supposed to see her in Hong Kong."

"Soong Aimei is an elegant lady, Mrs. Duke. We met and had an interesting evening at a friend's house. I helped her out when some goons took some pot shots at her and then tried to waylay us on the highway."

"What did you think of her?"

"Besides being beautiful, she is a strong person. It's entirely possible she could govern the R.C. in Taiwan one day, when the General gets his come-uppance. She sends her best regards and would like you to visit her in Hong Kong as soon as you can."

"Thank you, Geoffrey. That is good news. I shall try. You must have made a connection in Hong Kong. There is an unofficial request for you to return next week from someone at the Hong Kong Bank, reason not stated."

Duffy had been listening intensely, not missing a word or inflection. "That message came in this morning, Geoff. I forgot to tell you about it. Your old friend Abernathy has some unfinished business for you to attend to. He said it would only take two or three days around the fifteenth of the month if you can make it."

"No problem, if Madame Ambassador will give me another three days R&R."

"Do I have a choice?"

Duffy replied. "No ma'am, but courtesy dictates the protocol. Maybe one day Martine will write a book and tell us what he does when he's out of school. It should be very interesting."

"That's all I have to say, gentlemen, except the routine fax and telex communications. You might go through them, Geoffrey. Duffy has already seen everything, usually before I do." She smiled. "The book idea is intriguing. We could collaborate."

"You honor me, Mrs. Duke. Your reputation as an author is very impressive."

Geoff exited the main gate the next morning in his jogging suit. Light was just edging over the buildings. The air was still cool and damp from the night temperature.

"Have a good run, sir," the marine guard said, logging him out.

Geoff took off on the back street behind the embassy. He preferred it to the busy Jianguomen. The apartment buildings filtered the sun in intricate patterns and the boulevards had park-like dividers and pleasant shrubbery running down the center. This is China, he thought. Early morning, merging with the people of the street, joining their Taijiquan exercises. For a short time, the hardships, the politics, and the stress can be forgotten.

Three blocks from the embassy, a black Shanghai Special was parked on the street facing him. Exiting it was a familiar figure Geoff hadn't seen for five years.

Like déjà vu, the figure duplicated his memory of the man. A small man attired in Beijing casual wear emerged and waited by the back door of the vehicle. The full head of black hair was rumpled as if he had just risen from bed. A cigar dangled from the corner of his mouth.

Geoff's survival instincts made a quick appraisal of the area. Uh oh, hot shot. Wonder what Bubba wants this early in the morning. He has backup. Two more in the car and another vehicle across the road. Keep it cool. Let him make the first move.

The four men got out of their cars as Geoff approached. Fan Riqi spoke first. "Good morning, Commander Martine. It's pleasing to see you enjoy your reported run each morning on this route. You will forgive me if I interrupt you for a short time."

Geoff pulled up, bringing to bear as much height intimidation as he could muster by leaning over the smaller man. "Vice Commissar Fan Riqi, I believe. Your personal attention honors me. Two backup teams? My oh my. Are they Shaolin, or plain MSS goons?"

"You're annoyed, Mr. Martine? Regrettable." Fan smiled and extended his hand. "In another setting we could be friends. I'm a great admirer of yours. You're a very clever operator."

Geoff thought about refusing the handshake for a moment, and then decided an amicable relationship would be better. "Okay, Mr. Policeman, shake. You've something in mind? Surely, you didn't get up this early to tell me how much you respect me."

"Americans are so direct. We prefer more subtlety with our relationships and more time to enjoy the pleasure of intellectual contact. Mahn mahn, we say. Slowly slowly. I invite you to spend a short time with me, no more than an hour, I guarantee. We'll return you to this very place. No worse for the wear, I believe your idiom is."

"There are options, policeman. I could run and scream about diplomatic immunity. We could engage in somewhat of a confrontation, though I admit five to one is poor odds. On the other hand, it might be interesting to see the early morning show. What the hell, Commissar, let's go."

Fan held the car door open for Geoff and went around the other side to join him in the back seat. "We've met just once, Commander, as you may remember, outside the Embassy many years ago. You have gained rank since then, another stripe I believe you call it. Congratulations. I remain merely a poorly paid assistant to the Commissar. I admit I much prefer being called a policeman or a detective. My favorite American TV stars are Columbo and MacGyver."

"Detective Fan Riqi." Geoff paused, sat back in the seat and crossed his arms in contemplation. "That would make a fascinating TV series, especially if the locale were Beijing or Shanghai. I'll suggest it to my friends in Hollywood the next time I'm there. I would think the character of the French Detective Poirot would be more suitable than the old Charlie Chan however." Geoff conjured a smile and a wink, enjoying the repartee. "Would it be possible to learn exactly why you've kidnapped me? It's not considered good diplomatic form, you know. It would ease my mind a bit if I knew what this is all about."

"Patience, Commander, patience. We are going to visit a very special place in Beijing, an historic building that has never been seen by an American, to my knowledge. I must caution you, though. Don't be alarmed. We mean no harm to you. I reiterate my guarantee that we'll have you back at the embassy in good time. No one will even know you've been gone. We'll deny having met, if you lodge a complaint. We'll attribute it to your reputation as a trouble maker. You've caused us a good deal of embarrassment, you know, removing one of our worst criminals from under our thumb. Then, adding insult to lost face, your country saw fit to let him loose in the world to create more irritation for China."

Geoff smiled. "We do have a difference of opinion, detective. Our worlds operate under opposing ideas of government. You still haven't told me where we're going."

Fan unwrapped a cigar instead of answering and went through the ritual of lighting it. Geoff reached across him and wound down the window without comment. Fan's eyes rolled up to follow the movement. Geoff watched the passing scene, streets ghostly this early in the morning, more bicycles than cars. Workers going to their jobs, many with young children balanced on the front, or wives sitting side-saddle on the back.

There was no identification on the entrance gates. The compound was like a thousand other industrial, faceless buildings in Beijing. Double fences topped with barbed wire surrounded the entire compound, marking it as a special area. Uniformed local police guarded the perimeter and gate. Geoff noted the loaded guns, the personnel surprisingly alert.

"Qincheng Number One, Commander. Our most famous retention center for recalcitrants. It's here that we try to re-educate them in the proper way to think and act."

Geoff's mind was working overtime. Qincheng Number One? That's their prison for political dissidents. What's he going to show me? Relax, hot shot. Keep the mind clear. He's probably going to try to impress you with something. Once inside, you could disappear. No place to make a run for it either. The other car is right behind us. Assuming I get out of this, the boss will be pleased with an inside report of the Chinese Lubyanka. Fan knows what he's doing. He didn't get up to number two without having some balls.

"Very impressive, Commissar. I assume we are going in for a tour around the facilities? Damn, I didn't bring my camera. The boss would love to have a few snaps of this place. Don't suppose you have one to lend me?"

Fan laughed. "Very good, Martine, I like your sense of humor. The sight of a camera might incite the guards to begin shooting. Come, there is someone I wish you to meet. We'd like to impress you with our ability to react in difficult situations."

Inside the prison, Geoff emerged from the car and followed Fan into the building. The MSS detail waited outside. Four uniformed guards formed up ahead and behind them. Fan was tight-lipped. The entourage began walking lockstep through endless hallways, around corners, and up three flights of stairs.

The concrete walls and floor were dank, dimly lit. Toilet odor permeated the air. Geoff shivered.

They finally stopped before a door. There were no bars, and the door was unlocked, Geoff noted. The guards took up positions in the hallway. Fan opened the door and beckoned Geoff to walk ahead of him. High ceilings, unwashed windows, crude furniture and naked light bulbs made the room look like an ordinary Chinese business office. Against each wall stood four double tiers of bunks. A dozen men sat around a table in the center of the room. They started to get up when the door opened. Fan waved them back to their seats.

"Don't let us interrupt, Comrades. Proceed with your discussion. I have brought a foreign visitor to see how pleasant our re-education system is." Fan turned to address Geoff. "This is a rare sight for you, Mr. Martine. I'll explain. The men are all dissidents that sought the destruction of our system. We put them in this open room and suggest they talk to each other four times a day in two-hour sessions. They exchange all their feelings with each other and exorcise all their anger. Once a day, a group leader comes in and listens to their discussions. Eventually, they see how wrong they were and try to convince the others."

Geoff was shocked to see one man was Tsai, the Shaolin Team member from the Hong Kong episode. This was the purpose of the visit then. Fan was showing him how they could retaliate. "I am impressed, Commissar. How long does it usually take to persuade them of the error of their ways?"

"Sometimes a few months. Stubborn ones can spend years before they finally are convinced of the inevitability of the Communist doctrine. Then they go to trial, are found guilty of their crimes, and are released. You see they have already served their sentence by that time. Can you appreciate the system?"

"It would be very difficult for one raised as I have been, Commissar Fan, to appreciate your system. No, I cannot. The reason for your bringing me here is still a mystery."

"Come now, Mr. Martine. Don't you recognize Tsai? He did confess to stealing state secrets and turning over a certain recording to unauthorized parties. It occurred to me it might be you. You were in Hong Kong when this traitor was."

"You are well informed, Mr. Policeman. I'm enjoying your little game of tiger and prey. If you'll be good enough to point out the person you call Tsai, I will try to place him. It's difficult, though. I've such a poor memory. My mother often told me I couldn't remember to come in out of the rain."

Fan Riqi actually laughed out loud. "Another idiom. Americans have their special form of the English language. What must I do to jog that rain-soaked memory of yours?"

"Assuming you're looking for identification of some criminal and you regard me as an eye witness to the crime, have you tried the line-up method."

"You mean when the criminal is assembled with several others to be identified by the victim? We don't have that problem in China because criminals confess their crimes. Often the wife or family informs on them in the interests of the State. Would you be willing to tell us exactly what Tsai told you after he surrendered the tape?"

"I'd be willing to return to my morning exercise routine, Mr.

Vice Commissar. This prison of yours is very uninteresting. I'm glad I didn't bring my camera."

Fan shrugged his shoulders. Then he ran a hand through his hair and replied, "As you wish, Commander Martine. I had hoped you would be more cooperative. If you'll excuse me, I'm going to visit with this group of prisoners. Now that they have seen you, one of them may be willing to confess. My driver will return you to the exact spot we met this morning."

Fan Riqi proved as good as his word. After being deposited crisply back were he began, Geoff resumed his run by heading back toward the embassy. *Duffy and Lady Duke will have fun with this adventure. No use lodging an official complaint. He sure blew me off in a hurry. The big question is did he expect me to identify Tsai, or the reverse?*

The marine at the gate greeted him. "Long run, Commander. Any trouble?"

"Quiet and peaceful, thanks."

Duffy met him at the door. "Urgent coded message Geoff from Abernathy . Return to Hong Kong please in the next twenty-four hours. Special dinner arranged at the Leight House."

"Thanks, Duffy. Book me asap. I'll go clean up and pack. Show the message to the Ambassador with no comment other than I am on the way."

TWELVE
HAINAN ISLAND

15 MAY 1994

The Lear 25 Turbo Commander approached Hainan Island from the west at one hundred feet over the South China Sea. Geoff, in the co-pilot's seat, watched the instrument panel. The panorama of lighted instruments, each relating a bite of information, relaxed him. His right hand massaged his jade charm, while his left hand fiddled with the small radar screen.

Yuan, the pilot, concentrated on the constant beep of the radar altimeter bouncing its signal off the sea just below. It was easy to become disoriented at this altitude at a speed of 380 knots. Disaster was only seconds away if the nose dipped too low.

"We're inside the five mile mark, Yuan. You can take her up to twenty-five hundred. The civilian radar of Haikou Airport takes over from the military at this point."

Geoff turned and hollered back to Jimmy Leight in the passenger compartment, "Almost there. So far so good."

It was Leight who had requested his return to Hong Kong. Recanting original trepidations, the Hong Kong leader had taken him into his confidence and revealed the entire secession plan. Covert plans needed Geoff's expertise. Their friendship had blossomed in the days since then, as they shared each other's challenge for a free nation of Cathay.

The pilot pulled back on the wheel and exhaled noisily.

"Good, I've had enough of snuggling the waves." He tuned the radio to the specified air control channel. "I'd better see if we are welcome."

"Haikou, this is one zed five seven niner alpha. Haikou, this is one zed five seven niner alpha. Request permission to land."

A voice broke through the static. "Niner alpha, this is Haikou. Use north-south runway number two and taxi to the south-end repair hangar. Repeat: niner alpha, use north-south runway two, and taxi to the south-end repair hangar. South-east wind, ten knots. Welcome to Hainan Island."

"Roger, Haikou. I have the runway in sight. Will taxi as directed. Shall I switch to ground channel?"

"Negative, niner alpha. There will be no more transmissions. Over and out."

"They expect us, gentlemen," the pilot said to Geoff and Leight, who had come forward to join them. "We are to avoid the terminal and taxi to the south end of the runway. Radio contact is cut. Apparently, they want us kept under wraps. We have two more hours of fuel, enough to get us back to Hong Kong, Chief." He looked over his shoulder at Leight.

"Can you give me an ETD?"

"It could be four to six hours, Yuan. Geoff and I'll be taken to the meeting. Our hosts have promised guards for you and the plane. I suggest you stay inside the aircraft, set your perimeter alarms, and try to get some sleep. It's now twenty-two hundred. If we don't return by zero four-thirty, or you sense any danger to the aircraft, I order, repeat, order, you to leave. Return to base and report whatever information you have."

"Mr. Leight, the difficulty will be in leaving without you."

"There are other ways to get to Hong Kong, Yuan. Many people still arrive in a fishing scow or junque. If anything should happen to us, follow procedures exactly."

"Roger, Chief. Better go back to your seat and buckle in."

He put the plane, now at 1000 feet, into a long glide to the runway.

"Haikou isn't wasting electricity on this strip, Yuan," Geoff said. "Looks about one third of minimum international regs and we don't know how much is paved. Pilot and aircraft make the difference in places like this."

"Good aircraft though, Commander. Response to controls is excellent. Do you think you could handle this bird, Commander? I've had the auto pilot on most of the trip and she really does fly by herself."

"My only problem would be slowing down, Yuan. After shooting decks on aircraft carriers with the Navy's latest, I'd get lost on a strip this big. Maybe on the way back, we could share the stick and you'll show me her personality." The wheels glided gently onto the tarmac. "Smooth as an oil slick, Yuan," Geoff commented.

The aircraft braked quickly, turned at the first inlet road, and taxied as instructed to the ghost-like end of the runway. It then spun around ready to take off and cut its lights. In Geoff's mind, it looked like the famous airport scene from Casablanca. The dark night air was heavy with mist in the tropical climate. A black car waited next to the hangar, doors open to provide the only light. One man stood by the car, the interior lights framing him in the door. Geoff could see a man and woman in the glow, a few feet away. Eerie, Geoff thought.

Leight opened the door and the retractable steps automatically extended. He stepped down to the ground and Geoff followed a few steps behind as backup in case of trouble. Yuan kept the engine running for a few minutes in case they should need to retreat.

The greeters approached. "Ni hao mah, gentlemen. Welcome to Hainan Island." The woman spoke first. "You will forgive me if we don't use our names. These are dangerous times and we must be very careful. May our new nation be born in peace and suckle strongly at the breasts of its many mothers."

Leight smiled. "It's good to be born of strong mothers. The child, when weaned, is fortunate to have a gift of a golden spoon from a godparent. Please meet my nameless American observer."

"Honored to meet you, Mr. Golden Spoon," the woman said, with a touch of humor in her voice. "Welcome to the tropical paradise of Hainan Island." Turning to Leight, she said. "Will you need refueling, friend, or relief for your pilot? We have three armed men to safeguard the aircraft. They'll patrol until we return."

Leight replied. "No, we have enough fuel for the flight home. The pilot will remain in the aircraft and rest until we are ready to go. Is there any reason to expect danger?"

"It is better to expect it than be surprised." She motioned to three peasant-garbed men coming out to her from the shadows. "One of you patrols continuously around the plane. The other two take perimeter positions. If you notice anything, alert the pilot with your beepers. Two tones for suspicion and a continuing tone if there is serious danger. Your mission is to distract any attacking force until he clears the field."

The woman handed Geoff a small receiver. "Please relay the same instructions to your pilot – two for suspicious, continuous tone for danger."

Geoff took the beeper to Yuan in the plane. The pilot was waiting apprehensively at the door. "Good luck, Commander, I'll be waiting for you. Try to make it back before dawn. This place makes me nervous."

"Take the front seat, Mr. Golden Spoon" the woman leader said, pointing to the waiting car. "We'll have some whispers with your companion while en route."

Leight tucked himself between the two Hainanese in the rear seat. Geoff jumped in next to the driver, barely getting the door closed before they were in motion on an indistinguishable road. The driver, very sure of himself, flipped the lights on for only seconds at a time in the usual manner of Chinese night driving. Geoff heard snatches of the conversation in the back seat. His training took automatic note of the surroundings, marker points and distances as much as possible. The runway was north-south, just turned east out of airport.

He heard the sound of gravel spitting out from under the tires. Uneven dirt road, gate broken, not the main entrance.

And voices in the back.

"It was good of you to come."

"We are fortunate to have such friends."

Control tower in the side view mirror, three small horizontal lights. Eerie silence, not even a barking dog, as if there were no civilization.

"Are there others meeting clandestinely, as we are?"

"Mind if I open the window?" Geoff asked the driver, receiving a grunt of supposed assent in reply. "The air is damp. Expecting rain?" Geoff queried the driver, again receiving an indistinguishable grunt. Maybe doesn't speak much English. Better be quiet and let him drive.

"The clouds in the sky are as hard to count as the waves on the sea, but both are as restless as the people you ask about."

Rural highway, farm lands both sides of the road.

"How far do we go tonight to meet with your group?"

The single lights of homes far off the highway showed in isolated flashes. Otherwise, there was only the sound of air rushing over the surfaces of the car. No highway traffic, auto or pedestrian.

"Wenchang on the East coast, a little more than an hour's drive from here. We had to organize outside the capital. Many are loyal to the Party and General Tang Naiwa. Unfortunately, they have the guns and necessary vehicles."

The car drove on through the night, voices in the rear quieting to a murmur. Headlights winked on occasionally to negotiate a blind turn in the road. An hour later, the lights of civilization appeared ahead. Geoff chanced another attempt at conversation with the driver. "Is that Wenchang, our destination?"

"Yes sir. We're only minutes away. Sorry we couldn't talk on the way, but I had to concentrate on the road and keep an eye out for trouble. They may know we're meeting and could have intercepted us. My contingency plan had several side roads on the way for us to duck into. I'm a farmer here and know all the farm lanes in the area."

"Thank you, Farmer. My apologies for distracting you," Geoff replied.

"No problem, sir. Here we are."

Turning down a side street, the car stopped in front of a storefront to let them out. There was a concealed small panel, half the size of a door, in the night-shutter.

Geoff muttered to James Leight, "Judas Door, security for quiet entrance and quick escape." They crouched almost double to enter what appeared to be a food shop. Milling people crowded the large storage room in the rear. The hum of conversation quieted as everyone focused on the new arrivals. From the look of the debris and the smoky haze, they had clearly been waiting for hours on benches, chairs and floor.

The female leader introduced the group to Geoff and James. "These are the future leaders of the Independent Province of Hainan. Intellectuals, farmers, business persons, student representatives, work cadre leaders, even some politicians-to-be, all here to meet with you and learn first-hand of the general plans."

Then she turned to the group and broadcast her voice more loudly. "Friends of Hainan, these two gentlemen, who shall be nameless for the moment, are here to discuss the plan, advise you on contingencies that might occur, and provide whatever outside backup their governments will allow. This evening will be all too short, no time for speeches. Let's mingle and get to work."

Geoff followed Leight from group to group as the different entities explained their progress and asked about details of the program that might affect their particular involvement. The excitement of freedom charged the air, energizing everyone.

Three from the university reported that the students were in complete control of the student body and part of the staff. They would not go to classes, and would stay in contact and follow instructions, relayed by radio. Demonstrations as agreed would be without violence or interference with vehicles. Not a stick was to be raised, or a bottle filled with gasoline. They had learned the lessons of '89.

Geoff joined the communications group. Two young women excitedly explained their part. "We work at the postal telegraph center. My friend and I operate the equipment now and know how to immobilize it. If the military doesn't show, Chou and Wendy – oops, sorry, no names – are going on the air as a news team like the international stations we have seen glimpses of."

The young couple standing next to them chimed in excitedly. "We've already written pages of copy and background material to use. Other of the students have promised to range out and collect on-the-spot items for us to put on the air. Engineering has promised us handheld radios to communicate with."

Geoff agreed. "In 1989, there were only a few precious hours when the demonstrators tasted freedom of the press. Remember that equipment could be very important to the cause. Don't destroy it; remove parts that can be reinstalled."

"Friend." The question was directed at Leight. "Will we have any military assistance if we meet sustained resistance from the Communists?"

Leight replied with the low-voiced charm that made him such a charismatic speaker. "The central command for the new nation has commando units, called the Jade Leopards. Tough and fierce, they've been training secretly in the Philippines under Israeli ex-army officers. Our military, designed to be small and elite, is very efficient. One company of fifty men will arrive at Haikou airport at zero seven hundred on the fourth of June, after your air force defects and removes itself from the scene."

"What about the sea exposure? How will we control the three-hundred-and-sixty degrees of shore-land exposure?" an anxious voice interrupted.

"Amphibious craft will land another fifty men at Sanya, the southern tip. They'll be equipped with armored personnel carriers and assault helicopters. Each unit is equivalent in power and training to a normal battalion ten times its size. Once you have declared your independence, we assure you, the combined Commonwealth Naval Forces deployed in the South China Sea will back us up."

Six men and women introducing themselves as academics, professors and senior students were deeply concerned about the actual form of the new democratic government.

Leight explained, "There will be a general meeting of the New Provinces scheduled in Hong Kong in two weeks to define the new governments and elect temporary officers. A Constitution and government plan is already forming for presentation at the meeting. Hainan leaders, whose names must not be mentioned at this time, have been notified and will represent you."

Another group of civic workers asked, "Who will be in charge of the University, the city of Haikou itself? What help will we have after the island is secured?"

Leight advised, "Each military unit will have a small cadre of civilian civic advisers. Some of you in this room now provided data that backs up our plans. We believe that the vast majority of citizens, civic employees as well, will welcome democracy."

"My job is bus driver on the main Haikou route. I hope I can continue to work there and maybe the new government will accept my ideas for improving service," said one excited man.

Leight put a friendly hand on the man's shoulder. "We expect all citizens will want to continue on with their jobs until a new government can solidify."

"We are military, sir," one woman of a group of three said to Geoff. "We have a plan to kidnap the commanding General of the Hainan Army unit of the PLA. I'm a sergeant assigned to drive the general's car. Each morning I pick him up and drive to the HQ. The plan is to block the route and supposedly force me to drive to a safe house."

"That is a high-risk plan," Geoff answered. "Give me a quick outline with no names."

The young bearded man of the trio laid out the plot. "My friend here and I work a garbage truck. We hang onto the guardrails with a third man driving. We have timed the general's route to arrive at the corner just as they arrive. We will drop off our truck and enter the rear doors of the general's car with chloroform-soaked pads."

"Surprise should give either one of us a chance to put the general out before he realizes the trouble," the third member of the trio added.

"As I said, high risk, but what then?" Geoff asked.

"We try to convince the General to change sides. The present government calls it re-education," the woman answered. "I was arrested during the Tiananmen period for demonstrating here in Haikou. They sent me to a farm inland with several others for re-education for two years. They did educate me on how to re-educate the General," she said with a bitter smile.

"You have a point," Geoff said. "With the success of a takeover, military people have a way of enlisting themselves on the winning team. It's called self-preservation. You may persuade him, but don't use strong-arm brutality. State the facts and let him listen to the news coming in from Beijing."

The two hours went by so swiftly that Martine and Leight

had time only for a few more quick questions before they had to leave. Leight, checking his list of operational data, asked, "Are you sure the air force unit will defect? That part is worrisome to us. We don't want the unit destroyed, as it will be essential for our new air force."

The woman who had met them at the airport answered. "I can reveal that I am temporary head of the clandestine military forces in Hainan, a General without an Army. The planes will be airborne immediately after the declaration of independence, agreeing to take orders directly from me. Their mission is to defend against any mainland intrusion. The pilots are all young and Western-educated. There's one with us, if you wish to speak with him."

Looking through the crowd, the General-to-be beckoned to a young man in ill-fitting black pants and a red sleeveless undershirt. "Our friend would like assurance of the loyalty of your air unit."

The young man smiled at Leight and shook hands with him firmly. "Please excuse my appearance. Our new uniforms are being hand-sewn secretly now. They'll have Qilins embroidered on them with appropriate rank insignia. Like the Qilin, we have the wings of the eagle, the scaled body and fierce head of the dragon. Our symbol also shows the swift feet of the deer and the intelligent forehead of the unicorn. The helicopter units will have a turtle clutched underneath the body to denote their special power. The symbolism is self-evident, sir. Rest easy that we are solid to a man."

At a pause from the emotional and self-confident young pilot, Geoff commented, "Selections of the symbols for your units are well chosen. May they foretell success and good fortune for the United Provinces of Cathay."

"Thank you, sir," the young pilot said and continued. "We'll fly fully armed to establish contact with your Snow Leopards and support any action if necessary. There are two high-ranking officers we'll have to incapacitate. Suitable arrangements have been made for their safekeeping."

Smiling, he confided in a low voice, "It'll be easy to take them out of the action. They're addicted to a certain bar and jade-garden house near the air base. The women, offended at their brutality over the past years, have offered to see they remain incapacitated for the night and next morning. I believe it's called spiked drinks in your Western terminology."

Exhilarated at the plans of a new nation being formed, all were still aware of the dangers inherent within. James Shan Leight left a parting word. "May the Qilins fly high and breathe the free air of a new and cloudless sky."

The car was brought around and in minutes they were speeding down the highway back to Haikou.

"Hainan, Hong Kong, Macau, Shenzhen, Quandong – these are the United Provinces of Cathay? Who will join us after?"

Geoff listened carefully to the conversation in the back of the car. Jimmy, in the back seat with the General-to-be, was being asked a string of questions.

"Friend, why is the whole delta area of Quandong joining our new Cathay?"

"There is confusion within that whole delta area. Shenzhen economic area is small, only three-hundred-and-seventy-five square miles and a population of less than a half-million. Zhongshan has also been very independent. Being so closely knitted to Hong Kong's capitalism, they wish to be free of Beijing control."

Geoff, listening from the front seat spoke up. "Why is Quangzhou so important to the new nation?"

"Canton was practically a nation within itself for hundreds of years. The new name of Quangzhou is the mark of Beijing leaders. The population, still called Cantonese, would prefer to control the whole delta, whilst the other provinces just want autonomy. They've all had representatives at the provisional meetings. Fearing major repercussions and retaliations by the Zhongnanhai leadership if we fail, they're treading lightly on the dragon's tail."

Geoff turned half around to ask, "What would the economic reaction of Beijing be?"

"Quangzhou wants its original name, Canton, restored. They're responsible for a high percentage of China's trade with the outside world. The Politburo is not expected to accept secession lightly. That loss of income, plus the loss of Hong Kong and the others, will create a massive shortage of world currency in the coffers of the Bank of China."

The woman turned her head and shoulders to face Leight eye to eye. "Can you really expect the present Politburo of the People's Republic of China to endure defeat without retaliation?"

Leight, unblinking at the few inches of space between his grey-green eyes and her deep brown ones, hesitated and then replied, "There are other rumbles of thunder and clouds of uncertainty that may bring swords of lightning to change the whole world around us as we know it today."

Martine intently added, "Madame General, it is our destiny to foment the clouds, stir the thunder and strike the lightning in the hope of changing life for the better for over one billion people."

"Gentlemen, obviously there is much that you are not telling me, for which I do not take offense. The Dragon will have the equivalent of his hind legs and tail cut off, or actually die. Let us hope the offspring will create the better world you desire. You will have our hope and prayers, for which we will burn many paper dragons."

"Your comments are well taken," Leight said. "I can see the lights of Haikou now. We'll say goodbye. May the Immortals protect all your brave people."

The Hainan woman answered in farewell. "Thank you again, my friend. Some of us will perish in the battle, but the people of China will see true freedom for the first time in history."

Geoff checked his watch. It was four-twenty in the morning as the car drove up to the plane at the darkened end of the Haikou Airport. Waving the car away, Martine and Leight rushed over. The engines were idling. A nervous Yuan waited at the doorway, revolver in hand, a Uzi at his feet.

"I haven't seen the guards for a half-hour and no beeps on the receiver. If they've been taken out, we may have a noisy send-off."

As if waiting to be summoned, bullets whistled over the top of their heads. Yuan collapsed in front of their eyes, blood splattering the fuselage.

Geoff crouched, expecting the firing to continue. After a pause, he leaped up the steps and threw himself over the body of the pilot into the plane. He dragged Yuan into the aircraft and felt Jimmy jump in behind him. Then all they could hear were bullets whacking the fuselage around them. "Pull the door closed. I'll take the controls."

He crouched below the window line and rushed to the front cabin, slipped into the pilot's seat and pushed the throttles forward. The racing engines powered the plane down the runway. Searchlights suddenly illuminated the field as vehicles swarmed out onto the tarmac. In the sudden light, Geoff could see three bodies stacked like cordwood at the side of the runway – the remains of the guards somehow lured away from their posts and eliminated.

"Keep down, Jimmy," Geoff yelled as he pulled the seatbelt around him and reached for a set of headphones.

"All clear," Jimmy yelled. The instrument panel lit up, the green light signifying the door was shut.

Stumbling, he lurched into the co-pilot's seat, strapped in, and put on headphones so he could talk to Geoff over the noise. "Poor Yuan's dead. He took direct shots through the head and chest. Do we have a chance to get out of this, Geoff?"

Geoff pressed his lips together, forehead wrinkling down to compress his eyes into a sharper focus." They have forty millimeter cannon on the armored. All they need to do is land one shot on our tail and we've had it. But this baby can go from zero to one-twenty-five knots in about twenty-five seconds and that's time enough if a few of your immortals intervene."

From the side, they suddenly saw their black escort car swerve from the escape route they had taken, make a U-turn and head back to the field behind them.

"Oh no, they're going to try to run a block for us. They don't have a chance," Jimmy agonized.

From the other end of the runway, headlights blazing, a CAAC commercial plane lumbered down the path as if it were going to take off. To the men in the small jet, the Boeing 737 looked like a giant bird ready to pounce on them.

"I think they're trying to help us," Geoff said. "I'm going to turn on the east runway, just ahead at mid-field. We'll have to take a chance on a cross-wind takeoff."

As the Lear heeled to the right, the fugitives caught sight of the black car zigzagging directly into the military vehicles. Two jeeps in the lead both veered to avoid it, hitting the armored cars on each of their flanks. For a moment, it looked like the black car was going to escape through the middle of the vehicles and make a run for it off to the side road.

One armored car, ignoring the effects of the collision, turned slowly. It was like seeing an action movie suddenly going to slow motion. The vehicle turned toward the escaping car, which was silhouetted in the searchlights. The turret gun swiveled and belched a series of shells. They heard the cannon firing and the explosion on impact, overriding the other noises on the field. Geoff and Jimmy watched in horror as the car they had been in only minutes before ignited in a flaming torch of gas and explosives. Three bodies could be seen clearly in the light of the fire, flying from the car, rolling across the ground, each a ball of flame.

The 737 had now passed the east runway. Geoff and Leight watched from the side window of their aircraft. The chase vehicles were all over the field. They tried to recover their line of attack, guns belching, desperately evading the wings of the larger aircraft spanning the runway.

"Whoever our saviour is in the 737, he's one clever dude," Geoff said. They watched him weaving from side to side to cause evasive action by the military vehicles. One jeep was careening wildly over the turf to reach the east runway. An armoured vehicle, apparently blinded by the headlights of the 737, turned directly into it. Its cannon and machine guns fired aimlessly. The subsequent crash forced the 737 to turn away into the path of the other armored car. The plane suddenly exploded as the high octane fuel caught fire, engulfing itself and the vehicle enmeshed with it.

Geoff pulled back on the wheel. The Lear separated from the ground at a seven-degree angle. Pushing the nose down slightly, Geoff retracted the landing gear. The plane responded instantly, gained speed, and shot skyward.

On the ground on the far side of the runway, the remaining jeep turned to give chase, guns blazing uselessly at the distance, and then fell back into the fire-lit darkness beneath them. When the roar of the skirmish had faded into the growl of their engines, Geoff looked over at his friend. "Sorry about Yuan. He did all the right things to protect us."

Jimmy just shook his head, tears cascading down both cheeks.

"They are the first heroes of the new country. My friend Yuan, the General, her driver and aide, not to mention a brave civilian pilot, plus three more caught in the line of fire. It's only the beginning."

Geoff kept the Lear in a near vertical climb. On a whim, he turned on the radio. "Haikou, this is niner alpha requesting permission to take off. Haikou, do you read me?"

Choked with emotion, almost unable to get the words out, the voice came in: "Niner alpha, this is Haikou. The path of the dove is littered with the bodies of nightingales and vultures. Fly on the tips of the waves, as the eagles are scrambling. May the message you carry be worth the songs that were silenced."

Leight signaled to Geoff that he wanted to answer.

"Haikou, this is the dove carrying the message of freedom. We will burn many paper bird cages, and a Goddess of Mercy with a thousand arms will honor the nightingales who have given their lives. Thanks for the warning. We will take care. Niner alpha, tsai jian, sheh sheh. Over and out."

Unstoppable tears were flowing down the face of James Shan Leight as he tried to recover and control his emotions. The new nation would not be born without some loss of life, possibly even his. History related the bloody birth and afterbirth of nations seeking freedom. France, the United States, Israel, the host of new ones in Europe and the secessionists from the once mighty United Socialist Republic created by Russia. He said to Geoff, "Those poor people, I feel personally responsible for their deaths."

They took a last look at the field behind them. Barely discernable, the car was still burning, three tiny blips of fire nearby. Piled in a huge blaze were the 737 and the two armored vehicles, bodies strewn around them.

THIRTEEN
CHENGDE

20 MAY 1994

Wu Xian and Yang Yucie clumsily disembarked from the green railway car, each helping the other down the steps. Both carried black leather satchels. "It's good to be back in the mountain air," Yang said. "We can clear the stench of the city from our lungs and ease the ache of old bones in the mountain air."

Wu addressed the driver. "Thank you for meeting us. Please drive slowly. We wish to enjoy the scenery."

The two elders nudged each other and pointed to the wall of the Summer Palace rolling over the countryside. It disappeared for a time behind the hills, rising again as it circled the terrain.

"Restful and enticing," Yang commented. "I can imagine the imperials arriving on their elephants and sedan chairs. Like us today, breathing a sigh of contentment at the miniature Great Wall to give them peace and quiet."

"Yes, friend, Beijing was just as hot then when the Emperor led the annual exodus to this summer retreat as it is today. But there is a change in the picture from those days."

Yang nodded, "You mean the foot soldiers parading on top of the wall and PLA jeeps around the perimeter."

"For our Fourth Plenum of the Politburo," Wu Xian complained. "Just like at the Zhongnanhai enclave. They are giving us twofold protection. One level to contain the volatile leadership in case there is a reoccurrence of the Hu Yaobang or Zhao Ziyang problems; the other to keep the secrecy of the meetings inviolable."

Yang again nodding his head in agreement, "And we, of course, are the current volatile leadership, according to General Tang, our current Kublai Khan."

"Maybe the cool mountain resort atmosphere of Chengde for this meeting will cool the tempers of the hot heads in time for the full National People's Congress scheduled for the autumn," Wu Xian suggested.

"If General Tang continues his maniacal ranting after this meeting, we still have our retreat meeting at Beidaihe. There, the six members of the Standing Committee could still nullify his plans. It will be our last chance before the National People's Congress."

Guide Wang, the meeting person, opened the car door for them. "Gentlemen, welcome to the historically famous Summer Palace of Imperial families and their entourage. I will see that your luggage is placed in your room. Here is the schedule for the events. Please note there will be a short meeting after dinner tonight."

"Thank you, Guide Wang. We are familiar with the palace. There is no need for you to care for our small hand bags. We can attend to them."

"But Honorable Elder Wu," Guide Wang began to protest. Then, unable to make an obvious issue of the bags, she finished her sentence, "that is kind of you."

Wu winked at Yang when their guide went on into the hotel ahead of them. "Guide Wang was not too happy. Her team captain will also be unhappy because his team captain undoubtedly requested him to look for or plant some evidence in our meager luggage. However I'm sure they will look when we are at a meeting. Actually, all I have in the way of unusual articles is a packet of long beans I bought on the train. My favorite snack when reading."

"We could play a game on them, friend Wu. I saw a movie once where a single hair was placed on a luggage snap. Its loss proved a final factor of guilt for the supposed criminal."

Guide Wang followed them in after a short disappearance. Morose at first, she suddenly brightened and pirouetted in a circle on the new marble floor. "Look at all this, gentlemen. We have had one hundred workmen here for the past month. They refurbished the entire hotel to provide comfortable quarters for the senior leaders.

Modern plumbing with Western toilets have replaced the ancient latrines. An entire hotel staff was imported from Beijing, including new cooking equipment to set alongside the old charcoal-fired ovens."

Yang Yucie appeared thoughtful, wrinkling his forehead as he looked at the now happy young Wang. "Strange, I must say. Hundreds of thousands of Yuan spent for one short meeting of the Politburo."

"The elder statesman is wise," Wang said cheerfully. "Your observation is well taken. This renovation of historic sites is going on all over China in anticipation of the tourist years to come. My teacher at school predicts floods of rich tourists landing at seaports and airports in the next decade, providing untold millions of foreign currency revenue."

"And why does that make you so happy, little one?" Wu spoke in a grandfatherly tone.

"We are urged to learn languages, like English, French, German and others. Foreign school teachers are being hired for two year contracts. They are to teach those languages, especially the idioms and general speech called slang. Soon I will have tourists to guide, especially Americans. I hope to talk to them and learn the real facts about their country."

Massive carved wooden doors swung open on ancient hinges. The elite Mongolian guards were like their counterparts at the Zhongnanhai in Beijing. Their green uniforms definitely did not look like the Imperial uniforms pictured on the huge murals lining the walls of the entrance.

"Can you imagine what our arrival would have been like five hundred years ago?" Yang fantasized to his companion. "We would be entering a colorful, gay place with ceremonial trappings, music, and the excitement of our royal entourage arriving by elephant. And sedan chairs. Long lines of animal and human baggage carriers would follow behind us as we arrived for the summer."

Wu Xian took up the moment the day might have been. "You could have been the Keeper of the Royal Household and I might have been the Emperor's Humble Administrator of Foreign Affairs."

Soft lounge chairs in the meeting room gave real comfort. The hardwood and stone-inset furniture of the Qing Dynasty that had been there before had been relegated to a tourist's museum. The stables that once housed elephants now housed Japanese cars.

"We would kowtow to His Imperial Highness and crawl backwards on the floor as we left the audience chamber, if it were yesteryear, friend Yang."

"Do you remember the cartoonist who drew a panel depicting Politburo members getting off a line of sedan chairs, bareback coolies kneeling in the dust? Then the next panel showed the same group entering a row of limousines. The caption read: 'From the backs of the people onto the wheels of Japan.'"

"Yes, I remember. The Ministry severely criticized the artist, needlessly. The cartoon was very humorous to me. That's one problem with the Politburo today. Fear between us has replaced our sense of humor."

The two elders looked across the valley to the truncated pyramid buildings that reminded the visitors of Lhasa, Tibet. The Temple was a memorial to an earlier celebrated traveler. Long ago, the Panchen Lama, second only to the Dalai Lama in power in Tibet, had traveled on a diplomatic mission to the Emperor. Journeying the breadth of China on elephants and horses, the massive entourage spent a year on the road, exhausting many small villages en route. The baggage contained hundreds of gifts for the Imperial Throne, which was then in summer residence at Chengde. The politics of the time dictated the overtures of peace to the Manchus. The Panchen Lama arrived, presented his gifts, and then died a short time later of smallpox in Beijing. His entourage remained to build a temple to his memory, a replica of the Potala Palace of Lhasa, as a gift to the Emperor.

Looking at the replica, Wu remarked, "We have never solved the Tibetan situation. China's leaders have never condoned a truly autonomous region under our totalitarian government."

Yang added, "Many of our leaders show disdain for the Tibetans, saying they have prostrated themselves for their religious beliefs for centuries. That they throw themselves on their stomachs beneath the picture of a Dalai Lama and precious food and valuables are wasted on endless replicas of Buddha and his disciples. That they sit for hours in the stink of yak butter lamps. Yet every generation has risen against its conquerors, only to be subdued with arms and much blood-letting. We can learn from the Tibetans that the strength of faith is greater than soldiers and weapons."

Wu arose to walk back and forth, pondering out loud. "And yet today our problems are as massive as the ancient elephants were, old friend. One day we will replace the old ways with new systems that everyone can adapt to, but first we must rid our nation of those who would keep us in captivity. Such leaders are no better than the emperors of the world we just imagined ourselves in."

CHENGDE TRAIN STATION

Geoff stepped off the train at Chengde, a duffel bag in hand. A young man in jeans and a white shirt with a small blue button on the shoulder approached him. "Mr. Martine? I am with Luxingshe, China International Travel Service. Welcome to Chengde."

"Yes, I am Martine, but how did you know?" Both smiled, for Geoff was the only foreigner to get off the train. They watched the groups of elderly men disembark. Some were met individually; others followed a greeter to a bus waiting outside.

Guide Wang explained, "There is an important meeting here this week. The men you see are all members of the Politburo of the Communist Party. Those being picked up in private cars are the top bananas." He smiled knowingly. "China is a classless society, you know. What brings you to Chengde?"

"Official business of a sort," Geoff answered. "I represent the United States Embassy in Beijing. We have some important members of our congress coming to China soon. We want to arrange some travel itineraries for them."

As they passed through the station, Geoff noted soldiers stationed at several points. One at the gate asked for his travel permit, ticket receipt and passport. Slowly he entered the data in a log book, as if he had never seen such documents.

Two men in the same outfits that Geoff had seen in the Hong Kong battle – loose black slacks and black turtleneck sweaters, lounged alongside a car across the street.

Geoff and Wang watched the car with the two Shaolin men following them. Wang remarked, "The buzzards are circling. Special security, I suppose. We have a peaceful and happy resort ambience normally. When the Politburo arrives for its plenum, we are reminded of government controls. The tourists stay away."

With no sign that he had said anything out of the ordinary, Guide Wang escorted his charge to the hotel. Geoff checked in and they went up to the room together to discuss the tour plans for his stay. "Sorry about the inconvenience, Mr. Martine. The political meeting and the security for them will limit us somewhat. Unfortunately, we can't visit the Summer Palace, but we'll have ample time to spend in the Temple built for the Panchen Lama and to enjoy the second Potala Palace. There's also the Temple of the Ten Thousand Buddhas that you may like to visit. It's one of my favorite spots."

They visited the Temple of the Ten Thousand Buddhas that very afternoon. The replicas were arrayed in niches from floor to ceiling. Wang explained, "They were once made of pure gold, but the originals were stolen by a warlord centuries ago. Now you see plaster replicas, gold painted."

That evening, after dinner, Geoff lolled around the eerily deserted lobby of the hotel. He could remember the hordes of tourists swarming the hotel on his last visit. They had filled the halls, crowded the snack counter and tourist souvenir section, and made the dining room come alive with their voices, constantly complaining about the food.

From the window of his room later that night, he could see one black-clad watchdog sitting in the open door of a car parked in the driveway.

CHENGDE, 21 MAY 1994

Chou Shi reviewed the scene of the Politburo assembled in the room once used for royal audiences. Tapestries still hung on the walls, but the raised throne and attendant regalia had been relegated to the museum. Folding tables formed a square in the center of the room to accommodate the eighteen men assembled. He was satisfied to know that the meeting would be recorded with the new video sound equipment.

Liu Chinan addressed the morning session. "Let me remind you that we require a unified formal agenda for the Fall Congress. We're to prepare it during this plenum. Then the Standing Committee will review it in Beidaihe next week. These will be the last two official meetings we'll have before the Fourteenth People's Congress, the first since the Tiananmen affair."

Liu Chinan, the General Secretary, spoke eloquently, hoping to form a bridge between the hardliners and softliners. Without some agreement, the Fourteenth Congress would have nothing to stamp with their approval.

"It is time to get on with the modernization of China. The Wendingpai, Faction of Stability, still push for slow movement forward. They say we need five years, eight years or even a dozen years to accomplish the major changes. Right now China is suffering from lack of money caused by the past instability. Billions in tourist and business dollars, badly needed to pay for our Western goods and technology, have disappeared from our budget. Our coastal belt, the delta regions, are again clamoring for independence to bring back the rewards of the pre-insurrection years."

General Tang Naiwa and Cai Jixi, the Minister of the Central Commission for Disciplinary Inspection, pounded on the table seeking attention. Wu Xian stood up at his seat, that very fact signaling his request to be the first speaker. Secretary Liu recognized Wu Xian, with deference to his seniority.

The aged leader continued to stand by his chair to see better into the eyes of the group. He spoke quietly, as was his manner, while the others sat back, resigning themselves to half-listening. "General Secretary and members of the Standing Committee, supreme leaders of our country, we all know our ills. It's time to stop talking and begin doing something to cure our problems."

The room's air of indifference noticeably sharpened. Shoulders straightened and chair legs scraped as they were adjusted to face the impassioned plea of the speaker.

"For once in your lives, I plead with you to think of your country first. The people have spoken through their students and intellectuals time and time again. You all know what they desire and are entitled to, the same privileges as free men around the world. They want to think, act, live, read, and profit from their labor and initiative.

Scattered applause broke in and then quickly died as the hardliners took note of the sources. Wu took a sip of tea as he also noted the bent heads and embarrassed silence of the few supporters.

"Loosen their bindings, open their windows and doors. If we don't do that, history will overwhelm us, like the warlords of the past. There is one last chance, in a very small time frame, for you to act and save China from suicide before the fourth of June. Declare those freedoms immediately. Set the wheels in motion to assure the people we mean it this time. I predict that with freedom of thought and action, China, in one generation, could become a leader of the world."

Wu Xian sat back in his chair and looked around for a glimmer of hope, but could find it only in the eyes of Yang. Others, who would not speak up but agreed, turned their heads down, ashamed to face their friend. They were discouraged, Wu Xian thought. There is nothing more I can do here. Now, I must implement the alternative. There is no other way to save China.

General Tang was up and speaking before anyone realized he was overriding the Chairman's gavel. In his loud, coarse voice, he said, "I have just heard heresy, defamation of the very people in this room, criticism of the Party and its four basic principles. This is high treason and I call for Vice Premier Wu Xian's immediate resignation from the Politburo and the Communist Party. I insist that security place him under house arrest, until we can take suitable action on this traitor."

Raised voices getting louder threatened chaos as the group tried to digest the general's demands. The General Secretary pounded his gavel and shouted above the crescendo of noise. "You are out of order General Tang. You are out of Order, General Tang. The chair does not recognize General Tang."

Tang ignored the General Secretary, refusing to sit down or give up his momentary command of the room. He looked slowly around the gathered leaders, waiting to recognize and make note of anyone openly opposing his damning accusation.

Liu continued to pound the gavel, shouting over Tang's harangue until the General finally stopped, his Mongol features flushed, eyes burning with zealousness. Then he shouted, "Long live the Proletariat."

The General Secretary immediately gaveled a recess for lunch and rest until the late afternoon.

Chou Shi, the quiet Minister of State Security, put his arm around Wu Xian as they moved out of the room into the compound. He noted the curving spine and the slow, painful movement of Wu's legs as they walked.

"Don't worry, elder advisor. You won't be arrested, I promise. Tang likes to hear himself talk and we do need to hear from both factions to act for the good of China."

Wu Xian looked up at the younger man. Chou Shi was a full head taller. "The worry is for China, Comrade Chou. There are few days left in this body. Since Comrade Deng Xiaoping resigned his last post in the spring of ninety, I've learned to take each day as it dawns. My concern is for our country and where the body will lie after certain members of this group get through cutting her throat."

Chou put an arm through Wu's. "Respected Elder Wu, let us walk through the gardens to calm our thoughts. There are factions in our country; there are factions outside our borders, all with zealous concern for power over and above their concern for China. It will take more than words to outwit them. "

Wu interrupted, "There's a greater power than you all can imagine inside and outside our borders. It's greater than nuclear bombs, greater than the fierce words of our General. When the people explode, they'll roll over the party with a force ten thousand times greater than the Yangtze or Yalu Rivers in flood."

Chou replied, "We'll listen to your sage advice as if it were Confucius himself speaking, elder advisor. Will you join my table for lunch?"

"Thank you for your protection and kind offer, Comrade Chou, but I'll go to my room, have fruit, tea, and rest for the afternoon and evening sessions. They promise to be very difficult."

Chou watched him move lamely down the path, around the pool and garden, to his room at the far end of the compound. General Tang joined Chou. "The old fool! How dare he defy us so openly? Has he no worry about himself or his family?"

"Have care, Comrade General. One wok does not call another wok dirty to cover its own soil. It was unwise to demand arrest. The old one is not without teeth, though he seems feeble. I have competed against him at chess and bridge. The International Mensa Society saw fit to award him an honorary membership not too many years ago. The skin may be sagging, the back rounding, but he has a full heart and mind that can be dangerous to your plans. What have you heard from your associate in Taipei?"

Tang hesitated, caught off guard for the moment. How much did Chou Shi know? The Minister's sources were like a crystal ball at times. "The plan is formed and agreed upon. Yellow Dragon has made his move in Taiwan and prepared the next step. Depending on events in our own country, he will go forward soon. History will record it as the greatest military coup that China, or the world, has ever known."

Chou, realizing the General was evading his question, said, "Have caution, Comrade. The Yellow Dragon may swallow the Red Dragon, but be unable to digest the heavy meal."

"Are you well, honored sir?" the young female attendant asked as she held the door open for Wu Xian to enter the modest suite. There was an outer sitting room with the usual overstuffed couches, chairs, a small refrigerator in the corner, and a low carved table in the center with a glass top. Teapot and cups were on it, with a tin of tea leaves. Two thermoses of hot water stood on the floor near the table.

"Just tired, Amah. You need not worry about your elderly charge. At eighty and five years of age, the body does become weary in battle. Please peel some fruit for me and prepare a cup of tea. I'll wash and lie down in the bedroom."

Wu knew some of the staff to be students from the Foreign Trade University, Number Two. They worked during their terms to help service tourists. Often they acted as guides and interpreters. Those with language skills were assigned matching foreign visitors. The young woman carried the tray to him as if in offering to the gods and knelt by the bedside to pour reddish Pu Erh tea from Yunan Province.

"Pu Erh aids the heart, honored sir. May it bring many more years of life to you." Then she leaned in close to whisper into his ear. "There is a friend who might wish to visit with you, Honorable Wu, if you feel up to taking a walk soon."

Suddenly alert, the old one answered in a conspiratorial voice. "It's proper that I meet with this person. Is it possible without arousing suspicion from the guards who watch this humble person like an eagle hunting prey?"

"The guards are hungry, and will have to eat. I'll invite them in to share my rice bowl and bid them to be very quiet so as not to disturb your afternoon nap. If necessary, I will promise to walk with them in the gardens this evening."

"There is another exit then?"

"Yes. In ancient times, the concubines used many secret entrances to meet with their masters. In the bathroom there's a sliding panel behind the cabinet. It leads into a worker's shed where you'll find a common garment, a cap to cover your head, and a white dust mask used by the street sweepers. Take the barrow and broom, pretend to sweep the walk, and proceed down the left-hand path. You'll come to a stream that tourists visit. With good fortune, you'll find a stranger there who will converse in the Cantonese patois. He'll ask if you have ever heard the Nightingales sing. You'll answer, 'When the doves leave their cote'. I know nothing further, nor do I wish to know, honored leader. Please try to return before two-thirty so I can appear to wake you for the afternoon session."

"You are brave, young amah. You know you risk your life?"

"I'm but a nightingale, wishing for freedom, honored sir. It's impossible for me to sing and enjoy life inside a cage."

Guide Wang proposed the day's itinerary to Martine as they walked through the resort's gardens. "After breakfast, we will drive out into the countryside around the perimeter of the city. Views, especially of the Potala Palace replica from a distance, are much better. We see it thus as travelers have over the centuries. Lunch will be ready for us at the hotel and a brief siesta. We have permission to visit the palace gardens later today."

"Thank you, Guide Wang."

"Of course, Mr. Martine."

As they walked, the young guide quietly changed tones. "Mr. Martine, you have told me you are an aspiring poet. I've planned time for you to be alone to compose some poetry about China's future."

"That sounds very relaxing, Wang."

After lunch, they proceeded in the car to visit the royal gardens inside the walls of the palace. "Time for poetry, Mr. Martine," Wang said. "We're coming to a side road beyond the next curve that heads into the gardens. With good fortune, the car with the two black crows that has been our constant company has fallen back and will not notice us stopping for a moment. Please exit quickly. We'll pick you up in exactly one hour from now. Take the path where we stop. It leads to a small pavilion by the side of the stream. Historically, poets used to gather there in ancient times. You may find a dove in the area. Ask if he has heard a nightingale."

"Thanks, Wang. If I get back too early, I'll hide under a rock and write a poem for you."

Geoff slipped out of the car, which barely came to a stop for him. He played the tourist, camera hanging from the strap around his neck, a notebook and pen sticking out of a back pocket. He hid behind some shrubbery and watched the car following them pass on without stopping. So far so good, he thought to himself.

The afternoon was temperate, the sun high, the altitude of Chengde cooling the summer heat. No wonder the Imperials loved the area so much. Beijing in the summer is no picnic and probably was much worse five hundred years ago before air conditioning.

Following instructions, Geoff kept to the left turns and found the pretty pavilion. The stream nearby was moving slowly. He bent to release a lotus leaf to float downward, fantasizing of having been a writer in a previous life. He found himself remembering the story about ancient poets who floated their verses downstream on lotus leaves during contests. Winners were given wine and the poetry proliferated as the wine flowed.

At the pavilion, Geoff took out his notebook and assumed a reflective pose. There was no one around except an aged sweeper lazily moving a straw broom back and forth. A white gauze mask around his mouth and nose protected him from the dust.

The sweeper moved around the pavilion and leaned against the guardrail below Geoff, resting from his efforts. Geoff smiled at him.

"Ni hao mah, Xing Lao."

"Well, thank you, Barbarian. Are you a poet?"

"Only until the Nightingales sing. Have you heard them in this garden, old one?"

"When the doves leave their cote, poet, when the doves leave their cote."

"Can you tell me where and when that might be, Xing Lao?"

"It's said the dove can fly from villa two of the Central Beach Hotel in Beidaihe on the evening of the third day of June."

Geoff caught sight of a young man and woman walking up the path near them. The man was carrying a camcorder, taking pictures of the woman skipping ahead to stoop and pose by the flowerbeds. Without turning around, Geoff whispered out of the corner of his mouth. "We'll meet again under the palm trees. I'll provide a landing for the dove in a safe haven."

Geoff saw the camera rotating around the area, including the pavilion he was standing on. Boldly, he waved and smiled at the camera, impishly hoping the reviewer of the film might realize the smile was for him. It might divert interest from the sweeper if they had caught him in the picture too. He turned around as he got up. The Dove had flown.

"Honeymooners from Hong Kong?" Geoff asked as the young couple came up to the pavilion.

"Yes, but how did you know? Are you Australian?"

Geoff answered with a wry half-smile. "I'm an American with an Aussie accent. I could tell from your fancy camera. You had to be Hong Kong honeymooners or else some kind of spy for the MSS. Locals could hardly afford that equipment."

Geoff waved goodbye and sauntered down the path, taking a picture of the couple before they left. The car drove up as Geoff rounded the last corner to meet it.

"Did you find the pavilion, Mr. Martine?" Wang asked.

"It was beautiful, Wang. You were right. I floated a lotus leaf down the stream but forgot to put a poem on it. An old dove fluttered by and stopped for a short time until a pair of parrots came by. Do you suppose they were wild or domesticated?"

"Hard to tell, Mr. Martine. My guess is they would be a trained pair. I hope you didn't feed them anything."

"Very little, my friend. The dove had flown by the time they approached. Is it possible to get tickets on tonight's train to Beijing?"

CHENGDE, EVENING 21 MAY 1994

The television was playing the tapes of the day's recordings in a top-floor corner room of the hotel. "This is the one taken by the team in the Palace Gardens, Comrade Fan." Hu Banyi was sitting cross-legged in the middle of the floor surrounded by cables and equipment. He continually punched data into the laptop computer. "He's waving and grinning at us, with that lopsided smile, daring us to prove something. Watch him walking down the path, long legs moving like a lion stalking a prey. I wouldn't want to try to outrace him."

Fan Riqi, sitting under snowdrifts of dandruff, puffed on his cigar, blowing the smoke at a cluster of mosquitoes attacking him. "Is there anything else in the scene? Shaolin Twelve is an experienced team, but Martine slipped them when he wanted to, without trouble. We're lucky there was another team of agents stationed in the Garden, one of the two male and female teams we have. He had to be meeting someone, or he wouldn't be in Chengde."

He lifted a hand. "Wait, hold it. Back in the corner of that last shot, someone is walking away from the area. That was the person Martine met. Back the tape up and single frame."

"There's a bit of a wheelbarrow and broom handle showing. Note the bent shoulder of the man. It must have been one of our flock out on the loose somehow. Make a note, Hu. Check all the labor detail records of the groundskeepers. I'll guess you won't find anything. Re-analyze the Shaolin team reports. We have eighteen teams on duty around the area, one for each member of the Politburo. Someone must have missed one of our birds about that time."

"Comrade Fan," Hu said, after running the reports on his laptop computer. "Everyone is accounted for from the time the lunch break was announced until they returned for the afternoon session. Some were talking. The old ones were mostly napping and resting."

Sitting back in the deep upholstered armchair, Fan put his feet up on the ottoman, puffed a few clouds of smoke, scratched his crotch for diversion, and finally commented, "Comrade Hu, the lion is clever and somehow prevailed again. We assumed Martine came here to meet someone at the plenum. He did and therefore it has to be a softliner. That narrows our possibilities. Somehow he met one of our sheep. We can assume there is some devilment afoot. The only question is, who and what? Keep up the search, Hu. You have to come up with a tie-in somehow. Meanwhile, our Commissar is waiting for my report and I'll have to cook up something to keep him satisfied."

Fan reached the door of the room before Hu spoke up. "Comrade Fan. Do you really suppose a Politburo member plans on defecting?"

In response to Hu's expression of bafflement, he could only silently agree. He left the room scratching his head, preparing to face down his superior with no answers for his forthcoming questions, only a growing sense of excitement.

Martine will be at Beidaihe, the obvious place to escape with someone, as he did during the Tiananmen affair. It could be any of the six members of the Standing Committee, even Chou Shi. By this time next week, whatever is going to happen will happen, and I'm in the middle of it.

FOURTEEN
BEIHAI PARK

25 MAY 1994

People moved along the tree-lined streets leading to Beihai Park early in the morning. Bikes and baby strollers interwove with traffic. Sidewalk cobblers, markets with mounds of cabbage, bak choi, fresh fruit, stick ices, and small wrapped breads tempted the parkbound. There were long lines in front of the ticket windows to buy one-jiao entry permits. Purchasers moved happily across the white marble bridge to stay the day. The island was beginning to fill with families and lovers wandering the walkways, climbing the rocks, and paddling around the lake in rented boats. Chefs in the Fangshan Restaurant were at work preparing their myriad of delicacies for the day's patrons.

At precisely 8:45, four people who had appeared to be wandering around aimlessly joined the rowboat queue.

"It's a lovely morning in Beihai, sister," the youth said to the pretty girl joining the queue. "Today is a good day to come to the park. There are stormy days ahead, however, according to some predictions at BEIDA, my school."

"We students at CASS, where I'm a student, have been discussing the gathering storm clouds. There have been predictions from our social meteorologists of a high probability of thunder and lightning that could keep us out of classes completely."

The woman who had joined them in the line spoke up. "You students were talking about a potential storm. At the telephone and telegraph station on Changan where I work, bad weather is also predicted. Some on my team think that a severe storm could shut us down completely."

"Weather is important at my job also," the man standing with them said. "I drive a bus on a main route in the city. Other drivers and I are concerned about the same storm you folks have been talking about. We've decided to stop operating if the storm comes on the day expected."

Pointing to the boats out on the lake, the girl answered, "The people out there, paddling around the rock island, passing under the bridges, laughing and having fun, are taking each day as it comes. Troubled times are ahead, so they make the most of today."

"There's a long queue," the student from BEIDA said. "Suppose the four of us share one boat? If we wait for individual boats, it could be another hour before our turn."

The others nodded agreement. Each gave the young man a one yuan note to make the arrangements.

While waiting, the three of them talked about the families meandering around the park, most with an overprotected, often spoiled, single child. The elderly escaped small, crowded family apartments to wander in the sunshine. Hand-holding young couples worried about their future. Laughingly, the group pointed out plain clothes agents of the MSS who pretended to be tourists with new video cameras recording the scenery.

The girl giggled, pointing at a kindly Japanese visitor helping one of the identified agents. He was obviously confused about his camera's operation.

Winking, the young man said on returning to the group with the boat ticket, "They're not getting the most intelligent people these days, are they? You'd think they would train them to be a little less noticeable."

The CASS student laughed. "I've heard they have been having difficulty getting graduates to apply for the security divisions. It's the one career they must agree to serve, or actually apply for, well before graduation. There was a push at CASS to entice seniors to try for this rare opportunity. Films of action training for an elite cadre at Shaolin Temple were shown. They must join the party. That requirement turned off most of the prospective students. Two of my friends interviewed for the positions. They were treated to party dogma and ideology, couldn't swallow it, and backed off."

A few minutes later, the four people settled gingerly on the rough board seats in the boat. They tried to keep their shoes out of the dirty water sloshing around in the bottom. "Now we can get away from the crowd," the university coed said.

"Is the boat leaking?" the telex operator asked. "I don't swim."

The bus driver, who had done very little talking, piped up. "Don't worry, this lake is so shallow we can walk to the shore if the boat sinks. These boats date back to the reign of Pu Yi, the last emperor, older than my revered grandfather. At one yuan per person, they ought to give us better equipment. If the phrase that the free economic zones use, to get rich is glorious, is appropriate, I could think of a very good way to get rich right here."

"How so?" asked the BEIDA student.

"Design better boats with a theme, like dragons, turtles or whales, and rent them out privately, in competition with the park authorities."

"You're dreaming, friend. The chance for capitalism died with Deng Xiaoping."

"Not if the nightingales sing and our world changes from control to democracy," the CASS student answered fervently.

"The doves need to fly from their cote before that can happen," the BEIDA student replied.

The conversation had turned serious. Spinning the boat around with his oars to look around, the young man spoke. "It looks as if the crows are roaming elsewhere. I hope the day will come when we will have freedom from the constant surveillance. Think of the thousands of people hired by the government to watch over innocent citizens. How is the mood at CASS, younger sister? Are we assured of cooperation from most of your students and faculty?"

"Our latest count, little brother, assures us of more than eighty percent direct response and the rest willing to do everything except show their faces to the cameras. The reluctant ones are usually the sons and daughters of party members who might jeopardize their families. Strangely, many of them report that their parents agree that the government must change. And they are supposedly loyal party members."

"How much leakage and opposition?"

"There are always vermin who would squeal in delight at a chance to get even with an enemy or line their nest for personal comfort. The CCDI and MSS units that appear are so easy to spot they don't get much information."

"We think the government knows there is going to be a happening Thursday, the fourth of June, in memory of Tiananmen. They don't know exactly what we intend to do nor the total scope. We must keep them guessing with much smoke from the pot. When the dawn breaks ten days from now, we hope they'll be surprised. The advantage will be ours."

"That sounds remarkable," the bus driver said. "The students are superb and will lead a new China into the next century. How about the communications group, elder sister? Are most of your workers supportive?"

"Not only supportive, but anxious for the day," she answered. "They're fed up with all the senseless control over our systems by the Party's watchdogs. FAX division says they can't get a message out unless it praises some idiotic party boss. Our technicians continually alter the equipment at the behest of the cadre chiefs, trying to close some loophole in information leaks. Then they wonder why the system doesn't work half the time."

"What condition is the equipment in?" asked the bus driver.

"Many machines are down now, though I believe they could be repaired quickly if the techs really wanted to do it. We expect to control all the regular communications people and most of the technicians. The group leaders probably will stick with the government to start with, since most of them are old party hacks. They have little operating knowledge, and are more likely to foul up the equipment during an emergency than make it work."

"And you, Mr. Bus Driver, what of the labor group and their bid to form a union?"

"We agree amongst ourselves that we must form a union and have tried unsuccessfully for years to make it happen. Many of our leaders, arrested over the past few months, are in jail awaiting trial. Labor is a time bomb waiting to explode. The biggest problem is keeping our own members under control."

"What does labor plan to do?"

"We've studied the Polish group led by Lech Walesa and will follow their strategy of steady unrelenting pressure without violence. Our plans for the demonstration are different from 1989. Instead of leaving the buses on street intersections to be destroyed, we are simply going to immobilize them. All we need do is remove a few essential parts from the engines. Transportation will be shut down. Each driver will take a different part out of his engine, known only to him. There are so few spare parts around that service cannot be restored quickly without our help."

The older man sighed and played with an oar, letting his stress level come down. Excitement and the danger hanging over their heads showed in his flushed face. "Younger brother, BEIDA student, it's time the labor force joined your efforts. We've been afraid and very negligent in standing by while you fought and died for our rights."

"Uncle, we are students today and labor tomorrow. We are students today, teachers and intellectuals tomorrow. We are students today and dock workers tomorrow. We all have emerged from the same womb of China. One day the students of today will be the political leaders of tomorrow and must ready the people for a culture of freedom of thought, body and soul."

"Well spoken, student. You are our leaders, proved by the sacrifices of five years ago. Rest assured that labor and intellectuals will join hands. Dock workers in Tianjin and Shanghai, steel workers in the auto industries of Shenyang, and oil and coal groups from the Northern provinces have all responded to your trumpet calls."

"We students have plans to build a long marble wall in Tiananmen Square, dominated by a white marble replica of the crushed statue of freedom. Stone carvers will etch the names of the many thousands who died in all the Tiananmen revolts.

The other student nodded her head. "Americans remembered their Viet Nam dead in their tablet. It has been a mind-easing boon to the relatives of soldiers who died in that needless war."

The bus driver clenched his fists. "Yes, such a memorial will remind those responsible that we're people with family names and histories. The leaders consider us no better than cattle. Kill those who disagree. Bulldoze the bodies into mass graves at their whim and desire."

"You speak well, Uncle, but first we must win the battle. Then we can address the wrongs. What of the PLA? Is there any information about their cooperation or feelings about shooting us down again?"

The woman from communications spoke up. "The messages fly in bat-like clouds from the Zhongnanhai to the armies around the country. Recruitment is down, dissatisfaction rampant. It's my opinion they'll still follow orders. Until we can subdue their Generals, there is extreme danger."

"Then we must plan to meet again after the glorious Thursday," the bus driver proposed. "We probably have already been seen and pinpointed, exposing ourselves to arrest. That risk we take because of the importance of our task."

"You speak truth and hope, Uncle. It is fortunate we met to review the plans for that hope," the woman said.

The CASS student spoke up in an effort to change the conversation. "It is a lovely day for boating, and just think how lucky that we four strangers happened to join each other for the morning."

The others joined in with small talk as they rowed back to the dock. "The cabbage crop is so plentiful they are piling it up on neighborhood street corners."

"And cabbage does keep for a long time. Melons are due in soon and we can make summer melon soup, which my family likes."

"Bus driver, are they ever going to put new buses on the Changan route. The old ones are spewing all that bad smoke into the air. Beijing air is bad enough now and soon we will have trouble breathing."

"They keep telling us that a whole new fleet is expected, but not for another several years, so keep a mask in your pocket to wear if you are walking near the depot."

"My techs at the telephone center tell me there is a rumor that we may be able to have small phones to carry in our pocket, operating without wires. They are called cell phones and work somehow with satellites instead of the telephone land lines we now use. Can you imagine me sitting here in this boat and calling my mother in Tianjin to say hello?"

"Well, just look at the advance of computers in our large companies. If they miniaturize them enough, we could have them to carry around and do our school studies anywhere. You could sit under a tree and have a computer on your lap."

"Lap top computers. You're dreaming, young man," Uncle said. "But then I guess anything is possible. Our apartment complex just went together to buy one of those new television sets. They set it up in the entrance area so we can all see it like a theatre. It works, but we get the same picture on all three channels."

"Here we are," the CASS student said. "It was great boating with you all. Maybe we can meet again one day and renew our friendship. You can go ahead. I'll turn in the boat and sign off on it."

With a shrug of defiance, they split around the video camera pointing in their direction, deliberately jostling the suspected agent photographer as they crowded past him. The camera fell to the ground, bursting open. The tape fell out of a sprung door.

A crowd quickly formed around the screaming cameraman, who was on the ground fumbling for his equipment. Somehow the camera got kicked around underfoot like a ball in a rugby scrum. When a policeman came up a few minutes later, the man claimed loudly that he had been assaulted, and his expensive camera equipment had been broken. The film cassette had strangely disappeared during the melee, as had the four people he had been trying to photograph. "Go after them, go after them," he ordered.

The officer calmly took out a notebook and ballpoint pen. "Please give me a description of the perpetrators. Did anyone recognize them or see which way they went?" he asked the crowd.

Seconds later, the onlookers had dissolved as quickly as the four culprits. Meanwhile, the photographer pulled out a red plastic identification card, flashed it at the officer, addressed the police in general as stupid goats and hurried off. The broken camera dangled over his shoulder.

That afternoon in the office of Captain Yao Lin, Ministry of State Security, a chastened agent-photographer stood at attention in front of his leader, a broken video camera on the desk between them. "A group of thugs attacked me, sir. The police and a crowd of people watched. How can citizens and our own police stand by and watch hooligans do this to expensive state property?"

Yao Lin looked at the agent with contempt. "Numbskull. Idiot. Clumsy son of a sow. You are trained to be less obvious and to protect your equipment, especially the film. What do you have to show for the whole morning there? Where was your partner? You'll never get a promotion to a Shaolin Team with this on your record."

With a face-saving grin, the agent replied. "I have a tape, Captain. Two hours of filming taken earlier in the park. The cassette they spoiled was fresh. My partner went after the four I was trying to photograph. He will report back soon. I'm sure he can identify at least one traitor."

My neck is saved this time, Captain Yao thought. "Get in the projection room and see if you can identify the four from the previous shots. We need to find and eliminate those people quickly. Exactly what were they doing that made you suspicious? What made you suspect treachery?"

"My training, Captain. Watch for strangers that are suddenly close. There were four individuals queuing for a boat and suddenly they went out together."

"For your sake, I hope you are right. Review the tape thoroughly and call me the minute you have any of them identified. If you have done your job properly, we will know exactly if they match previous contacts."

Three hours later, Captain Yao Lin entered Vice Commissar Fan's office with four photographs in his hand, enlarged to show a group of people in each. Red circles had been drawn around one face in each shot. "We have a positive match, Comrade Fan. These were the four people who entered Beihai Park individually this morning and a half hour later were out in a boat together. Unless that fool agent was trying to cover his sow-mother's ass, these people are important leaders of next week's demonstrations."

"The question is how good is the identification. There are hundreds of reports, photographs, video film, and voice tapes from the past two days to review. We cannot afford to be spending time chasing a wild panda. How do we know he didn't pick out just anybody to save his skin?"

"He did do that at first, Comrade, so we had to use a little incentive on him to make him concentrate. We finally tied in the boat they used, blew up that frame, and then ran the rest of the tape until we got close-ups of the four. Two have been positively identified from file photos. We are working on the other pair for prior record."

Fan sat back in his chair, propped the four photographs up on an easel on the desk, relit a cigar, and then commented. "The two look like typical students with their tight jeans and carnival t-shirts."

Yao smiled. This was going to be better than expected. What luck to catch the four of them together and two already recognized. He pointed out and elaborated on each.

"This one is Sun Qili from Beijing University, BEIDA, whose folder is thick with reports going back to the '89 riots, when he was a freshman. He was a hunger-striker that we brought in after the shootings, excuse me, the affair. He did nothing overt except starve himself, so we held him six months for interrogation.

"The young girl student is from the Chinese Academy for Social Sciences, CASS, Chen Lishu. Her chop is on several posters and we have one other photograph where she turned up in Tianjin with a group of students. It was at a memorial service for Hu Yaobang in 1989. As for the other two, they are too old to be students. We are running them through the files again."

"Pick up the two you've identified at once, carefully, away from their universities. We don't want to alert the other students or start an early demonstration on their behalf. It's important to make sure they are in custody over the fourth of June, so we can find out what the hooligans are up to this year."

"Yes, Comrade Commissar. We expected the students to assemble in Tiananmen Square by this time, working up to a larger affair by the anniversary date. Actually, there are only the usual tourists. PLA patrols have been assigned in the evenings as usual. The weather is beautiful, but a strange air hangs over the area, like the quiet before a storm."

"For once you are right, Yao." Fan ran his fingers through his hair and brushed ash from his shirt. "The Western Nations plan to run documentaries, reviewing the eighty-nine affair. It's very difficult to keep news within China with today's technology. The world views our demonstrations with satellites."

Fan continued, releasing all the pent-up frustrations of the previous week. Chou Shi and the mad General had been at him every day for data. "The sky is full of surveillance by every major country in the world, including ours. They'll see you blow your nose in the gutter, scratch your ass, and will count the bullets if a gun is fired. They see our every move above ground and record some of the movement below."

The unusual flare of temper subsiding, Fan sat back and pointed to the photograph of the older woman. "This woman, I know her. I've seen her somewhere at work, but I can't think where. Make some enlargements of her and the other unidentified man. Pass them around the unit and the police stations. Someone must know them."

BEIHAI PARK, 26 MAY 1994

On Monday afternoon, Sun Qili was led into the Vice Commissar's office. One wrist was handcuffed to an agent, the other suspended in an arm sling and tied to a belt at his waist. A plaster cast covered the arm from wrist to elbow and a large unbandaged bruise showed raw and ugly on the side of his head. Fan looked up menacingly at Yao and the agent, who shrugged his shoulders. "The hooligan resisted arrest, Vice Commissar. He fought back and had to be subdued."

"That's... a... lie..." Sun said, spitting it out like an oath. "Your two goons broke my arm and slammed my head against the sidewalk before they even talked to me. If I had seen them coming, there would be a few broken limbs of theirs."

"Take off that handcuff and untie the arm sling, Yao. We will talk about this arrest technique later. We trained your agents to take a person without a single bruise. Suspend this team until we can have a proper inquiry."

"Comrade Commissar," Yao started to explain. He was going to have to answer for this later. "It wasn't a Shaolin team that made the street arrest. It was the control unit that had taken pictures of them at Beihai Park yesterday. They were angry because this hooligan broke their camera, losing them much face in front of the people."

"That's all, Yao. We'll review this stupidity at a proper time. How about the girl? I suppose our unit had to rough her up also because she was dangerous."

Sun Qili started to explode from his chair, shouting. "What did you do to her? Fascists! Nazis! How dare you treat honest, unarmed citizens like this?" Yao Lin and the agent pushed him down in the chair. He struggled and grimaced with pain as they clamped his shoulder tight.

"Sit, young man, and be quiet while I try to find out what happened, or I'll have them chain you to the chair. Now tell me, Captain, what happened to the girl?"

Sun tensed in the chair. Yao let go of his shoulder and stood up. He looked harassed and sweated, as he always did when he was in trouble with his superior.

"There are no bruises on the young woman, Vice Commissar. She complained loudly that she was hit on the buttocks and stomach by the officers. She didn't like being strip-searched. The woman was more adamant than this one, Comrade Fan, when questioned. Both deny knowledge of a demonstration at Tiananmen on June fourth, or other demonstration plans. Obviously they're lying."

"Obviously," Fan said dryly.

"There's one problem with the girl. We've had an inquiry from a Politburo member about her. One of her classmates saw our arrest unit force her into the car. She's a friend of the official's daughter, also a student at CASS. The esteemed Vice Premier wanted to know what the charges are against her, and where she is being held. I denied knowledge of the incident, saying his daughter must be mistaken."

"The Vice Premier, Wu Xian… and you played word games with him? Ex-Captain Yao, are you out of the little bit of mind you had to start with? Leave me alone with the prisoner. Phone the Vice Premier. Apologize, and tell him you now have information about the young woman. She is in Qincheng #1 prison for making a sign criticizing the Party. Release will be in a few days after some ideology instruction. You will make sure, personally, that no harm or further intimidation comes to this woman. Understand?"

Yao left the office chastened and muttering to the agent leaving with him, "When General Tang takes over, we will handle these hooligans properly. Only broken bones and bruises will prove to them we mean business."

Sun Qili, sprawled arrogantly in his chair, was massaging the shoulder Yao had clamped so hard. "I suppose all that good guy stuff was for me. Comrade... stinking policeman.... Well, I won't buy it."

Fan ignored the snarling remark. He leaned back and pulled out a lower drawer of the desk to prop his feet on. Then he stared eye to eye at the young man. The tape recorder in the drawer was on, and a monitoring video camera concealed in the wall molding above him watched the office. A guard watched the proceedings from the monitor.

"It's too bad that we didn't let you all die of your hunger strike in '89, instead of sending in the hospital corps to rescue you. You should appreciate our PLA. They lost more than three hundred men. Not one demonstrator lost his life during the clamp down."

Provoked again, this time beyond endurance, Sun stood up and pounded the desk with his one good fist. "Lies, lies, lies. You slaughtered thousands of us and you damn well know three soldiers, not three hundred, lost their lives. I saw the blood of my friends and the whole world saw the blood of my friends. One day, you fascists will answer for their deaths."

Fan, seeing that he was getting someplace by building up the anger in the student, continued to prod him. "You are foolish, student. You've been taken in by false pictures from the foreign press, have heard untrue stories from the Voice of America. The only people who died then were our own soldiers. The demonstrators burned their vehicles and overwhelmed them. They are nothing but armed thugs and hooligans."

"Armed with what, Comrade... Vice Commissar? Sticks, stones, words, against cannon and automatic rifles. Even now your men knocked me down, stomped on my arm to break it, and smashed my head against stone. With a broken arm, they feared me and had to put on handcuffs, laughing at my pain."

Fan laughed, seeking to aggravate the student even more. Sun lunged across the desk, swinging his one good arm wildly, but hit only the cigar. Hot ashes flew across the room with the vehemence of the strike. Fan leaned back out of the way, calling out for help.

Sun continued to rant, as the guards pulled him back into the seat, away from the desk. "You and your men fear me, a student with but a voice to defend myself. You are right to fear me. My name and the names of the other students you killed will live long after you and your proletariat are buried deep and nameless. My son, though just a seed now, will carry my name on. Generations will follow, while yours will dissolve in the wind."

Fan's head itched unmercifully. He longed to scratch it. Resisting the impulse, pursuing the anger in the student like a relentless bulldog, he interrupted the tirade. "And this time, you are going to come out with more and more people to fill Tiananmen Square, Chang An, Jianguomen, Xidan avenues so they can mow you down like wild dogs? For academics, you think like two-year old children stamping your feet for a two-fen ice cream."

Sun, rubbing his shoulder again, sat and smiled slyly. "Wrong this time, security man. You're fighting a whole country and you won't have a chance to use your clubs, guns and tanks. Threats of imprisonment and re-education will accomplish little. You had your chance during the early days of Deng Xiaoping. We believed in his modernization and the sympathy of Zhao Ziyan. You've lost our trust completely. You could have controlled a few thousand dissidents. How are you going to contain two-hundred-and-fifty million people demonstrating against you?"

Pleased with himself at gaining this important information, Fan questioned the student softly for a few more minutes, then rang for Captain Yao. "Keep him in Qincheng #1 for a few days, isolated. We don't want him harmed or word to get out where he is. Do you understand, Yao?"

Yao was leading the prisoner out when Fan called out. "Just a moment, Student Sun, another question. You mentioned something about your seed already developing. That wouldn't happen to include Chen, the young lady from CASS?" Sun Qili blanched, then flushed as anger swelled. He tried to throw himself at Fan, restrained all too eagerly by Yao. "Rodent, slime, excretion not fit for the fields. When one-hundred-and-fifty-nine Universities lead two-hundred-and-fifty million people, the wave will engulf your precious General. This chamber, wherever it is, will burn in the hell that it created. I'll live the next few days to see your China disappear from the face of the earth and ours will rise like the Phoenix to become a new nation.

You are too late, Vice Commissar. The nightingales will sing again in a free air."

After he had removed the prisoner, Yao came back into the office. "Excellent performance, Comrade Commissar. What did you find out?"

"It was no performance, Yao. What you and your men did was stupid and outright dangerous to the mood of the country. A mere spark could explode China, tearing her apart at the seams, impossible to recover." Fan was speaking quietly now, thinking of the information divulged by the student in his anger. He must tell Chou Shi. One fourth of the population was going to act. A ground swell larger than the whole of Europe was about to drown the nation.

FIFTEEN
BEIDAIHE

FRIDAY 30 MAY 1994

Vice Premier Wu Xian and his daughter Mei Lei, each carrying a black valise, picked their way through the encamped crowds at the Beijing Railway Station. More than a dozen pairs of tracks fed out from this central core of China to the four corners of the Nation. Family groups, infants, running children and mounds of personal luggage entangled the sidewalks, curbs and parking areas outside the station.

The people were dressed in a hodgepodge of clothing from silks, clean and neat, to rags, torn and soiled, emitting the stink of unwashed bodies.

Travelers arrived and left the station by car or van if they were officials or visitors. They moved on foot, bicycle, pedal carts or buses if ordinary citizens in this classless society.

In spite of the new rules for cleanliness, garbage spilled everywhere beyond the capacity of the clean-up crews. The constant hacking coughs of China's eternal bronchial problems produced indiscriminate globs of sputum at the curbs. Only the deluge of summer rains washed the pavements clean for a short time.

Entering the cavernous station, Mei Lei showed the bored gate attendant their tickets. The crowds were thinner inside, as only those with paid tickets could enter. "It's early, Father. We have two hours before train time. I think it's better if we go to the V.I.P. lounge and have some tea. I know you prefer to mingle with the people, but the wooden benches will be very hard to sit on. Please?"

"All right, Mei Lei." Wu Xian smiled at the lovable young woman he was so proud of, the only flower of his second, late-in-life marriage. He thought less often in these troubled times about his first wife and family, lost when the Nationalists burned his village to the ground. Mei Lei's mother, only forty to his sixty years at their marriage, had not survived childbirth, the strain too much for her years. This spunky young woman and his love for China gave purpose to his life.

Mei Lei, a student at the celebrated Chinese Academy for Social Science, had made the contacts for him through friends at school. He had never questioned how. In the code of clandestine society, he did not need to know. The secret meeting with the American at Chengde had gone well. If they succeeded in extracting him, he would insist on the Americans taking her with him when they left the country. There would be no place in China for her without her beloved father. They followed the crowd to the long escalator going up to the concourse level of the station and turned left at the top. The main stream of people went ahead into the gate areas. An attendant at the doors of the lounge, bored and unsmiling, checked their tickets to make sure they had paid for soft-seat passage, thus entitled to use of the exclusive waiting area. This special room contained cracked leather lounge chairs, soiled cocktail tables, a hot water urn with tepid green tea, and a very malodorous toilet.

Mei Lei sat her father down with the luggage and went to bring hot water for tea. She used a pair of clean screw top drinking mugs brought for the trip containing the Pu Erh tea he liked best. Disdaining the lounge tea, she took boiled water from the worn, dented thermoses stacked on a counter.

Mei Lei thought, It is pleasing to see father freshly alerted about the impending adventure. Gone is the pretend senility he saved for the meetings. He now looks at the world with bright eyes and only the tiniest wrinkles at the corners. Hope. I love the smooth waxen cheeks, round face, the tender smile seeping from thin lips, seen so seldom these past years. I share the ache of his old bones each time he winced getting up from a bed or chair, and his frustration at trying to bring China into modern times.

Democracy now reigns over much of the world; even Russia

shows halting progress. My hope is for father to see China become a true democracy before he dies. There are a few years left.

Wu Xian closed his eyes and rested. Mei Lei looked around the room. German tourists were in one corner, attended by a Luxingshe guide explaining the rules of train travel. Since the resurgence of Germany, the Germans had become world travelers, starved for most of their lives of visiting the outside. China welcomed any tourist money in these times.

Two Western businessmen sat together, glumly not talking to each other. A few pairs of middle-aged and older couples were whispering together, not daring to strike up a conversation with strangers. Other men in pairs and threesomes, all carrying identical black valises, talked and wandered aimlessly around, apparently on official business to the other provinces of China. Many had teacups filled with the watery tepid green tea supplied in the lounge. Few drank more than the first sip.

A man and a woman entered the lounge with the brash, wonderful effrontery Mei Lei loved in the easily recognizable Americans. The man had greying red hair with a cowlick begging to be brushed back. He was tall with a handsome, craggy face. The woman, almost as tall, had mousy-colored hair primly tied back. Her large glasses roamed the room like television news cameras seeking the center of action.

Mei Lei thought, wouldn't it be wonderful to walk boldly into a train station or airport terminal without worrying about which pair of men or women were watching your every move. Walk up to a counter and buy a ticket for wherever you wanted to go without having to show a permit or identification card. Freedom: described in the Western dictionary as the condition of being politically free. Would she and her father finally taste it?

Geoff quickly took in the room with a sweep of his eyes. Emily, his backup, also assigned by CIA Headquarters at Langley, was a staff secretary at the embassy. "Let's sit over here, Em. They won't call the train for another hour. Would you like me to get you a cup of tea?"

Looking at the decrepit thermoses, she answered. "Ugh, no thanks. I'll go dry until I get out of here. This train station is really something. Every time I come here it's more depressing. Can you spot the goons?"

"They could be any of the black bags. Try not to be obvious, but catch the pretty young girl with the elderly sleeping man. I've a strange feeling that I've met the old one before. They look different from mere vacationers and could be attending the meeting coming up in Beidaihe. Take off, Em. I can handle it from here. I'll stay in touch." Geoff gave her a peck on the cheek and watched the prim figure march out.

Mei Lei was watching, wondering how she would react if that man put his hand on her hip as casually as he had on the woman with him. Whispering love talk probably, though they looked ill-matched. There was little opportunity for sexual exploration at school. She was the daughter of a Communist Party leader, set apart from the crowd, dangerous to associate with. None of the young men took any liberties with her. She understood little when the other women students joked amongst themselves about their experiences. The American kissed the woman in public. How casual the Americans are. How wonderful it must be to express your feelings openly.

When Emily Forbes had left, the room quieted. Finally, the attendant went around announcing the departure of the Beidaihe-Shenyang-Chongchun-Harbin train. Geoff roused himself from the stupor of a nap, noticing the old one had been awakened from a similar pose by his younger companion. Geoff put the duffel bag strap over his shoulder and joined the file of people going out of the room. They went down the concourse to the gate plainly marked with train number 1362.

His train waited on track four. Down the steps to the underground tunnels beneath the tracks and up again to the departure level. Geoff checked his ticket. Car 9, Seat 12. The train attendant smiled when he double-checked at the car. "Beidaihe?" He showed his ticket and she nodded yes, motioning him aboard. Locating the seat, he set out a book, walkman, and two cassettes of Montavani to occupy him en route. The duffel went into the overhead rack and he settled himself against the window.

The older man and young woman walked slowly by to the next car forward. The face now came into focus, recognized from the files he had gone through before leaving the embassy. The elder was Vice Premier Wu Xian traveling on an ordinary train, without an entourage. He compared it to the Vice President of the United States, who moved only with a retinue of guardian agents, staff, press and hangers-on. There were only two of the pseudo businessmen following Wu Xian and his companion, probably a Shaolin team sent to keep him under control, not for protection. China is a strange country. Will I ever fathom it entirely?

The train jerked and began to roll. Ceiling fans were turned on and music began blaring through the static of the speakers. "Turkey in the Straw." Geoff smiled to himself, no doubt one of the few Western music tapes they had, selected especially for him. He recognized people from the waiting room who had entered the same car. The German tour group settled in with a great deal of noise and their national guide.

The attendant came by with papered tea portions, requesting the customary two fen, and supplied a clean-looking cup and cover. She pointed to the thermos under the tiny table.

"Sheh, sheh." Geoff thanked her and emptied both packets of loose tea into the cup. He filled it with steaming water and let it steep. The man and woman in the seat across the aisle from him glanced over from time to time, but made no effort to return his smiling nod or start a conversation.

He mused to himself. Not like five years ago when China's open-door policy pervaded. People would speak the few English words they knew, exchange pleasantries, often fruit and snacks. Now there was the fear of contamination with a foreigner instead of the joy of visiting. Too bad.

Precisely at six-thirty, as scheduled, the train pulled into the station marked Beidaihe in English and Chinese. Through the window, Geoff saw a young woman with the blue Luxingshe button sporting a bright print rayon blouse and blue denim skirt. Knowing his car and seat number, she waved to him as the car pulled to a stop right in front of her.

As Geoff emerged from the car, the woman introduced herself. "Mr. Martine, I am Wang, your Luxingshe guide. Welcome to Beidaihe." She quickly appraised the tall American. A friendly smile started down from his eyes, emerging as a wry grin. "It's been a long time since I've had an American tourist to guide. I hope you will stay for a while."

Geoff actually laughed as he acknowledged the greeting. "Are all guides with Luxingshe named Wang? It seems I have met most of your family from time to time, traveling through China. Thank you for meeting me. I believe you want these travel orders," he said, handing her the CITS travel packet.

The pretty oval face leaned back to take in the tall American and broke out in a laugh. Her hair braid, extending below her waist, swung cheerfully with the laughter.

"Wang is a very popular name in China, like Smith, in America. You may call me Cha Cha, if you like."

Geoff chided, "Now that isn't a Chinese name. Where did you pick that from?"

"From an American couple I guided many years ago. They said I was so effusive, I reminded them of a Latin American singer. Our car is waiting over there for us, but I do have some bad news."

"Don't tell me. All the hotels are full and I have to sleep on the beach."

Wang giggled, holding her hand to her mouth. "The sea turtles would lay eggs nearby and the crabs would surface and pinch you. I couldn't get a villa at the Central Beach Hotel, as you requested. The officials have taken all the deluxe accommodations because of some meeting here. There is a comfortable room in the hotel building close to the beach, however, that I think will be suitable."

As they crossed over the tracks and then through the station gates, Geoff noticed the Vice Premier and his daughter had gone ahead, met by a black limousine. At the car, another man of his generation greeted them effusively. The three climbed into the car. The two guardians jumped into another car and swiftly followed.

Geoff took in the whole scene and glanced around to see if he could catch sight of the team that was probably following him. Two youths sitting on motorbikes a couple of hundred yards from the station were the only possibilities.

Geoff's instincts went into high gear. Little danger of losing me en route from Beijing. It was simple to have someone pick up my trail on arrival.

Wang, anxious to keep the American around, was describing the possible recreational activities in the area. "If you stay the whole week, we'll take some trips into the country. One day in particular, I'd like to show you Shanhaiguan, near Qinghaungdao, where the Great Wall begins at the sea. In Beidaihe village itself, you might find it interesting to visit the open market and the shops. This is a seaside resort with many souvenir shops, and a friendship store."

Geoff interrupted. "I'm familiar with China's Friendship Stores – they sell only imported goods and China crafts, isn't that right? Locals are not allowed to buy there and only the tourist foreign exchange currency can be used. Cha Cha, if you need to buy anything there like Kodak film, I'll be happy to get it for you."

"Thank you, Mr. Martine. I love Coca Cola and that is the only place available. But we do have an old bakery called Keisselings left over from the German settlement years. They serve ice cream and Sacher tortes."

Geoff smiled. "Then you're not completely deprived. You'll have to take me there. What else have you got planned for us?"

"Well, for exercise, we can walk for miles down the beach."

"How about fishing?" Geoff asked. "Is it possible to rent a boat, or go out with the fishing boats?"

"I will ask my leader. No one has requested that adventure before."

"Rest is really what I came here for, Cha Cha. The diplomats have their enclave here, I know, but I didn't want to get caught up in any parties or get involved in political discussions. By the way, how's the food at the hotel?"

"You will find it excellent, Mr. Martine. Lots of fresh crab, which we are famous for, and other seafood caught daily. The locally grown fruits and vegetables are delicious. I'm sure you will find it most satisfying."

Checking in at the hotel, Geoff filled in the usual foreign visitor's form, surrendered his passport to the desk clerk and followed Wang toward the beach. The air was tropical. Palm trees, sandy soil, and lush greenery filled the space around the buildings. "What about the night clubs and discos that were just beginning five years ago? Foreigners were allowed to dance and the locals watched us."

"The government cancelled them, as evils of the Western world. It was too decadent and turning our people in the wrong direction."

Geoff detected a note of wryness in her voice as they walked down the path to the room. It was hard to imagine this vibrant young woman never dancing and swaying to rhythms or enjoying the fervid beat of modern youth music. He noticed the limousine drawn up at the entrance of Villa #2 as they walked by. "Is that an official coming in for the meeting?"

"Yes, he is an elder we all respect, Wu Xian, the Vice Premier. He has been known to fight for the modernization plans of Deng Xiaoping. The young woman is probably his daughter. The other older man is another member of the Politburo. I don't know his name. I've been told there will be six important men, the Central Committee of the Politburo, and we are to keep our guests far away from them. No pictures, no casual talk."

The two guards who had followed Wu Xian now numbered four, Geoff noted. They noticed Wang and her guest stop for a moment to watch the arrival of the officials. Two of the guards started over toward them, waving them to keep moving. This was not the time to cause a scene or draw attention to himself.

"Come on, Cha Cha, let's not annoy the local black crows. What are the rooms like in the villas?"

"Reception room, bedroom and bath, very luxurious, larger than my home where my parents and grandparents share the apartment. We can stop by Villa #4, still empty, and have the room boys show you around."

"Good idea, Wang. In case I return next year, I'll at least know what they look like inside."

They stopped by the empty villa and the two room boys joked with Wang while Geoff looked casually around. The usual front room contained an overstuffed sofa, lounge chairs, tables, tea necessities, and a small green refrigerator in the corner with a lock on it. The bedroom had twin beds. In the bathroom, an ancient porcelain tub on claw feet crowded the walls. It was big enough to soak in, rusty stains coloring the once white ceramic. A double-panel storm shutter opened to the garden from the bathroom window. Geoff mentally noted the escape route.

Wang led her charge up the steps of a sagging wood building with a screened porch. His was the first room inside the building entrance, simply furnished, tourist minimum. The single bed had a pad on top of a hardboard base and mosquito netting hung from the ceiling. "It'll be just fine, Cha Cha. I'll get a good rest. I can manage for dinner and the evening. Why don't you come over in the morning and we'll discuss the side trips? Please let me know about the fishing trip. It's important."

"Actually, my Father and Uncle own fishing boats, and go out nightly. You could go with them, if I can get permission for you."

"Quiet as you can, Cha Cha. Don't ask if someone is listening nearby. I don't want to get you into trouble. Tell your Father it will benefit him in American dollars."

"I'll speak to Father tonight," she said in a whisper. "The dining room stops serving at eight o'clock and it's past seven now. You'd better go right over."

"Yes ma'am, on my way. I'd invite you to have dinner with me but I know it's against the rules. Good night. See you in my dreams."

"You'll have to explain that idiom to me tomorrow, Mr. Martine. Sleep well. I'll see you in the morning, unless," she giggled, "if I meet you in your dreams first."

At dinner that night, Geoff watched the two ministers and the daughter come into the dining hall. They went into a private dining area behind a series of screens.

Two legitimately honeymooning couples from Hong Kong joined Geoff at his round table and he bought them Dynasty wine to wish them well. They had been to Shanghai, Beijing, and Tianjin and were enjoying the beach here. A train would take them south, to Quangzhou, in two days to wind up their trip. There was no mention of politics, or of the expected demonstrations.

Geoff wondered if they were oblivious to the historic times that might occur while they were in China, or the fact that they might actually be part of what might happen. It was possible they were equally suspicious of him, so he offered his business card with the impressive embossed Great Seal of the United States on it.

"I will be in Hong Kong in about ten days. If you call and leave a message for me at the Shangri La Hotel, I'll pop for a dinner at the Spring Deer Restaurant on Mody Road. It will be fun to reminisce about Beidaihe."

After dinner, Geoff walked the lighted streets down the beach roads, enjoying the cool evening, the smell of the sea and the tranquility of the area. Most of the town's guests were also walking the seaside road in pairs and groups, talking quietly. He could see the two bikers a distance back keeping an eye on him. Wu Xian and his daughter were back in the crowd, trying to look for him unobtrusively.

Geoff took a quick left up a grassy footpath and waited on the trail for his trackers. He heard the motorbikes whiz by and then double back, stopping at the path entrance. Quickly shifting off to the side in the dense foliage, he watched them come up the trail, whispering to each other and then separating.

A quick neck chop immobilized one man. Moving across the path, Geoff circled to catch the other agent on his way back. This must not be a Shaolin Team. That was too easy. That should take care of them for an hour or so. After all, I don't want to start a war yet.

Assuming there was no backup team on the lookout for him, Geoff walked boldly across the road, crossing a few feet in front of Wu Xian and his daughter, who were mingled with the other walkers. He left his sandals for a marker, drew an arrow in the sand, hunkered down behind a big rock on the beach, lit a cigarette, and leaned back to wait.

The squeak of dry sand signaled the approach of someone. "What do you see out there, American?" The voice was a soft singsong in lightly accented English.

Geoff sensed her closeness, smelled the fresh night sea air on her skin, and caught the tenseness in her breathing. She crouched down on her heels next to him. He pulled her closer to get under the shadow of the rock. The girl made no move to shy away as knees and thighs touched.

Answering her question, Geoff said. "I see the calm waters of the Bohai Sea, where the fish swim freely and the crabs crawl sideways over the bottom waiting to be taken to the tables for our dinner."

"And... what do you hear, American... in the quiet of the night?"

Enjoying the melodious voice and the subtle prompting, he was slow to answer, prolonging the moment. "I hear the endless pounding of the surf making its musical drumbeat on the shore and the dulcet tones of a nightingale soothing and gentle in the night."

Mei Lei was also taken by the moment. There was an electric current running through her body, flowing from the nearness of the man. The repartee with the stranger, the full moon, and the thrill of adventure produced an excitement she had never known before.

"The Immortals say, the nightingale will sing when the dove flies from his cote. The words are centuries old and written on the steles of the scribes recording history. Tonight, the world changes; the words come alive. Two doves must escape, hoping to return one day to their nests, and the nightingale desires to fly with them. Do you think it possible, American?"

"It sounds like you sing a new twist to an ancient tale, nightingale. Your doves may find it more complicated to return to their nest than to gain freedom in the first place. Also, I hear two doves and a beautiful young bird want to fly away? Preparations are necessary and the danger multiplies with the number in the flock."

"Yes, we are aware of the dangers that surround us and wish your help to free ourselves. Returning will have to be another flight at another time, I hope in the light of day and aided by a gentle wind from the West."

"So many were not expected, lovely song bird. I must confirm the changes. It'll be too dangerous for us to meet again, so look beneath this rock tomorrow night. If there is one stone, I can only take the Shou Lao; if three, we sail into the dangerous waters together. We will set the exact time of departure later, on the night you have asked for. The doves must rest well, for the flight will be arduous."

"As you wish, American. The ravens are thick in the trees. Watch carefully, for they will be very angry when they see the cote is empty."

Unable to see her face clearly in the shadows, Geoff lifted a hand and very gently, sensing her tenseness, touched her cheek with his fingers, tracing down to the chin, and around to the other cheek.

"Watch out for the black ones, sweet nightingale. May there be a time soon when you will sing freely."

Mei Lei covered his hand with hers, squeezing it for a moment, and then disappeared, like a bird frightened from a perch, winging into the night.

Geoff waited for more than a half hour, and then returned slowly to his room. Two black shadows followed him openly, mounted on motorcycles. He could hear the angry revs of the engines as they criss-crossed behind him. The indignities they had suffered earlier would have to wait for revenge.

BEIHAI PARK, FRIDAY MORNING 31 MAY 1994

Fan Riqi read the report the next morning. The team following Martine had been waylaid and attacked by a large group of students, dragging them off into the bushes, their quarry lost for more than an hour. He summoned Hu Banyi and Captain Yao Lin.

"Hu and I are going to Beidaihe today to take direct charge of the operations there. Captain, you will remain here and keep in hourly contact with us."

SIXTEEN
HONG KONG

31 MAY 1994

High up in the Bank's towering structure, Oliver Abernathy looked around the boardroom table. This was the most secure room in the building except for the vaults below ground. Elevators, halls, and escalators were monitored. Internal security in the central control room was coordinated with the Royal Navy Secret Service and Hong Kong's Police force. The HKPD were covering the perimeter of the building, the entrances and the streets for any unusual activity. The RNSS were in plain clothes and deployed at various strategic points. Each person at the table had entered at a different time, to diverse offices throughout the building and was then escorted to this room.

The boardroom of the Hong Kong Shanghai Bank was impressive. Tinted windows revealed a panorama of the waterfront bustling with its traffic of the Star Ferry, freight barges, junques, and a composite of seagoing vessels from around the world. Small boats darted fearlessly between them, like water bugs. Across the narrow strip of water, Kowloon swarmed with people, buses and cars in the daily frenzy of commerce.

The room bore the quiet elegance of conservative banking. A massive polished rosewood director's table dominated the center, suitable for twice the number of people now using it. Leather chairs embraced occupants who could swivel, tilt back or nap quietly with feet propped up on the foot rail of the table if the meeting became too tedious. Leather folders, Mont Blanc pen sets, and transparent porcelain teacups decorated the twelve places. Camcorders in the four corners of the ceiling were ready to record every nuance of movement and every whisper. Remote control buttons imbedded in the arm of the Chairperson's seat could guarantee privacy or record the detailed history of a meeting. In front of each two persons, a delegate and a second, was a calligraphic sign, beautifully lettered in English and Chinese, labeling the Provincial District they represented: Hong Kong, Quandong, Shenzhen, Macau, Hainan, and Formosa. Taiwan adopted the ancient name Province of Formosa. Liu Guohua and Soong Aimei represented the government in exile.

Abernathy, for Her Majesty's Government, and special envoy, former Secretary of State James Baker for the United States, honored guests, were sitting away from the table near the door. Designation as temporary Masters at Arms justified their presence as unofficial observers. Thus, their governments had given tacit approval of the Congress for the birth of the new nation, the United Provinces of Cathay.

James Shan Leight, merchant, selected with the approval of the three major Hongs, the commercial groups, Jardine Matheson, Hutchison Whampoa and Swire Pacific, gaveled the meeting to order for the host Province, Hong Kong. Proudly Eurasian, born of two worlds, an English father and a Nepalese mother, he spoke in the clipped accent of his father's country. "I declare the Provisional Constitutional Congress of the United Provinces of Cathay open. Hong Kong welcomes the delegates and especially the new and gratifying addition of the Province of Formosa."

"Mr. Chairman, may I make a motion?"

"The chair recognizes the delegate from Macau."

"Macau moves for the nomination of James Shan Leight, delegate for Hong Kong, as Provisional President of the United Provinces of Cathay for one year. We expect to establish an electoral process within that period."

"Formosa seconds the motion, and moves the nominations be closed," Soong Aimei spoke up.

"The Province of Hong Kong is deeply honored. Is there any discussion?" Jimmy looked at each delegate and their seconds. "Will the secretary please call the roll for a voice vote? All in favor will answer: shir for agreement, and bushir for denial of the motion."

"Guandong?"

"Shir."

"Shenzhen?"

"Shir."

"Macau?"

"Shir."

"Hainan?"

"Shir."

"Formosa?"

"Shir"

"Hong Kong?"

"Humbly, shir."

"The motion is carried unanimously. Let the record show that Hong Kong's delegate is the Provisional President of the United Provinces of Cathay. The first order of business will be to approve the date and time to declare our independence. It's our intention to officially announce the formation of this nation Thursday, the fourth of June, 1994. We will call an international press conference to inform the world. Each of you will be present at that historic moment.

"Plebiscites within the provinces will elect democratic governments within the provisional constitution. The purpose of this meeting is to agree on the form of that document for ratification by the provinces."

Abernathy leaned over to his counterpart, Baker, speaking quietly so as not to disturb the meeting. "What do you think of their chance for success, or survival, I should say?"

"Not easy, Oliver. Macau, of course, is a cinch. Portugal couldn't care less and has been anxious to unload its colony for several years. Even the Chinese haven't shown much interest in it, except as another gateway to or from their heaven. They will have to be careful, though, that the gambling interests don't take over. There are some rough and tough people over there who would like nothing better than to preempt a territory like that for gambling, vice, drugs, whatever. Protected under the umbrella of a legitimate new nation, they could do anything they wanted under this autonomous theory."

He lowered his voice even further as one of the delegates flicked the two men a sideways glance.

"China will of course be the major obstacle to any change. Keep in mind how much the Taiwan situation has boiled and bubbled to no real solution. The residents of these various entities are the key, in my opinion. For instance, Shenzhen is so much a part of the Crown Colony now that the people are interchangeable. They don't even want to be part of the People's Republic like Quandong, a separate province. If the new nation exists, the joint ventures, with Hong Kong participation, will then be free of the regulations and political pressures put on them by Beijing. 'Profit is glorious', as Deng Xiaoping said."

"Go on, Oliver, so far we're of a like mind."

"Thanks. It's about time the US guessed right in Asia. They've been missing the boat for the past century. Hainan is something else. They are independent, fiercely capitalistic in nature, entrepreneurs favoring independence. They can be the fruit basket for the United Provinces of Cathay if they allow farmers ownership of land, as promised. There is a serious problem, though."

Baker interrupted, "Hainan is a very important part of China, a military bastion of the South. If the PLA starts shooting first and asking questions after, there could be a lot of blood spilled. Would your Prime Minister send ships and troops in there to help them?"

Oliver shook his head. "It's not the Falklands. We have no ownership prerogatives in Hainan. Hong Kong... maybe. In either event, the UK has a bona fide treaty agreement with China, effective in three years. We can't throw that over without a fuss around the world at our honesty and integrity."

"Guandong Province, principally Canton, is a knotty problem," Baker continued. "It's my opinion that the Zhongnanhai are going to fight with everything they have for that money maker. The territory is impossible to defend against a land assault, with such a long mutual border. You're going to have to tell me what you think will happen in Hong Kong. In view of the pact, what can Whitehall and the PM do to support their views?"

"A knotty problem indeed. Knots fashioned into enigmas, tangled with emotions," Oliver answered. "There has been no official word to my office at NAVTEL, or here at the bank. I can assure you, though, that Hong Kong would delight at the elimination of the thousands of applications for British citizenship with their requests for right of abode. Remember the Vietnamese and Cambodian refugees still in

Hong Kong? They're waiting for the United Nations to come up with an answer. The United Provinces of Cathay will have some land for them to spread out in by taking over the New Territories."

"Solving a few birds with one stone," Baker agreed.

"The problem is more basic than that," Oliver explained. "It's my guess that the new nation, because of the racial mix, will become severely ethnic and racist after formation. Cathay, for the Chinese, will be the rallying cry. Like everywhere else, we have our hotheads and rabble-rousers. That's a problem Jimmy will have to fight through. It won't be easy."

"You can say that again," Baker drawled.

"How about Formosa?" Oliver asked. "Any news on the fangs of Feng, the mad General?"

Baker replied, "We're watching that closely. General Feng has to keep his gun loaded to stay in power. Madame Soong is one smart lady and we think she and Liu have some aces up their Mandarin sleeves. If they get control of their island again and team up with Hong Kong... watch out. A Hong Kong-Taiwan tie-up amounts to a mighty total of trade dollars. The three major Hongs alone account for fifty billion dollars of cash flow. With a clean government and real democracy, there would be no rivaling that combination in all Asia."

Abernathy listened to the speeches for a moment and then turned back to Baker. "In five thousand years, the Chinese have never adopted the principles of Confucius or democracy. They've always reverted to guns and power, from one lord and master to another. Look what happened when China blew their chance five years ago. The nation reverted down practically to the Imperial days before Sun Yat Sen. I wish them good luck this time. Maybe we'll be the generation to see the Dragon finally run out of fire and pull a plow in the field. Can you imagine what a billion people could produce if they were free?" He paused and cocked his head, holding up a hand. "Listen to this speaker; he carries a great deal of weight."

The delegate from Guandong rose, Kung Demai, a seventy-seventh-generation descendant of Confucius. "Delegates to the Provisional Committee to form the United Provinces of Cathay, I am honored to be here at the birth of this nation. You also honor my ancestor, K'ung Fu Tze, Confucius, and the fulfillment of his dream of twenty-five hundred years ago. His thoughts, as related in the Book of Analects, reflect what you are trying to do here now.

"You have my brief of the proposed Constitution at your places. It is a declaration of the same freedoms that have made the United States and the Commonwealth Nations so successful. We propose a tri-cameral, Executive, Congressional, Judicial form of government. The leaders will be responsible to the will of the people, as soon as we can teach our citizens the power of democratic voting."

The tall, angular man with his ancestor's long nose, wispy beard, and sotto voice, took a sip of tea and continued. "Each Province is autonomous and will house the National Government in rotation for five years. That Province's Governor will be the automatic President during the term and provide the various ministry heads. By this method, no one Province will dominate and deadly layers of bureaucracy will not accumulate, actually starting over each governing cycle.

"The basic principle is that the Provinces will be united for economic advantage, with one currency, one stock exchange, one central bank, free trade, and unfettered borders throughout the territory. It has similarities to the European Common Market, the British Commonwealth of Nations, and the United States, without the burden of large debt and bureaucracy. Taxes will be based on the very successful Hong Kong flat tax system, with a maximum of fifteen percent income tax. Five percent will go to the federal system, the other retained by each Province. Free trade in and out of our entire nation will make it unique in the world.

"The Judicial Branch will have life appointments, with one system of laws governing all the Provinces. Each will have two members on the Supreme Court, appointed by the Governors. Lower courts will be under local jurisdiction.

"The senior members of the Provinces' elected Congresses will form the National Legislative Branch. Representation based on the total votes cast in their individual territories will generate voter participation. Political parties will have to get their members to vote to have a share in the local and national governments."

Kung Demai nodded abruptly and resumed his seat.

Next, President Leight introduced Security and Defense, chaired by Hainan. "This officer, a newly appointed general, is also the head of Hainan's air unit. In fact, he is the son of Madame Zhen Ailing, the previously unnamed leader who organized our trip to Hainan. It was her people that allowed us to escape with our lives, sacrificing her own. Please let us take a moment of silence to commemorate the first lives lost in the formation of our new Nation."

Zhen's son spoke solemnly into the silence. "Two of our foremost leaders, a dedicated car driver, three men acting as guards, and the personal pilot of our Chairman gave their lives on that fatal morning."

The man, his voice choked with emotion, paused to collect himself, then continued. "Their sacrifice saved the life of our President and the secrecy of our plans. On the day the United Provinces of Cathay announces itself to the world, the names of these brave people will be proclaimed as heroes. A monument will be built in their honor in Haikou, a replica of the Statue of Democracy that was built by the Tiananmen students five years ago."

Everyone stood and applauded softly, most with their own tears pouring readily from the intense emotion of the moment.

When the sobered group took their seats again, the delegate continued with his speech on security and defense. "No one can accurately predict the reaction of the Politburo in Beijing to the dismemberment of China. My father, General Zhen, was executed three years ago for voicing an opinion of democracy. The expected demonstrations of the people and violent reaction by the mad fools in the Zhongnanhai will provide the cover we need to establish ourselves. We expect another blood bath by the military in subduing those who disagree with them."

Murmuring sounds bemoaning the loss of life echoed around the room as the members nodded acceptance of the inevitable.

Zhen paused as a wave of emotion filled the room. Then he continued. "There will be a total emptying of intellectual, technical and academic talent directly into the arms of our new nation. We welcome the addition to our wealth and to our defense forces. There is a bold secret plan by the Hainan-based air wing to form our own air defense and attempt to enlist other selected air units of China. I'm not at liberty to tell you the details, but if successful, the flower tiles will be in our mahjongg row."

Applause and shouts of "hear hear" complimented the positive hopes of the future.

The defense minister waited for the room to quiet. "We have trained elite attack squadrons from the Viet Nam refugees, unregistered immigrants and our own dedicated youth. The Snow Leopards have Israeli retired military instructors. Their tactics are designed to make swift maximum-force attacks with sophisticated weaponry. Formed and disciplined in the Philippines, these forces are standing by and ready today. They will have their first action in Hainan, if need be. Delegates... the United Provinces of Cathay does have a defense force you will be proud of."

Shenzhen Province, previously nominated by Leight to the tasks of a Foreign Office, reported briefly. "We hope to be recognized as a nation within minutes of our announcement in order to give us the status of our declared independence. China will raise a cloud of protests and try to bar our entrance to the United Nations. The momentous changes in other parts of the world the past five years are in our favor."

The voice of the Foreign Office temporary secretary grew in volume as it filled with emotion. "Friends that I have met from other once-free economic zones in China have heard the swelling rumors of our destiny. The mighty Chang Chiang Yangtze areas, delta Provinces of Shandong, Jiangsu, Shanghai, Shejiang and Fujian are in the same position we are in Shenzhen."

The incensed minister pounded on the table for emphasis. "We were promised economic freedom to trade. Investing with foreign countries promised to yield desirable results. The repressive hardliners then bound our feet as they have their women for many centuries. We, as a group of Chinese Provinces, cannot walk crippled and sorely abused."

Applause and shouts of agreement filled the room again, until President Leight signaled for attention to introduce Soong Aimei. The room quieted as all eyes and attention centered on the famous and beautiful representative of the Province of Formosa.

Fingering the Jade Kwan Yin at her throat, Soong Aimei stood behind her chair, reflecting for a moment. "Our plans to retake control of our country are in the making now. Fortunately, most of our island population is on our side. The coming demonstration in China is in our favor. We fully intend to take our place in the new nation of the United Provinces of Cathay. Like Phoenix, rising from the ashes, the ancient name of Formosa will once more be a free and prosperous entity.

"The future is bright, but we cannot ignore the clouds, my friends. We all have hopes and dreams, but remember the realities of existence. There is much work to be done and we cannot afford complacency to creep in. Thank you for including the Province of Formosa. May our new flag, yet unsewn, show the blue of a clear sky and the waves of the sea. The emerging figure of Longevity, Shou Xing Lao, standing on the back of a turtle, guarantees us a double wish of long life."

James Shan Leight watched his good friend gracefully return to her seat, applause continuing for several minutes. Her classic face was serene, emotion trapped underneath the calm exterior. "The delegate from Formosa speaks plainly. Birthing is painful and can be very dangerous. We would do well to heed her words. Walk slowly and carefully. Our plans can no longer be considered secret, so it is best we not collect in one place together again until the declaration. We shall meet at 6 a.m. in the ballroom of the Mandarin Hotel Thursday morning next for the international press conference before the audience of the world."

The Provisional President looked around the room, memorizing faces, absorbing the moment in history. "The Chair will entertain a motion for adjournment."

"So moved," said Guandong. "Seconded," said Shenzhen.

"All in favor will signify," said Leight. A chorus of "shirs" answered.

"The first meeting of the Constitutional Congress of the United Provinces of Cathay is adjourned."

SEVENTEEN
KAOSHIUNG, TAIWAN

2 JUNE 1994

The Military Operations Headquarters of the Republic of China in Taiwan faced Fujian Province across the straits on the mainland of China. General Feng Qizi, newly self-appointed Dictator-President of the R.O.C., strutted around the war room dressed in the full regalia of a General of the Air Force. Decorations covered the full left side of his chest.

Accompanying General Feng was General Tang Naiwa, Minister of the Central Military Commission of the People's Republic of China, dressed in the uniform of the People's Liberation Army. The mainland General had arrived after midnight in a Chinese Air Force jet fighter from Wenzhou Air Base.

A large map dominated one wall of the room, depicting the whole of China from the USSR border in the north to Hainan Island in the south. Japan and Korea were the demarcation in the east; Afghanistan the western border. Off the southeast shore, the outline of Taiwan radiated lines from Kaohsiung to pinpoints on the mainland.

Feng pointed with a long rod. A red light at the end followed his descriptions. "General Tang, the yellow lines are the attack routes of our planes and ships to hit those army units you have designated as defecting or enemy. The green lines lead to the units under your control that will join with our forces to subdue the opposition. Our planes will leave the ground before dawn, awaiting your final signal that air-warning systems have been nullified. The ships and landing craft are leaving at dusk tonight, in sequential waves depending on the distance they have to travel. They'll hit their designated targets here, here and here by dawn Thursday. On your transmission to our officers on the assigned secret radio channel, all units will move in to secure the coastal area from Dalien to Xiamen." The small red dot followed the route south to north.

Tang broke in when Feng paused. "Only myself and two other trusted officers have the new radios you supplied that have the range to communicate with your invasion military. What do you expect to happen after the coast is secured?"

"Within three hours after daybreak, you can announce complete control of the coast and demand the surrender of forces inland to the western border. You and I can then meet in Beijing to announce the abolishment of the Communist Party and the heroic takeover by the Kuomintang in the name of our departed leader Chiang Kaishek. We will declare China a republic with freedom for all. Martial law will be immediately declared to protect the people. The world will be glad to hear China is rid of the bumbling idiots of the Proletariat, replaced by our benevolent Republic."

"Our forces will be waiting to join you, General," replied Tang. Under our joint leadership, more than one billion people will produce goods and services that can supply the world at the cheapest prices. We know China can produce everything from nuclear weapons to buttons for their shirts. With the contracts coming through our offices at the special branch of the Bank of China, we will become the richest men the world has ever known. Dissenters cannot leave, because there is no place for them. Look at the Vietnamese boat people returned to their country, unaccepted any place in the world."

"What about the rumors, Tang, of secession by Hong Kong and the Hainan Island group?"

"There is no muscle to their dreams, General Feng. Hong Kong cannot stand alone, so we force England to keep their original agreement. In 1997, we will take over all that wealth without a fight. Let them run the island and build the new airport for the time being. We will work our own people into the banks, hotels, business and transportation facilities, then dump the garbage into the sea. As far as Guandong and Hainan are concerned, some purging is necessary. We may even have to fight certain units of our own army, but that is immaterial clean-up work."

Both walked around the operations room, studying the data from the banks of monitors. Logistics, weather, locations of equipment, personnel rosters, local maps reproduced for the landing units, all humming like a well-oiled machine. They sat in a corner lounge area. An aide brought a beautifully decorated porcelain bottle of the infamous maotie liqueur to toast their plan. "To a unified China, Feng, gombei."

After the two generals drank their toast, Feng said, "There is one item in the data output that worries me, General Tang. Your MSS Minister, Chou Shi. You reported him on our side sometime back and then have not mentioned him in any of the secret communications. His Ministry is strong and covert. I don't like someone standing around ready to throw a knife into my back."

"Don't worry about that dung-brained ox," Tang boasted. "The minute you land, I'm closing off the entire Zhongnanhai complex, putting everyone there under house arrest. The Standing Committee, including Chou, will be at Beidaihe for the plenum. I'm part of that group, and I will take personal charge of their capture and return them to Beijing. We'll have to decide later if any of the Politburo will be of use to us in the new administration."

"What you are telling me then, Tang, is that the entire Politburo will be at the Zhongnanhai, except the six members of the Standing Committee, at the time we launch our attack. You are wise to keep them so tightly under control. Question? Where will you operate from, at the critical time? Which hotel suite will you have and where will the communications' headquarters be?"

"Communications will locate me, Feng, do not worry. Actually, my plan is to take over the five Ministers at Beidaihe during the night, so as not to create a fuss, and then fly them into Beijing by helicopter. That will put me in early enough to oversee the Zhongnanhai operation. I'll leave nothing to chance or accident. The key officers that I trust will welcome your forces, but they do not know the general plan. They will then open and execute sealed orders, delivered to them late Wednesday afternoon."

"The student demonstrations are organized for Thursday. What do you intend to do about them?"

Tang thought for a moment, trying to decide just how much this man should know. "We hope they do something, because it will disguise our plans. The fools will tie themselves up in their senseless plot. Days will pass before they realize they have been bypassed. My orders are to do exactly what we did before. Ask them to disburse, threaten them if they don't, and then go in and kill off a few. There will be some dead, of course, but it is a good military exercise for my armies. There are few enough times when they actually shoot anything other than paper targets."

On the return flight, Tang had time to mull over the visit, think through some questions Feng had put to him and decipher what was actually going on in the man's mind. The key was obvious. Feng had insisted on knowing where he would be. Feng planned to take him out along with the Politburo.

Of course, he had suspected that fact long before, when negotiations began. Tang also knew he must counter the move before it began, as in all good battle plans.

There is no way I am going to share power with Feng. The man is mad. I'll take total control of China, including Taiwan. It is fortunate the coup was successful. A coup to replace a coup has more validity – fewer of the enemy to conquer. Everything is clearer now, like the dawn beginning to light up the sky. The spirit of my ancestors, the Great Khans, will glory in my accomplishments.

The solution came to him in a flash of light as the sun broached the demarcation line between the sea and the sky. Clouds formed in the early morning humidity. He knew now what he had to do on the morning of the fourth of June.

General Feng addressed his immediate staff after Tang left. "There are some changes we must make in our plans. General Tang Naiwa is dangerous, bordering on lunacy. He must be removed." He addressed the military officer in Army field uniform. "Colonel, do we still have one of their MSS Shaolin team under deep cover?"

"Yes, General. Fortunately, they are now in Beidaihe."

"Have our control get orders to them. They are to eliminate General Tang by midnight Tuesday and hide the body. His disappearance will confuse the military staff. The headless dragon will thrash around, unable to think, while we win the battle."

"Admiral Zen," Feng addressed the beribboned naval officer in the gold decorated cap standing by. "Can you get a destroyer to the Bohai Sea, offshore from Beidaihe, by early Thursday morning?"

"It will be tight, General, but I can divert the Suzhou from the invasion group and have her underway immediately." He turned to the computer behind him, punched up the craft's tech log and entered some data. "If I get them underway by 0900 this morning, they should be standing off Beidaihe at midnight Wednesday, barring weather problems."

"Very good, Admiral. I want them ten miles offshore with a rocket boat and attack team on board.

"Now comes the tough part." He addressed an officer with air force wings on his chest above the many bars of activity ribbons. "Colonel, we need two fighter planes that once belonged to the mainland air force. You can use the ones brought in by defectors over the past years. Equip them with extra fuel tanks. They will need the code identification signals Tang left with us. Compute a flight plan to put them over Beijing at precisely 0600 on the fourth. They'll take out the target assigned, refuel at the airbase as if they were part of the general invasion plan, and return to base. The pilots must be our finest. Arm the planes with the new laser-guided bombs. We need pinpoint accuracy with no possibility of collateral damage. To answer the question on your faces, I am not planning to bomb the Palace and the Forbidden City. The bombers are to make consecutive runs to ensure success and bring back photographs of the hit."

The Colonel saluted and left, leaving behind an aide, Major Dan Shen, security advisor in charge of covert affairs. This officer replaced a particular former aide. Feng did not tolerate subordinates who could not carry out orders. The escape of Soong and Liu was a crime punished by summary execution.

"Major Shen, did you find out who our mole is in the MSS?"

"Yes sir. It was simple. He identified himself last week in his phone call to the control in Hong Kong. He is Captain Yao Lin, aide to the Vice Commissar, Fan Riqi. He has been doubling to General Tang and us for sometime now. Control advises that the captain has offered a series of floppy discs containing the entire files of the MSS, and video tapes of the most recent Politburo meetings."

Feng let out a loud bellow of a laugh that caused everyone in the operations center to look over. "The captain must be a real pile of camel dung. I suppose he would like some sort of compensation for all this information?"

"Yes sir. The price requested is five hundred thousand US dollars in cash, delivered to him in Singapore on the fourth of June."

"That makes it easy, Major. Promise him anything he wants... after his team gets Tang out of the way for us. Fake the money, have our men pump him dry and then delete the vermin from the roster." General Feng smiled. "Never trust a traitor."

Feng Qizi, self-imposed ruler of the Republic of China, felt smug and satisfied as he went over to the large map display. Taking up a red marker and measuring stick, he carefully drew a bright red line from the southwestern tip of Taiwan to the heart of Beijing. He then drew another line from the same source over the water in two legs: north from the east coast of Taiwan to a point between the Korean coast, Yantai and Dalian, then west to the Bohai Sea. Two more attack points added to the battle plan.

He sprawled in a director's chair pulled up in front of the map and, with an electronic pointer, reviewed every designated line and mainland contact.

"Thursday morning, I'll sit right here, release the orders to attack and watch the green lights go up on the board as the reports come in. I just love it when a good plan comes together."

EIGHTEEN
BEIJING/BEIDAIHE

TUESDAY 2 JUNE 1994

Patrick Duffy brought the message from Beidaihe into the Ambassador's private quarters early Tuesday morning. Mrs. Duke was having tea and toast by the window. She wore a silk robe ornately embroidered with a multi-colored phoenix bird, symbol of the Chinese Empress.

"Sorry to disturb you, Madame Ambassador. It's a message from Martine."

"No problem, Mr. Duffy. I was already awake when you called. Is there a change in the plans?"

"Let me read it to you. See if you interpret it the same way I do. Knowing that the MSS monitor all communications, Geoff and I agreed to use open language in case he had to contact us. The message is short. HI THERE PATRICK HAVING GREAT TIME CAN YOU AND EMILY ESCAPE FOR A COUPLE DAYS. SEE IF ROOM ON TRAIN FOR TWO MORE. HAVE BOSS APPROVE R AND R CHITS. ACCOMMODATIONS TIGHT HERE ADVISE ASAP SO I CAN BOOK. RGDS GEOFF."

"And you read that how, Mr. Duffy?"

"Martine's got two more passengers and needs an okay from Langley. I suggest a personal call to Geoff's friend. The MSS listens, in spite of protocol. A scrambler would alert them to dangerous traffic. A regular call will confuse them."

In the Telephone and Telegraph Building on Changan Avenue, area code 532 activated to record the number dialed and the conversation. All foreign embassies had a 532 prefix and were automatically taped for the MSS to review.

A laconic voice answered the Ambassador's ring to Washington. "Kelly here. Who's singing this time of the night?"

"Lena here, Andy, in Beijing. I need a favor. A friend of mine has to have a couple more seats on Northwest's Thursday flight. Their office here is giving me the fully booked line. First class preferred, but they will take business if necessary. Have them get right on it and let us know through the Northwest Beijing office. I'll give them the names when they call me. Can do?"

"Might be a problem, Lena, waking up the President of Northwest this time of the night, but I'll get right on it. Regards."

"Thanks, Andy. I appreciate the service."

BEIDAIHE

"You look puzzled, Hu. Don't tell me there is a code problem you can't solve?"

"Comrade Fan. I ran the communications of the American Embassy through my decoder program. They are in plain language, no code used. That fact alone makes me very suspicious. Would you care to look through the transmissions? Your friend Martine sent this one from here. Soon after that, Beijing relayed a telephone conversation that the Ambassador had with a number in Washington. It's supposedly to a friend, but that number was used by Martine before this."

Fan got up from his desk in the back office of the Central Beach Hotel. They had commandeered it on arriving in Beidaihe and set up all Hu's computer equipment. He went over to look at the communications Hu had established with the Beihai Park headquarters through the modem on his laptop Toshiba. "The message from Martine is a thin disguise, obviously a sham. He's toying with us, not bothering to use the phone scramblers. Two more of something. It has to tie in with his mission here. We suspect a defection; it could be three. Assuming it's a major player, we must watch each of the six committee members.

"Maybe I should just go over to Martine's breakfast table and ask him? On second thought, alert the Shaolin Team to keep a closer watch on him. The man has an uncanny ability to evade them anytime he wants. The next twenty-four hours should be very interesting."

At the breakfast table, Wang brought the reply to Geoff's telex. Geoff was sitting alone, horn-rimmed glasses on, hair neatly brushed, dressed in bright yellow shorts. A white t-shirt with Chinese lettering for Shanghai completed the tourist outfit. An empty rice bowl sat in front of him and he was methodically peeling hard boiled eggs.

"Please have a seat, Cha Cha. Would you like a bowl of congee? I could order an American breakfast of bacon and eggs for you?"

She giggled. "No thank you, Mr. Martine. I've had my breakfast of pickled vegetables and rice at home. Your office in Beijing answered your telex. I hope it's good news."

"Tell me, little one, what comment did your office or my two shadows have when they read it?"

"Mr. Martine, are you in some kind of trouble? How do you know they read your message?"

"By the nervous look in your eyes. They're blinking. You don't like the attention they're paying me, do you? I work for the American Embassy in Beijing. They are suspicious of all Americans, so don't worry."

"You're right though," Guide Wang admitted. "Two men came in last night and inquired about you. They showed my group leader some important identification and she told me to tell them everything I knew. There's not much to tell. We've spent very little time together so far."

Wrapping and un-wrapping her long braid around her hand nervously, Cha Cha continued. "They were mean and warned me not to say anything to you. I'm frightened. My team leader told me the men are from some secret police organization. 'Be careful,' she said to me. It's not just me at risk; punishment for non-cooperation will affect my family as well. Losing my job as a tour guide would be the least of the trouble they can cause."

Geoff looked into the wide, dark eyes, sensing the danger she felt. The young ones all felt rebellious, but they could only go so far before it affected where they lived or worked. He smiled to ease her concern. "Not to worry, Wang. Remember there's a big meeting coming up, with some very important leaders. The men you talk of are security people wondering why there is one solitary American here on vacation. Americans are seldom known as terrorists, but your leaders worry about everyone. Tell them whatever they want to know except our secret about the fishing trip. I don't want to get you or your family in trouble. How did they react to my telexes?"

"Oh, I forgot to tell you. They read and re-read both yours and the answer several times, very concerned. When I left the office, they were still going over copies of them."

"Well, let's see what the office has to say." He picked up the dispatch.

LADY BOSS OKAYS R AND R FOR BOTH OF US STOP RSVD TRAIN THURSDAY SOONEST STOP EMILY WANTS SEPARATE ROOM TKS RGDS.

"That doesn't sound too complicated. Can you get a couple more rooms for Thursday?"

"Very difficult, Mr. Martine. I asked the desk clerk, who had to ask someone in the back office. They agreed to give me another room for the lady and will put another bed in your room for your friend. Will that be all right?"

"Fine, Cha Cha. Maybe you can take all three of us for a tour around Beidaihe."

Geoff and Wang watched the VIPs enter the dining room and go to the private area behind the screens. Wang tried to identify the leaders for Geoff. Apparently the others had arrived this morning by plane.

"There's Wu Xian and his daughter, who came yesterday. She looks so worried about her father. According to my cousin at Xidan University, he's a softliner, one of the few left in the Politburo. The other elder with them, I learned, is one of our Vice Premiers, Yang Yucie. A Long Marcher, he is almost the last of Chairman Mao's original cadre."

A tall, round-faced, heavy-set man came in next, dressed in a military uniform, accompanied by two others, all apparently officers. "That is General Tang Naiwa," Geoff said. "I recognize him from all the publicity he received during the Tiananmen Massacre."

Wang identified the General Secretary, Liu Chinan, without any trouble. Geoff recognized Cai Jixi, Minister of the CCDI. He explained, "As Attaché, it's my job to observe protocol and know who the upper crusts of the Communist Party are."

Last to walk in was the one member people knew little about, as his name was rarely mentioned in public. The MSS warned the media time and again to delete anything said, reported, rumored or even thought about the Security Apparatus or its personnel. Chou Shi walked in alone far behind the others, looking around the room. His eyes met Geoff's for an instant only. Geoff could sense the recognition, an ever-so-slight hesitation in his step.

"There they are, Mr. Martine. The six members of the Standing Committee of the Politburo, a rare sight for you and me to see. I assume you notice all the ravens and crows around the place."

"The only problem with all the black pants, Cha Cha, is identifying the pair watching me. It looks to me like they have guardians to match each member of the Committee."

"To change the subject, Mr. American, today would be ideal for taking the trip to the Great Wall. The sky looks a little overcast, but the rain should hold off until late afternoon."

"All right, Sunshine, off we go into the wild blue yonder, clouds and all. Are my shorts and sandals appropriate dress for the occasion?"

"Perfect and you promised to explain about "see you in my dreams", "wild blue yonder", and "giggle puss". Oh, and be sure to bring your camera with an extra roll of film. The sea coast and the old portion of the Great Wall are memorable."

Martine mentally recorded directions as they drove while Wang talked on, describing the area, names and famous places. "This is the industrialized area north through this factory town called Qinghuangdao, and soon we will be in a park and see the Great Wall," she said.

"It doesn't look like the Great Wall I saw near Beijing," Geoff commented. "There, I saw assortments of vehicles, masses of tourists, and bad-smelling toilets spoiling the historic sight."

Here Geoff noted, there was a massive uncluttered mound of earth on the edge of the sea stretching far off into the countryside. He and Wang were the only other tourists walking up the steps to an original section of the Great Wall of China.

Down below them, two motorcyclists pulled into the parking lot behind their car. They looked up to see their quarry. Geoff waved to them mischievously and nudged Wang to wave also. The two watch-dogs didn't wave back, turning instead to talk to the Luxingshe driver who had stayed with the car.

"You see them talking, Mr. Martine?" Wang said. "You must not say anything in the car that you don't want repeated to those guards. The driver is a member of the Communist Party and takes pains to stir up trouble. He enjoys reporting to the authorities on anything that's against regulations. Now, on with the tour. We are actually at the village of Shanhaiquan, the Eastern point of the Great Wall, extending right into the Bohai Sea. This section dates back to the year 1381, during the Ming Dynasty."

Looking down the grassy mound, eroded by six hundred years of weathering, Geoff could easily follow the shape and direction as far as he could see in the distance. Fantasy took over for a few moments, as he imagined himself a charioteer racing his war cart down the wall, reining and whipping his team of four horses. He was hurrying to save the lovely Mei Lei and her father, who were hanging on for dear life in the back of the chariot. If they could reach the sea before the Mongol hordes caught them, they could escape in the waiting boat.

"Mr. Martine, Mr. Martine, are you listening? You seem far away."

Geoff shook his head back to reality. "Just dreaming, Cha Cha, of what I would have been doing here six centuries ago. Now what was it you were telling me?"

They walked toward a round structure built like the watch towers along the wall. It served as a museum and souvenir shop. When they entered, Wang explained the series of antique drawings framed and mounted along one wall. "The paintings depict a beautiful love story. May I tell it to you?"

Geoff took out his glasses, carefully wiped the lenses, and put them on to study the pictures. "All China has stories, but the ones I favor are tales of love. Please tell me, Wang."

"Once there was a fair young maiden who had been born by stepping out of a gourd, as you can see in this first picture. Two families found her. Both wanted to keep her because she was beautiful, so they shared raising her. When she grew up, she fell in love and married a handsome young man. The local wicked general pressed the husband into service to help build the Great Wall, interrupting their idyllic life.

"The beauty went to visit her husband in the winter to take him a heavy coat. Sadly, they told her he had died in a construction accident. Not believing he was dead, the wife searched the wall for weeks. She cried so profusely that part of the wall washed away. The wicked general sent for the woman who had caused such havoc to his fine project and immediately fell in love with her.

"She reluctantly agreed to marry the general and to stop crying the wall away if he reburied her husband in a suitable place and erected a monument to him. After her demands were satisfied, the beauty led the general and his party to a rocky place near the sea for the wedding. The heartbroken woman then diverted their attention for a moment and threw herself into the sea rather than marry the wicked general."

Wang finished the tale with tears in her eyes. "The story is really much longer, as you can see by the drawings. Every time I tell it to visitors, I become sad myself. It reminds me that even today, China is in the control of wicked generals, and will have to commit suicide to escape."

Wang and Geoff walked far down the wall, a surface wide enough to accommodate his imagined team of horses. "Is it possible you are more than a tourist, Mr. Martine?" Wang asked quietly.

"Why do you ask, Cha Cha? I couldn't have enjoyed a tour more than this one."

"The men in the office who questioned me about you have followed us ever since your arrival. Has it anything to do with the fishing trip you want to take? My father and uncle, the fishermen, agreed to take you, but my group leader refused permission without a reason. Why don't we meet the fishermen on the beach early tomorrow morning when they come in with the day's catch? They sell right on the pier just below the hotel. I'll meet you there and translate. They don't speak English. If they take you out, it will be without my official knowledge. The boats leave late at night and return by dawn, so you can be out and back before anyone is aware. The only problem is how to draw off the scary crows who are following you."

Geoff looked at the serious, concerned face and took the jade amulet from his pocket. Holding it in his fingers, he stroked the smooth, time worn surface. "You are taking chances for me, Little One, and I appreciate it. We hope the fingers of the ancient one that I'm holding will protect us. Important events are taking place in your country. One day soon you will know the small parts you and I played."

"My friends have discussed the anniversary of the Tiananmen Massacre and believe there will be another demonstration. Have you heard anything in Beijing about it?"

They turned to walk back down the wall toward the rotunda as Geoff replied, "There is much talk in Beijing about everything. Tell me, why do you talk about the Tiananmen Massacre? I thought your leaders said only a few soldiers died and some hooligans were punished?"

Scornfully, Wang answered, screwing up the smooth skin of her brow in the only angry look Geoff had seen on her face. "We know that was all lies, though there is little we can do about it. Someday, the truth will be written, but meanwhile there is much support for the students. Our group leader told me strikes may stop the trains and service in the hotels. Even the fishermen, Father tells me, will beach the boats on Thursday. It will be the fifth anniversary of the Tiananmen Massacre."

MIDNIGHT 2 JUNE 1994

The Shaolin teams changed shifts on the porch of Villa #4. Bored and tired, the two who had been relieved expressed surprise at their replacement. "You're a different team than the one that usually spells us – where are they?"

"They're unhappy at having the night shift. We rested on the beach today and offered to switch. The night air is cooler. We like it much better than following the top bananas around and sitting in front of a meeting hall twiddling our thumbs. Is there anything going on, unusual noises, or wild animals?"

"Nothing but the noises of Kublai Khan snoring. He likes the window open, so you will hear the nose music all night. You're welcome to the assignment. The aides are in the right side rooms. He's alone in the left."

Watching the two leaving, the new team heard them talk. "I haven't seen those two around before. Have you?"

"Yes, they were on the road following the American today, riding motorbikes. Someone said they're extra teams imported from Guangzhou to help for the plenum."

General Tang was lying on his back snoring loudly, arms by his side, when the two guards entered the bedroom chamber. Each went to an opposite side of the bed, slipping a garrote out of a pocket.

Tang was dreaming of riding across the Mongolian Plains on a fast pony. An army of warriors followed him, screaming insults at the enemy and waving long rifles. Suddenly a snake flew up from the ground, wrapping itself around his neck. Frantically he tried to wrest it free, grasping with both hands at the constriction around his throat.

He awoke suddenly pulling at what he thought was a serpent around his neck. Instead he felt two wires inexorably tightening from either side. Two expressionless faces watched his eyes to see the moment they would roll up in death.

The garrotes were given a final twist, digging into the soft flesh, oozing blood to the surface. Air stopped flowing into the lungs of the General. The eyes rolled up in his face, tongue protruding.

After cleaning their weapons, the men quickly wrapped the body in a terry cloth sheet from the bed and slipped it out the bathroom window in the rear of the villa. It took less than half an hour to carry the dead General out to the hole they had already dug in a ravine nearby. They packed dirt rocks and brush over and around it so animals would not disturb the area.

Whispering to each other as they trudged back, they gloated over the ease of accomplishing their task. "First time we have ever used a double garrote. Did you notice it took a lot less time to quiet him down?"

"A good technique. We'll just keep it to ourselves in case we need it again. I wonder who the order came from to take this ugly out? Yao Lin isn't in the habit of giving us much inside information."

"Must have been pretty high up in the party. I understand he was a real heavy in this group. How quick will they miss him, do you think?"

"When the morning relief team comes on, we'll tell them the General took off jogging down the beach and ordered us not to follow him."

When General Tang Naiwa did not show up for the Standing Committee meeting at ten that morning, the overall feeling was good riddance. Maybe he would stay away for the rest of the plenum, relieving the abrasive tension he always created.

Chou Shi took a walk in the late afternoon, prowling a radius of a half mile around Villa #4 into the semi-jungle area. Fan Riqi reported that the team assigned to the General could not locate him. The night guard said he went jogging early in the morning. Chou questioned his aides. The General did Tijichuan – he never jogged. Stopping by a recently disturbed area in the ravine, he watched a line of large ants descend into a small mound. An identical line streamed out of it, going off into the tangle of brush nearby.

"Tsai jian, General. I wonder what chain of events is beginning."

Fan Riqi confronted the mystery of Tang's disappearance with annoyance but no sympathy. Kidnapping was a possibility; a professional execution more probable. Had the American done it? More likely one of the other members of the Politburo. The only other experts were his own Shaolin teams. Yao Lin? Yes, Yao Lin was involved.

NINETEEN
BEIDAIEHE

EARLY MORNING 3 JUNE 1994

Wednesday's dawn was just beginning to open the sky when Wang knocked lightly on Geoff's door. "Come on, lazy American, the fishing boats are already coming in to the pier."

Geoff strapped on his money belt and pulled on a light sweatshirt over shorts. Then he stuffed into his pocket his wallet, jade fingering piece, a penknife and the handful of coins that had accumulated since his arrival in China. A wide leather belt held the case for Ray Bans and canteen. Canvas boat shoes completed the outfit.

"Okay, Little One, on to the beach."

A dozen boats were tied up at the pier or had been grounded in the sand at the shoreline. Buyers anxious to be the first to buy the day's catch greeted them eagerly.

"The fishing fleet, Mr. Martine," Wang said. "Generations have brought food in from the sea, handing down the same boats and the same netting trapping techniques to their sons. My father and uncle are the last of the Wang family to be fishermen. I'm an only girl child, considered not suitable or strong enough for the task. My male cousins don't respect or want to be fishermen. We call then Geihu; they think they are businessmen, independent tradesmen. Actually they listen to Western rock music all day and want to set up private enterprises to make money without so much physical hardship and danger. The sea can be very hazardous. It's taken many lives from Beidaihe over the years. One of my cousins is a student at Xidan University in Beijing. When he comes home, he fills our minds with all the advantages of the democratic Western world."

The boatmen were busy slinging heavy baskets of fish and crab up onto the pier or the sand. Bicycle vendors were negotiating for the day's catch to fill the deep baskets attached to the rear of their wheels. Geoff recognized people from the hotel trying to bargain with the crab men. In a few minutes, the hustle and bustle was over, with only a few housewives and tourists buying up the leftovers.

Calling down to one boat, Wang hollered. "Was it a good catch today, father and uncle? Did you keep anything special for our table tonight?"

With big smiles and waves, they held up two large fish with the golden red color of snapper. Geoff guessed the weight to be ten pounds each. "For your Mother to steam with ginger and spices. Who is the barbarian next to you? Does he wish to buy one of these beauties?"

Wang translated the question. Geoff answered, "Tell your father I wish to buy a fish and have the hotel cook it for me. He must give me a good price because I'm an American tourist."

Laughing, Wang translated. "He says the price is five yuan and that the hotel would charge three times as much for such a splendid fish."

"Sold. Now for some more delicate arrangements." Geoff switched to the local tongue. "May I get in the boat and talk quietly with them?"

Wang nodded yes, shocked to hear Geoff talk to her in Chinese. Up to this moment, she'd had no idea of his ability to speak fluent Mandarin, let alone the local patois of the region.

Nimbly, he grabbed onto the gunwales and vaulted over the beam onto the deck. Wang held herself back from applauding, lest she draw attention from others on the beach. The performance was as good as that in the Ninja movies sometimes shown in town, she thought.

She tried to overhear what was being said, but Geoff and her father huddled together like conspirators, ignoring her completely.

When Geoff climbed back up on the pier, he had a satisfied smile on his face, and held the fish up so everyone, including the watching black ravens, could see. They had suddenly appeared, looking frustrated at having lost their quarry while they dozed in the early morning.

"Don't look so worried, Cha Cha. Your father and I understand each other perfectly. Pretend, for the benefit of the two crows sitting on the rail over there, that we have been negotiating for this fish. Wang the elder has agreed to take me fishing tonight and promised to bring some heavy lines for sport fish trolling. It should be a memorable experience. You can meet us tomorrow morning to see how well we did."

Wang's wrinkled forehead and troubled eyes showed the agitation going on inside her head. "You didn't tell me you could speak Chinese. There is another brick to the house of mystery around you. I should go fishing with you tonight."

Picking up the fish, Geoff took her elbow lightly, steering her down the pier to the shore. "There are many events stirring under the waves, Cha Cha. Surely you, who have lived by the sea all your life, know that. For the moment it's better that you concern yourself with instructing the chef to prepare this great fish for myself and the two Hong Kong honeymoon couples. Do you suppose he knows the recipe for steamed Mandarin fish that your father was talking about for your table?"

Geoff turned his back to the shore, leaned over and spoke quietly. "You must not go tonight. It would only throw suspicion on you if anything happens. Now brag about our bargain as we pass the two crows. Laugh about me jumping into the boat to make a deal for myself and how much I probably overpaid the fishermen."

Wang put on a good act in front of the crowd gathered around the pier, embellishing the story so much that Geoff almost burst out laughing. They passed by the two agents lounging against the rail, listening to the joke on the American. Geoff affected a gangling gait, cowlick hanging over one eye, and dragged the fish along the pier like the bumpkin he was portraying.

"You were great, Cha Cha," Geoff said. He concentrated on being natural, at ease, playful, while the excitement of the coming adventure built up inside him. Time tightened the drawstrings on the unknown future.

Wang negotiated the preparation of the fish with the hotel chef and disappeared, wishing Geoff a pleasant day on the beach. She pleaded a headache from all the excitement and the events of the past two days.

Later that evening, Geoff passed Wu Xian and his daughter in the entrance of the dining room. He intercepted a slight smile and nod from the woman. She had seen the three pebbles left on the beach. He acknowledged her smile with a wink and wrote ten in his palm with his finger to indicate the time they were to meet. Mei Lei answered with another nod.

TWENTY
BEIDAIHE

10 P.M. 3 JUNE 1994

An overcast sky hid the full moon and blanketed the stars. Winds, predicting a rising storm, were already strong. Geoff crouched in the middle of a clump of tropical bushes, contemplating the rough evening in store for the old ones. He smiled to himself, remembering how easily he had escaped from the bikers assigned to watch him. They were going to be an angry pair when they discovered he wasn't still down on the beach drinking with the Hong Kong honeymooners.

The two couples and Geoff, after finishing off the fish for dinner, had hiked down to the beach with a dozen cans of Tsingtao beer. The watch team followed lazily on their bikes, not bothering to conceal themselves, and hunkered down across the road from the beach.

The impromptu partygoers made a beach fire with some drift-wood in the crook of a small jetty near the water, protected from the wind and the road. The Hong Kong honeymooners were alive with the joy of newlyweds in the sensual tropical ambience. Laughing and giggling with the gaiety of the mildly drunk, they chased up and down the beach, splashed in the water and settled down next to the fire.

Geoff smiled as they cuddled in sand chairs around the fire. "I'm not as young as you folks are, but it's wonderful to see you all so happy and free for the moment from the problems in your part of the world."

"We are a mixed part of the world, American," said Shova, an Indian girl with a small diamond piercing the right side of her nose. "I'm Indian and my parents are not to happy with me marrying Benny."

"And you, American, is there a romantic woman in your life?" Benny asked.

"Not married, but I am falling in love with a wonderful young woman I met when I arrived in Beidaihe. Like your mixed love life, there is a problem in mine. You saw the two bikers back on the road. They follow me around to make sure I don't get into any trouble. As a diplomat, I'm not allowed any privacy. We have a date for tonight at ten and I'd like to slip away from those guys on my tail. I have an idea how you could help me if you will."

The honeymooners were delighted to join the romantic game to the hilt. They laughed, pretended to get drunk, and addressed Geoff in a loud voice long after he had slipped into the water and swum back to the pier.

The kids from Hong Kong had promised to stay on the beach until well after midnight, or until the beer ran out. Geoff slipped back into his room and changed into his hunting outfit, as he called it.

The wide heavy leaves of the banana tree waved around him like elephant ears. Three huddled figures, wrapped in black plastic rain ponchos ballooning and whipping in the wind, came down the path. The two heavier figures crouched over and walked slowly, bent into the wind. The smaller third person followed, turning from time to time to look back.

Damn, they should have come one at a time, a few minutes apart, to make it harder on the watching team and easier for me to counter. Here come two of the goons, flanking out on either side, far enough back so the girl won't spot them. Double check, hot shot. Make sure you've accounted for everyone. This pair would have alternating duty watches with their counterparts. One team is out on the town or sleeping. Watch for a reserve back-up following them. Okay, looks clear. All I have to do is remove these two and we can get on with the show.

Geoff had prepared himself: a jogging outfit and a dark grey turtleneck for nighttime concealment. A wide leather belt holstered a throwing knife at his back. A waist pack contained a miniature lithium battery flashlight, a compass, a red Swiss Army tool-knife, and plastic wrapped packages of currency. A second knife was strapped to his left leg just above the ankle. Special running shoes were fitted with horseshoe-shaped razor edge steel clips on the toes and heels. The greying red hair was confined in a sailor's black knitted hat.

He waited on the path as banana leaves undulated in the wind around him. He checked his watch: 2150 hours. Still ten minutes to the time he had agreed upon with the fishermen. They should be at the pier waiting now. Double check again, hot shot. Make sure there isn't a second team following the first. Okay. Time to move. Both these guys are in front of you.

There would be little chance for finesse or niceties with the black-clad bat men. Fan Riqi's team would be ready for the showdown. A dark shape moved ahead of him. No, it was veering off to his right, apparently trying to encircle the three escapees. Geoff assumed their orders were to intercept the fugitives and return them to the villa. The committee would deal with them later.

Instead of following the one he saw, Geoff took off to his left to locate the other man. It would be better if he knew where each was before he attacked. He could just make out the three figures hurrying toward the pier, slickers blowing around them in the wind. The road was the only barrier between them and the pier. Geoff located one guard, running hard around the trio, crouched low, exposed for only a moment as he crossed the road. Apparently, he intended to meet them at the entrance to the pier while his teammate came in from the other side.

Geoff accelerated as he ran, pulling the waistband knife with his right hand. He crossed the road. The guard stood up at the pier directly in front of the three approaching figures. Twenty feet away, Geoff stopped, planted his feet, took careful aim and flipped the knife through the air. The blade pierced the jugular. Blood gushing, the body crumpled without a sound. Suddenly, flaring pain starting in his wrist shot up Geoff's arm, announcing the shock of broken bones. He had seen the foot flying through the air at him out of the corner of his eye, but had refused to relinquish concentration on the knife throw.

Damage control, hot shot. The other bird must have cut back and followed you. Right arm's out. Ignore the pain, roll out and counter.

Throwing himself sideways in a trained reflex, he rolled in the direction of the blow to get under the expected follow-up. Geoff saw the shadow of the figure land and swing around. He struck out with his foot and caught a kneecap with the steel tip of his shoe. The man grunted, dropped to the ground and rolled away. Geoff sprang to his feet and spun like a top to gain force. He struck at the head with his toe and heel as the body passed over him.

Another grunt of pain proved he had caused damage, but then vise-like arms whipped out to clamp Geoff's legs and bring him down to the ground.

The three fugitives were shocked at the body in front of them, blood running out on the ground, hands still twitching for the knife. They watched the battle knowing their lives depended on their protector killing the other guard.

Geoff's good left hand chopped at his foe's bloodied head even as he tried to roll out of the grip. The man rolled with him, trying to dodge the blows, and clamped his arms tighter to break the leg bones he was squeezing. Suddenly, the Shaolin fighter freed the leg grip and brought his one undamaged leg under him for leverage. In one smooth, well-practiced motion, he whipped out a garrote to circle Geoff's neck.

Caught unprepared, Geoff was pulled backward on top of his enemy, the wire digging into his throat. With all the force he could muster, Geoff kicked the steel heel plate of his boot down into the man's groin. Then, arching his body, he slammed the back of his head into the agent's nose. The wire relaxed for just the second he needed to force a hand under it. With the pressure relieved, he flung himself free, spun to his feet and gave a final steel-tipped kick to the head of the groaning figure.

The anxious audience of three heard the crunch of steel meeting bone and then there was silence.

Mei Lei rushed over as Geoff slumped to the ground, massaging his neck. "Are you all right, American? What can I do?"

Geoff looked up at the sound of the worried voice. Taking deep breaths, he replied. "I'm still alive, though slightly damaged. I just need a little time to catch my breath. We can't afford to alarm the others. Get going to the boat, quickly."

"You're hurt, American. Let me help you," Mei Lei said.

Geoff forced himself to stand up and shook himself back into control. "You can play nurse later, nightingale. Get the old ones aboard the boat and caution them to walk carefully on the rotting boards of the pier. Send the fisherman for the bodies. We must leave, quickly now."

Used to carrying the heavy baskets of their catch, each fisherman took a dead body over his shoulder and carried it out to the boat without a word. Geoff rubbed his sore neck, moaned softly, exploring the damage to his wrist. He hung back to kick sand over the blood stains. It was dark and with luck the expected rain would wash out the rest of the evidence he couldn't see in the dark. The fishermen dumped the bodies into large fish baskets and threw tarps over them. After throwing off the mooring lines, they poled their boat out through the shallow tide water.

"When will the rest of your friends take to the sea, Fisherman?" Geoff asked, grinding his teeth at the intensity of pain in his wrist and arm.

"Soon, American. You can see the shadows now forming along the shore. We usually go out between now and midnight, gather our catch, and return by daybreak to sell it. It's normal for us to separate from the group. The others know we are independent and seldom fish with them. Can we reach your friends in three hours?"

"With luck, fisherman. I wouldn't want any harm to come to you or endanger Wang. She knows nothing of our plans, I hope?"

A form detached itself from the dark well of the bow deck and a soft voice whispered next to him. "You're injured, Mr. Martine. Let me help, or you'll be in no condition to find your friends."

The fisherman shrugged his shoulders, acknowledging Wang. "She's always been wild, with no respect for the decisions of her elders."

"Wang, dammit, what are you doing here? If they catch us, it'll be sure execution, or even worse, torture. Your father and uncle are willing to take a chance, but you shouldn't be here. I've a good mind to throw you overboard and let you swim to shore."

Wang's brows drew down threateningly and she reacted in a way he wouldn't have expected of the humble young woman he had come to know. Angrily, she barked out, "I give the orders and you'll do as I say. Father, start the engines and let's get moving. Woman," addressing Mei Lie, "hand me that bucket of ice and come with me. Uncle, give me your chopsticks and that reel of fishing line. Sit, American, and let me see how badly your wrist is broken. Why are you rubbing your neck?"

Geoff just shook his head in resignation at the pain and the orders ripping out of her. He settled himself in the bottom of the boat and let the two women work on him. They functioned quietly, by feel, in the dark of the night, complicated by the roll of the boat. Geoff gripped the gunwale and bit down on a piece of soft wood Wang gave him. Efficiently, she explored the fingers, wrist, arm and elbow.

"Maybe some cracks here and there, but the bone is not broken through at any point." She laid the chopsticks along the underside of the wrist, and wrapped the fishing line tightly around it. "Keep the arm buried up to the elbow in the ice for now. It'll dull the pain. Now, let me see about your neck."

Geoff felt soft fingers tenderly explore the raised welt from the garrote. "It's going to get a lot sorer, Wang, and there will be a bright red line from the garrote. Do you have any Tiger balm, the stuff that comes in the red can?"

"Father has some. There is always skin breaking on a fishing boat. It will help the soreness." Wang applied the salve, feeling the welt. She enjoyed massaging the man's skin and sensed a strange exhilaration. The physical touch and the smell of danger induced sweat-stirred emotions. "From the look of the bodies over there, your wounds are minor compared to theirs. Now rest while I take care of our passengers."

Wang spoke softly to the two elders and moved them to the bow of the boat where she had been hiding earlier under the forward decking. "Sit on the pillow seats we have fashioned for you, honored ones, and pull this tarp over the opening. We don't want the other boats to start counting our extra fishermen. Woman, hunker down next to the American and try to keep him warm. There'll be cold, wet weather in the open sea and he may go into shock from his wounds. Our dragon slayer is in greater pain than he's letting on."

Mei Lei inclined her head gracefully.

"My name is Wu Mei Lei, Wang. Your father must be very proud to have a daughter as strong in mind and body as a son. We're very appreciative of your efforts on our behalf."

Wang shrugged her shoulders, jealous that she had assigned the woman to keep the American warm. It would be pleasant to be close to him for the few hours they had. Being with Geoffrey Martine yesterday at the Great Wall had generated some physical reactions in her body that she couldn't control. Severe punishment awaited any woman accused of consorting with a foreigner, but somehow she found she did not care about the risks.

Wang shrugged her shoulders. "From what I can guess, Mei Lie, it must be very important to China to have your old ones complete their mission. I'm happy and proud to be of some help."

"My father struggles to change China for us and the future generations. History will record this event and your part in it."

The putt putt of the ancient marine engine merged with the faint sounds from the rest of the fleet heading out into the Bohai Sea. "When will we fish, Father? If we come back with empty baskets, the other boats will laugh at us and become suspicious."

"Our friends will share their catch on the way back, fearless one. Only the hiding places of the fish are secret from fellow fishermen. We're all of the same mind and fear for China. This is the first time we can do something to help. Meanwhile, find out from your friend what heading we must take. What will be the signal, in case he faints or goes into shock?"

"I'm awake, fisherman," Geoff said as he struggled upright to join the conversation. "Take a course 135 degrees east-south-east and watch for three red lights flashing twice every fifteen seconds about ten miles from shore. Do you suppose we could find any sharks out here? We need to dispose of some black crows."

"Not to worry, American. We have some extra lead weights that will solve the problem as soon as we are far enough from the other boats. We will bleed some fish to cover any stains in the basket on the return trip."

The fishing fleet spread out, vague outlines in the night. They motored away from the other boats, now a half hour from shore. Suddenly, searchlights lit the sky, coming from the shoreline. The land was invisible, but the lights could be seen for miles.

"Patrol boats," Wang said. "They're heading toward the fishing fleet. What happened to the crows that were following you for the past two days? The pair here in the basket is a different one."

"Well, Cha Cha," Geoff managed to put a little lightness in his voice. "I went swimming and they stayed where they thought I was. The Hong Kong kids assumed that you and I had a hot and heavy date tonight. The only problem is that it turned out to be true and not just a story. We can dance, though the floor isn't very smooth."

Wang giggled, and although Geoff couldn't see too well in the darkness, he knew she had her hands up to her mouth trying to stifle it. "What does hot and heavy mean? That's another American idiom you'll have to explain to me."

They all watched and listened, trying to see through the darkness and follow the noise from the patrol boats. Geoff quietly said, "Fisherman, shut off the motor. They'll hear our engine even at this distance. We can drift with the current until the patrol boat disappears. The sea swells will make their radar ineffective."

"Will your friends wait, American?"

"We have a one-hour window; from twelve-thirty to one-thirty tonight and then they'll return tomorrow at the same time if we don't show. Will we drift far off course?"

"Fortunately, the wind is rising again, blowing south with the current. We may have to double back east depending on how far we have drifted."

The lights of the patrol boats dimmed as they moved farther away. The sea increased. Only the wind behind the boat gave them enough steerage to face the build-up of water.

High-powered boat engines sounded from seaward. The occupants of the fishing boat crouched down, fearing a larger Navy Boat called in for the search. A grey shadow passed by no more than 200 feet away, throwing off a high V-shaped wake.

Geoff shouted out over the noise of the wind. "Start the engine, Fisherman. That's a Navy Rocket Boat and will have radar. We want them to think we are just a fishing boat. It is on a mission, judging from the direction it's coming from. There will be a mother ship out there somewhere who won't want us to identify them. Let's get back on our course and maybe we'll miss them."

Geoff went forward to the two elders under the bow cover. "There is one of our submarines waiting out there to meet us. The plan is for the sub to take you two and Mei Lei aboard. Transfer will be difficult due to the heavy seas."

The huddled forms spent the next half hour talking about the future and the wonder of the aid of the United States naval craft. Geoff returned to his ice bucket, the pain returning in spasms.

"Only forty-five minutes lost, American," Wang's father said. "We still have time, provided the sea doesn't worsen."

Uncle had not said a word since the adventure started. Now he whispered to his brother. "The patrol boats will know we are missing, Brother. The country is still under martial law. We could be in much trouble."

The two fishermen settled at the tiller in the aft of the boat, talking into each other's ears over the noise of the storm. "I fear only for my daughter. She is far too young and bright to spend the next years in prison subject to torture and indignities. The reputation of the MSS is fearsome. Let's concoct a story of an engine breakdown and the storm blowing us way off course. Did you recognize our two passengers? Their faces are familiar."

"They are the elderly White Eyebrows. Must be important, Politburo, for the patrol boats to chase them."

Uncle came back sharply. "I wonder, Brother, why are we doing this? Maybe you can enlighten me?"

"The American gave us five thousand US dollars and promises another five thousand if the mission is successful. That is equal to more yuan than we can earn selling fish in ten years. With capital, we can leave for Hong Kong by sea, your family and mine. Malaysia is possible, or Indonesia. They'll accept us, since we have funds to bribe the patrols. They are fond of the US hundred dollar bills. Provisioned and with cover from the sun, we could motor for many days to safety and live the rest of our lives as free men. At worst, we could easily change the dollars on the black market and make our homes and retirement in Beidaihe very comfortable."

"You are a dreamer, my brother. Getting mixed up with the State Security is very dangerous. If we do escape, what about the pirates we have heard about in the South China Sea? They could be more dangerous than the MSS. If we do get away from Chinese waters and the pirates don't get us, can these two old ones, the Lao Xings, do something for us in a new life?"

"You are full of questions only the future can answer, Brother. Let us first get by the next few hours. Meanwhile, tie some metal to the dead ones there and let us dump them over before they catch us with their bodies. That would be disastrous."

The fisherman beckoned Geoff to the tiller. Carefully, Geoff pulled his arm out of the iced water bucket and moved to the stern. He held the tiller clumsily while the two old fishermen effortlessly picked up the wicker baskets and dumped the heavy chain attached to the bodies over the side. Geoff braced the tiller under his injured arm and pulled out the pocket compass and flashlight with his good hand. They were right on course.

The two aged mariners, using only their old gimbals compass, steered without benefit of the stars in the stormy night. They negotiated the sea by instinct, as if they had sophisticated navigation equipment inside their heads.

Winds continued to build up; the boat heaved and rolled in the increasing swells of the sea. The two elders emerged from the bow niche to breathe fresh air, sick with the tossing of the shallow draft vessel. Wang comforted them and supplied oranges to keep their mouths moist. Mei Lei huddled close to her father and Yang, all three of them unfamiliar with the miserable sea.

"How far do you reckon we are from shore, Fisherman?" Geoff asked. "We have twenty-two minutes left to make contact."

"Patience, American," Wang's father answered. "I'd estimate nine miles out now, twenty minutes more to rendezvous. The Dragon King of the sea is very angry tonight. Maybe he will relent for a few minutes and allow us to see the signal and make the transfer safely. What craft do you expect to meet us?"

"A black shark, Fisherman. A long black shark that can disappear beneath the sea in seconds if we don't spot the signal."

The fishing craft rode high, then burrowed deeper into the belly of the waves. The wind increased and the crests of the waves grew taller. The sea threatened to swamp them at any moment. The old ones sat close to the gunwales, holding on in desperation. "Not much farther," Mei Lei said, moving over next to them to give encouragement.

All eyes were focused on the sea, searching for the lights. Geoff checked his watch constantly, the luminous hands moving inexorably slowly. He announced the countdown in a loud voice over the sound of the wind, holding fingers above his head. "Six minutes... five minutes... four minutes... three minutes... two minutes... one minute... thirty seconds ... this is it. My friends, if we keep going, you won't have time to rejoin the fishing fleet. The shark has probably sounded already."

There was no sign of the signal lights. The two elders talked of suicide. Their absence was too obvious. They would never be free again if they returned.

The fishermen hated to turn back. Repercussions would be nasty, explanations disbelieved. Wang's father shouted from the rear of the boat. "American, I can give you ten more minutes, because the wind will be at our backs returning."

Again the countdown. This time they all marked together. "Four minutes... three minutes... two minutes..."

The boat reached the top of a swell and they saw three red lights blinking on top of a long black silhouette riding the sea not five hundred feet away.

"Quickly, over to the submarine," Geoff shouted. He flashed his light, two... three... two... in succession, then repeated it. He caught the brief flicker of a return signal. Time moved agonizingly slowly.

Alongside the craft they could hear shouted commands from the conning tower. Preserver-clad sailors could be seen at the rails dropping bumpers alongside. They reached far out to grab the small boat's ropes thrown up to them. The swells raised and lowered the fishing boat against the towering steel hull. Mei Lei was numb and sick with fear, wondering how they were to get aboard.

A megaphoned voice from the conning tower sounded loud and clear over the scream of the wind. "We're tossing you life jackets with breaching lines attached. Strap them on firmly and just stand up on the seat of your boat. We'll take it from there. Happy to see you. Glad we could wait the extra minutes."

Three orange, padded jackets with nylon ropes attached thumped down amongst them. Wang and Geoff with his one good arm, following instructions, strapped them on Wu Xian, Yang Yucie, and Mei Lei. The two fishermen attended the ropes with the rising and falling boat, one forward, one aft, trying to keep it from crashing against the side of the sub.

"Take one," Geoff hollered and waved at the sailors above, jerking on the line attached to Wu Xian's jacket. They held him upright on the seat of the boat with difficulty. The fishing boat plunged suddenly down and away from the submarine as the sea dropped from under them. Wu pulled out of their arms, hanging in the air. They looked up to see the sailors hauling him over the rail.

"Take two," Geoff hollered again, as he repeated the action with the other old man, desperately supporting him with his good arm. Wang held on to Yang's legs standing on the rolling seat. The boat separated from the submarine again. Yang dangled out of their arms, only to crash between the hulls as the next swell threw the boats together. They heard a fearful crunch and saw the orange jacketed figure caught between the two crafts right in front of them.

"Eeyah!" The scream penetrated the storm. The figure fell free and lifted to the deck above them when the boats parted. Mei Lei screamed in Geoff's ear over the roar of the sea and wind. "I'm afraid. He's dead, isn't he?"

"On with you now, he may be all right. The jacket could have saved him. It's your turn. Jump clear when you feel the rope tighten over you. Brace your feet against the side of the submarine when you're free of the boat and walk right up the side of the sub. There are strong arms waiting for you. Remember us, Nightingale. We'll meet again when China is free."

"Take three," Geoff hollered as loudly as he could. The woman flew out of his arm. He saw her swing safely in the air, her feet rappelling up the side of the submarine.

At the same moment, the two lines attached to the fishing boat flew off at the shouted commands coming from the conning tower. The fishermen immediately put the craft into gear, their backs to the wind, and headed away from the big boat. Geoff heard a final shout from the skipper. "Roger three, good luck. There's a bogy destroyer in the area. Don't think they can see you in this sea, but be careful anyway. Norwest should take you away from them. Happy landings."

A clank of metal resounded as the hatch slammed shut, and the long shark-shaped craft sank beneath the sea like a mythical monster.

Geoff's wrist ached. He felt Wang pushing him down onto the seat, holding tightly to his good arm. She braced them both against the roll of the sea. His neck was sore and raw from the wet sweatshirt abrading the garrote wound.

The bottom of the boat was awash with water. Uncle bailed frantically with an old hand pump.

Geoff checked his watch. Only ten minutes for the transfer. The Immortals willing, the old man would live with a few broken ribs.

They were twenty minutes off schedule, but the fishermen were right. The wind at their backs increased the speed, giving them a chance to arrive with the fleet at daybreak. They'd play the game of a tourist gone fishing with his Luxingshe guide. The broken wrist could easily be explained as an accident in the heavy surf.

The wind eased off somewhat. Clouds separated to reveal a scattering of stars. Tensions in the small fishing craft subsided with the satisfaction of the task completed. Geoff stripped off the wet shirt with difficulty around the wrapped arm and settled with Wang out of the wind under the small bow deck. The canvas pillows, brought for the passengers, cushioned them from the wet and cold. A tarp kept them warm inside the snug niche.

"We'd better redo that wrist of yours," Wang said, using Geoff's small flashlight to see. "It looks like the fishing line and the swelling from the wound are cutting the chopstick splints right into the flesh." Gently, she held his arm in her lap, feeling the swollen flesh with her fingers. "We are fortunate the bone didn't separate. The bandage held it in place. Hold onto the light and the splints. I'm going to re-wrap it with your shirt instead of the line." Tenderly, she untied the existing wrappings and replaced them with strips cut from the wet shirt.

The pain eased off somewhat with the pressure released. Geoff said, "Thank you, Cha Cha. A little neck massage with your essential balm and I'll be as good as new. You're a wonderful nurse." He turned the flashlight to her face for a moment. The strain of the past hours showed in the trembling mouth and the eyes straining to stay open. He put his arm around her to comfort her and ease the after-shock she was enduring.

Wang, luxuriated in the strength and warmth of the man's body, imagined him as a lover and husband. She sighed and the tension trickled away, replaced by the tingling sensations of ying and yang attraction.

Geoff propped his bad arm on a pillow to ease it and twisted around to make Wang more comfortable against his bare chest. For a while, they both dozed.

Uncle shook them awake to the sound of motors around them. Geoff, with his one good arm, boosted himself up onto the bow to see their boat heading into the center of the fishing fleet. The shore-line was a grey shadow in the emerging dawn. Friendly boats came alongside and dumped fish and crab into their baskets. Thumbs-up signs and quiet words proved the unwritten camaraderie of the sea.

"How are your wounds, Mr. Martine?" Wang looked up at him, surprised at the obvious physical recovery.

"Good shape, considering everything that happened," Geoff responded. "Remember our story. You're simply my tour guide giving in to the whims of the tourist who wanted to go fishing. We hit bad weather and I broke my wrist."

With Wang's help, he put what was left of the damp sweatshirt back on. She buttoned the wind collar to conceal the neck wound. Geoff gave her a thank you kiss on the cheek. "There's sure to be a welcoming committee. They can't prove anything, if the other fisher-men keep quiet."

Wang's father spoke, a full smile spreading across the weathered, gentle old face, the first since Geoff had met him. "We can expect trouble when we return, American. My friends said the patrol boats that followed the fleet were looking for our passengers. We can ex-pect a reception committee. I've weathered many storms and the satisfaction of bringing in the catch is worth the aches and pains of the effort."

"You've done well, Fisherman," Geoff said. He removed the plas-tic-wrapped bundle attached to his belt and handed it to him. "A small reward for changing history."

Stuffing the bundle into the wide maw of a large fish nearby, the fisherman carefully stowed it under the deck in the bow. "We accept the money for the future of our families, American, but I must say we'd have done the same for nothing. Saving the lives of our honored elders may prolong the life of China."

The fisherman pulled on his straggly beard in thought, and then turned to Geoff again. "If we decide to take a long voyage one night, is it possible to have someone meet us in another port to assist our landing?"

"With good fortune, Fisherman, you may not have to take that voyage. If ever you do, I'll give Wang a US phone number to call. Mention this night, which we will call 'the night of the fishermen,' and you'll be taken care of."

Geoff recognized the man standing at the end of the dock watching the arrivals as they pulled into the pier. A disheveled jacket and loose-fitting trousers gave the illusion of a Charlie Chaplin tramp without the mustache.

"We meet again, Commander Martine. Did you have a successful fishing trip?" Fan Riqi extended his hand to help the obviously damaged American from the boat.

"Mr. Fan, how pleasant to have you meet me. What brings you to Beidaihe? If I hadn't broken my wrist, it would have been an interesting fishing trip. I enjoy the sea."

"About what time did you leave, Commander?"

"Is there a problem? It must be important to bring out the Vice Commissar of the MSS."

"My questions, your answers, please, Commander. Suffice it to say there is an important meeting taking place here today. Two of the participants are missing. You have the unfortunate bad luck to have been in Chengde a short time ago and here during the trouble. Strange coincidence, wouldn't you think, if you were a policeman like me?"

Geoff replied. "Our boat has been out since late last night. How could we possibly know anything about the troubles you're investigating?"

The two adversaries had been talking in English. Fan now turned to Wang and spoke out in rapid Mandarin. "Get your guest over to the medical clinic and bring him back to the dining hall at the hotel immediately." To Geoff, in English, he said. "Your guide will get you medical attention for the wrist, American. We'll meet for breakfast in the main dining hall. Perhaps you'll remember something to help me."

BEIDAIEHE, 4 JUNE 1994

Geoff, escorted by Wang, walked to the dining hall. It was nearing 6 a.m., the sun just clearing the horizon to announce a clear day.

"Apparently, you're a very efficient barefoot doctor, Cha Cha. The x-rays showed the bones cracked but in perfect position." Geoff waved the plaster. "With a bath and fresh clothes, I feel much better. He replaced the freshly bandaged wrist in the muslin arm sling. A turtleneck cotton shirt covered the other wound. "I'm not sure I know what to do with this sack of leaves and roots they gave me for medicine. Do you chew them or just paste them on your forehead to relieve the pain?"

Wang laughed and turned around to walk backward facing Geoff. "You're making fun of our rural dispensary. Brew the ingredients as a tea. Drink it to restore the strength lost during the accident." She pirouetted in a carefree mincing dance. Geoff was happy to see the pretty face relaxed, released from the tensions of the past night.

The tables were set with boiled eggs, toast, fruit, pickled vegetables, and diamond-shaped pieces of sponge cake. A large pot of congee was at the side of the hall with a big serving ladle and a pile of rice bowls alongside. There was no one else in the room. Wang checked the kitchen and returned shaking her head. "Deserted. There is no one here."

Geoff motioned her into a chair. "You must be very hungry. Please share my zhaofan. Surely the protocol can be broken on such an auspicious morning. There's not much surprise on your face regarding the missing staff. They're on strike too, I suppose?"

Wang spooned out bowls of the rice gruel for both of them. "It's the plan of the Nightingales. Everyone is supposed to stay home, including me. We should find a radio and hear what is going on after breakfast."

Vice Commissar Fan Riqi and Hu Banyi came into the hall, wheeling a cart with a large television set on it. Hu pushed it over to the wall near the table and plugged it into the power and antenna outlets. Not a word was spoken as the four of them sat on the edge of their seats and watched the picture of a flotilla of grey-painted naval ships coursing gracefully through the sea.

The picture changed to a close-up of an impressive aircraft carrier in the center of the fleet. The Stars and Stripes rippled grandly from the top of the mast.

The picture changed, replaced by the familiar face of Joan Rogers, darling of the NBC news team. Hong Kong Harbor framed the background. "This is Joan Rogers speaking to you from the Mandarin Hotel in Hong Kong. We're expecting a special momentous news event. Please stay tuned."

On screen, Rogers closed her mic with a hand and leaned aside to talk with someone out of range of the camera. Her perfectly coiffed head nodded once, then she turned back and opened the mic again. "There's a slight delay. A superimposed special telecast is coming in, live from the USS America, aircraft carrier underway in the Bohai Sea off the coast of China."

TWENTY-ONE
BEIDAIHE

0600 THURSDAY 4 JUNE 1994

Fan Riqi's itchy scalp remained unscratched, the cigar in his right hand unwrapped. Hu Banyi's mind, like the hard disk memory of his computer, was humming quietly, retrieving data and getting ready to update with the new input coming over the television.

Geoffrey Martine cradled his broken wrist, trying to massage the sore muscles inside the cast. The scene coming over the screen on board the carrier USS America was familiar. He had taken off and landed on that deck more than a hundred times.

Wang, surprised to be sitting at a table with high officials of the Ministry of State Security, nervously began to eat the congee. The history unfolding via satellite on television was secondary to her instant recall of the pleasant sensations that had taken place in the boat only a short time ago.

CNN'S Ginny Chen described the scene. "The USS Aircraft Carrier America is underway in the Bohai Sea off the east coast of China. A historic ceremony is about to take place."

The video replay showed the flight elevator bringing a small group of people up from the hangar deck in a dramatic exposure to representatives of the world news media seated in front of them.

Geoff, without asking, was switching channels to get the best view and sound of the scene. In a moment of camaraderie, he explained to Fan the competition between the stations and reporters. "Ginny Chen is Hong Kong born of Cantonese parents, as you might know. She is in her element, a wise choice by CNN whilst Rogers at NBC with no Hong Kong or China experience is struggling to find ground for her audience."

"Thank you, Commander, for the information. I know of the

Chen woman and her family, but I don't understand the competition between the two women."

"Capitalism, Vice Commissar, capitalism and to a degree, entrepreneurism. Each of these women competes for personal audience recognition, which has a direct relationship to the two elements of salary and ego."

On screen, Chen continued. "The audience is a pool of international reporters, equipped with earphones and tape decks set to hear and record the event in the language of their choice. English, French, Japanese, Russian or German is available, also Mandarin Chinese. Representatives of the media are pool selected, by their peers, to record the momentous occasion and inform their respective countries."

The cameras focused in tight on the four people on the stage who were emerging from below decks. Ginny Chen continued her commentary in a hushed voice, dramatizing the scene. "The people you see left to right are: United States Special Ambassador James Baker and Vice Premier of China Wu Xian. The young woman next to him is his daughter, Wu Meilei. The naval officer is Admiral Bud Crockett, Commander in Chief of the Seventh Fleet, Task Force One."

Background shots picked up the immediate surroundings of the long decks and aircraft tucked neatly along the sides. The ungainly superstructure at one side of the deck housed the command of the ship.

Sailors in dress whites lined the rails, facing the platform, legs spread to answer the roll of the sea, hands clasped behind their backs. Visor-capped chief petty officers with rows of hash marks on their sleeves spaced themselves between their details. The ship's operations and flying officers flanked the press corps. Summer whites and gold braided caps lent authority and dignity to the proceedings. Broader shots of the cameras picked up the surrounding sea, decorated with the graceful flotilla of warships rolling in their protective positions around the carrier, the flagship of the Seventh Fleet.

"The time there is 6 a.m., dawn in the Bohai Sea, tomorrow morning in China, Thursday the fourth of June."

Geoff switched back to the station with NBC's news team and

Jane Rogers. The screen was filled with the old news scenes of Tanks on Changan Avenue and the tumultuous crowds in Tiananmen Square.

Rogers was doing fill using the old footage of 1989. "It was five years ago on this day that we showed you these scenes from Beijing. They recorded the Chinese Army shooting down innocent students and bystanders to take forcible possession of Tiananmen Square."

In Atlanta, Georgia, it was 6 p.m., daylight saving time, Wednesday, the third of June. The program director of CNN frantically made last-minute decisions for the evening news programs. He faced four live screens to juggle and project to a worldwide audience. Ginny Chen was on a balcony of a suite at the Mandarin Hotel overlooking Hong Kong Harbor watching her monitor. She would pick up on whatever was projected, ad libbing descriptions from her own memory.

Another lead was coming in from the ballroom below her. The United Provinces of Cathay were ready to proclaim their new nation. Media representatives from all over the world waited for James Shan Leight to lead the entourage of Provincial leaders onto a stage. Scheduled for 6 a.m. Hong Kong time, the telecast had been delayed by the dramatic event coming in from the Bohai Sea.

The team of Brokaw and Gumble was in the New York studio signaling frantically for a live mike. Rogers already had astronomical ratings whenever she was given airtime. This was no time for second lead.

The fourth screen showed the President sitting at his desk in the oval office of the White House, patiently waiting for a signal to speak regarding the events happening on board the America.

In the Central Beach Hotel dining room, Wang gasped and reached for Geoff's good hand at the sight of Wu Xian and Mei Lei on board the ship. Geoff silenced her with a slight shake of his head and squeezed her hand.

Fan Riqi turned at that moment to say something to his antagonist and caught the expression. "There's no need to hide your evening's adventures, Commander. The picture we are viewing is self-evident. We now have to see what will happen within our own government. You are either in very deep trouble, or will be a national hero."

The scene flipped to the deck of the carrier. CNN's director, with a fine sense of history, let the dramatic moment speak for itself. Cameras focused on the gray-haired senior diplomat James Baker as special envoy approaching the microphone. Baker moved a little uncertainly with the roll of the ship's deck and grasped the podium firmly to steady himself to address the audience in front of him and around the world.

"People of Asia. People of the European Continent, the African Continent, and all the Americas. People of Australia, New Zealand, and the Islands of the Pacific. Citizens of China, and people of Chinese origin who live apart from the motherland. Today the United States of America takes another step for mankind, for freedom."

Pausing, taking strength from the intense attention of the immediate audience and very conscious of the millions of listeners around the world, the Special Ambassador continued. "A leader of China has asked the United States of America for refuge. In jeopardy for his life in his country, Wu Xian, senior member of the Politburo and Vice Premier of the People's Republic of China, requests sanctuary until it is safe to return home."

Turning dramatically to face the three people behind him, Baker extended his hand to the small, stooped, owlish Chinese gentleman rising from his chair. He approached the Ambassador and warmly gripped the extended hand. A radio tech hurried over to pull a two-step stool out for him to stand on. With the two people now equal in height, Baker turned back to the bank of microphones.

"People of the world, I bring you, with extreme pleasure, Vice Premier Wu Xian of the People's Republic of China. Formerly General Secretary of the Communist Party, once Premier of China, a comrade in arms and Long Marcher with Mao Tsetung, he is now a Vice Premier and member of the elite standing committee of the Chinese Communist Party. Wu Xian, the United States welcomes you to their sovereign territory, the USS America. The President, speaking from the oval office in Washington, will personally address you."

The large television monitor in front of the dais showed the beaming face of the President, with the overprint caption at the bottom: LIVE FROM WASHINGTON, D.C. 6:08 P.M.

"Vice Premier Wu Xian, it's my understanding that you have requested asylum for Yang Yucie, your daughter, and yourself. As President of the United States, I hereby grant the three of you asylum in any of the sovereign territories of the United States, until you feel safe enough to return to your homeland."

Clinton's charismatic smile filled the screen as he continued. "We welcome you wholeheartedly to the United States. Hillary says you can even use the Lincoln bedroom in the White House if you need a protected residence. Our sincerest wish is that China will change soon to allow you to return in peace to the land of your birth."

Special Ambassador Baker shook hands with Vice Premier Wu Xian again and dramatically indicated the stage was his to use.

Wu Xian took a firm grip on the microphone stand, seemingly as physical support for the weary body. In a voice as firm as the grip, he spoke. "Mr. President, we accept gratefully and humbly the asylum you grant for us in the great United States of America. That decision will shed light on the hope of freedom and democracy to the one billion citizens of the People's Republic of China. It is our intention to cause the reflection of that light from China to all democracy-hopeful people around the world."

The dean of the press corps stood up and began to applaud with a slow, measured beat. Row by row the media arose and joined her. Baker was already clapping, as was Admiral Bud Crockett, rising to the occasion resplendent in his white uniform. Colorful ribbons filled the chest of his jacket. Wearing a uniform cap thick with braided gold thread, the admiral represented the full power and authority of the United States of America.

Like a ripple of firecrackers, the sailors around the railings of the America raised their hands to join in, preceding their officers by seconds. Mei Lei, next to the Admiral, put her palms together in front of her face, stood and bowed to the accolade, tears flowing down her cheeks.

Geoff, watching the scene from leagues away, felt himself part of it and stood. He clapped his good hand flat against the table in unison with those aboard the ship. Wang stood with prayer palms together like Mei Lei, identical tears flowing openly down her cheeks.

A camera focused in on the beautiful oval face of Mei Lei, framed in square-cut silken black hair. Her tears were tiny lights reflecting the rising sun. This was the shot used in the Atlanta studios of CNN, held for fifteen seconds. It was destined to remain in history, to be shown with the memorable picture of the lone demonstrator, five years before, facing an oncoming tank in the streets of Beijing.

The whispered voiceover of Ginny Chen was saying, "Mei Lei, the daughter of Wu Xian, who we understand escaped with him just a few hours ago. It is known that the Premier and his daughter were at the seaside resort of Beidaihe less than twenty-four hours ago attending a meeting of the Politburo elite.

"It's now 6 a.m. Thursday, aboard the USS America, somewhere in the Bohai Sea, off the east coast of China in international waters. Two important leaders of China have defected. The President has welcomed them to the United States territory of the USS America."

Hu Banyi raised his hands to clap with Geoff, but held back after a glance from Fan. "Don't let emotions replace our immediate responsibility, Comrade."

A map insert flashed up on the screen, showing the large body of water pinched by Dalian in the north and Yantai in the south. It was on latitude directly east of Beijing. An arrow pinpointed Beijing, then Beidaihe.

Wu Xian stood at the podium, shaken by the spontaneous accolade. He bowed several times, the smooth skin of the austere face breaking into a soft smile. He waved his hands, palms out and downward, to quiet the crowd, each time increasing the crescendo. Finally, the people in front took their seats. The sailors around the rails assumed at-ease positions. All attention was riveted on the speaker.

"Sheh sheh ni, Mr. President and all of you. Thank you very much." Wu waved in a slow undulating motion to cover the people seated and standing in front of him. "Thank you from the bottom of China's heart, for it isn't this old body you have to applaud and honor, but all China. With good fortune, we will impose on you for only a short time, Mr. President."

With a mischievous twinkle in his eyes, he added, "Mr. President, I understand many good friends and celebrities sometimes occupy the Lincoln room. I would hesitate to dislodge anyone. Maybe, if I stayed for a short time, the hallowed bed would give me the sagacity and resoluteness of its original user, though I would be using only half its length."

Wu's face sobered, now speaking in his native tongue. The interpreters scrambled to their microphones. "In 1911, Sun Yatsen released the people of China from the slavery of the Imperial Manchu. In 1949, Mao Tsetung, our Great Helmsman, fought and secured the release of the people from the despotism of the Kuomintang. On this morning, five years ago, a horrible tragedy befell our nation. Tanks and armored vehicles stormed Tiananmen Square to spill the blood of thousands of our finest minds and bodies. That raid spread like a verminous disease throughout the country. The people returned to the bondage of fear and oppression. Unreported thousands are still imprisoned through the desire of certain leaders to keep their power.

"This day, on the anniversary of that terrible event, recorded in history as the Massacre at Tiananmen Square, our people act again. They are listening now, through the channels of the Voice of America and the BBC, poised to act on my signal. Our young intellectuals, straining again at the yokes enslaving them, stand ready to repeat their demands for freedom. Sadly, the military, mistakenly called the People's Liberation Army, stand ready, ordered to shoot.

"It was for this that I defected, unable to sway my peers from repeating an act that can only result in the Suicide of China."

Gaining more strength of spirit and voice, the small man looked taller, stood straighter, years apparently melting from his body. He spoke to China through the voice and eyes of the cameras and microphones in front of him. "Citizens of China, I hereby resign from the Communist Party and address you. Peasants, farmers, workers, group leaders, managers, entrepreneurs, minorities, even those that believe in the socialism of Marxist-Leninist-Maoist thought, join with us. The students, academics and intellectuals will form a new government. Together we can throw off the bindings of domination, whether Imperialism, Nationalism or Communism."

The speaker paused, spent for the moment, watching the audience of reporters glued to their earphones, listening for the translations to catch up, hands scribbling madly on the tablets on their knees.

The cameras wandered to seek faces and expressions: the Admiral whispering to Mei Lei; Wu's inscrutable features.

Admiral Crockett sat calmly, with a proud smile on his face for the Navy's success in bringing out the aged leader amidst the fearful danger of the night's storm. The submarine captain had briefed them on the struggle to get the three people aboard. The other octogenarian, in critical condition, was in the ship's sick bay below with broken ribs and internal injuries, awaiting transfer to a Hong Kong hospital.

A young officer came up to the Admiral, leaning over to whisper in his ear. Crockett held up his hand for him to stop and motioned Baker to go with him to the rear of the platform.

Geoff watched the side scene, and caught the expression on Baker's face. His smile had disappeared. Crockett disappeared from the scene. He returned to his seat, obviously distraught.

While Wu Xian paused for a moment to refresh, the long night of strain visible on the aged face, his voice weakening perceptibly, Tom Brokaw broke in. "You are listening to a special Nightingale broadcast, the code name used for this historic nationwide demonstration in China. Wu Xian, the Vice Premier, calling himself a dove released to fly free, is speaking. He urges a general strike to offset any Army ploy to shoot demonstrators."

The Vice Premier re-affirmed this. "People of China, the students, the nightingales, will soon be singing, and the doves of peace will fly all over the land. Let me tell the Politburo at Zhongnanhai and Beidaihe what your plan is. They were anxious to know and would never guess.

"Comrades of the Politburo, wherever you are. The students are staying in their living quarters on the campuses. They avoid the streets. They disdain flags and statues. They abstain from their classes. They wait patiently and peacefully for you to step down. They desire the basic freedoms of body and spirit.

"Leaders, you call yourselves, but your tenure is short. Millions of workers will stay at home until you change our political and government structure. There will be a shadow parade. A parade of minds you cannot challenge with guns and tanks. Today, the workers of the plants manufacturing the guns and tanks have quit.

"Cadre leaders and officials, stay home. Your factory is noiseless; the fires are out. Your work place must convert from politics to profits. When our new plan becomes effective, each factory will have autonomy. The labor force will own the production unit, through shares of stock. They will elect their most capable managers and market their goods in a free and open society.

"Transportation workers, communication workers, shipyard workers, miners and service people are striking today. They will organize unions to protect their interests and provide an incentive for the improvement of products and lifestyle."

Beginning to weaken, Wu's face and posture showed the toll of the long night's physical effort. The terror of lifting to the deck of the submarine and descending into the bowels of the ship had taken its toll on the aging body. Geoff could see the strain in his sagging mouth and his eyes shrinking into their sockets.

Baker walked up to the leader and whispered to him before he began speaking again. The camera came in for a close-up, revealing to the worldwide audience the worried looks on their faces.

Wu Xian turned to his audience again. His shoulders had drooped and the body curled within itself, shrinking. His voice dropped so low that the technicians fumbled to increase the volume enough to catch the words.

"My People of China, our world is spinning amid your efforts. Stay in your homes and listen for television and radio news. Cataclysmic events have pyramided on your efforts. Our country is in a state of shock, nerves rattled from the tremors of changes occurring. It will be necessary for the tranquilizer of time to take effect and calm us."

Geoff looked at Fan and then Hu. "What's happening? There must be something going on we don't know about."

"Commander Martine," Fan replied "We have received reports via our Beijing headquarters. A naval force is enroute from Formosa to our southeast coast. I can tell you Beidaihe was attacked last night by a small force from the sea. From what we can reconstruct, a rocket boat landed just after midnight. Apparently a special team was able to take out three of our teams and when they left, the Premier and Cai Jixi were dead.

Geoff broke in, "Yes, while in the fishing boat, we saw the rocket boat five miles offshore. Frankly we thought it was your boats trying to locate us."

Fan continued. "Not ours, Martine, not after you and the passengers we assume you had. Apparently they had detailed information of the residence of the ranking members of the Politburo. They searched the villa occupied by Wu Xian and Yang Yucie and found it empty. We know where they went. Thanks to your efforts, their lives are spared. Minister Chou Shi was seen taking the last train out of Beidaihe south just before midnight."

"What about General Tang Naiwa? I saw him here a couple of days ago."

Fan shrugged. "We found his body yesterday, garroted. It was about his death we were going to question you. The CIA could have ordered his assassination and you were a logical choice. Judging by the other events, it's possible Tang's murder was an inside job."

Geoff shook his head. "Sorry, policeman, I'm a fighter. Look elsewhere for the assassin. But you must have some background. Let me try to get through by phone or telex to our Ambassador in Beijing or even Washington."

"You're welcome to use our communication facilities, Commander. You will soon see on the TV that your carrier and escorts are preparing for battle. Radar on our east coast reports a large invasion force enroute from Kaoshing. This would be led by a General Feng, an old Nationalist still trying to take over the mainland. We have a mole in our department, it seems."

Hu Banyi went off to see if he could get any more information from Beijing. Wang excused herself to be with her father and uncle. Geoff mused at the thought of himself and Fan Riqi being the last two humans on earth. Deadly antagonists a few hours ago, now watching the morning news having breakfast and talking freely with each other.

At CNN, microphones mistakenly left open during the confusion added a clamor of voices to the scene on board the America's deck. Ginny tried to describe what they were watching. "There is chaos as Vice Premier Wu Xian suddenly cut off his speech and retired with Ambassador Baker. We're trying to find out what dire information came through."

Ginny Chen's voice came through excited and patchy. "Get me on, get me on. There's a lead coming over the telephone that an invasion fleet from Taiwan is landing right now on the east coast of China."

The screen showed the media on their feet, screaming at the ship's information officer and the participants. The retreating figures of Wu Xian, James Baker and a worried looking Mei Li paid no attention to their shouted questions. The ship's press officer took over the microphones, trying to quiet the melee. "Patience, patience, please. The communications center below deck will release whatever news is available. Please take your tapes and earphones with you and proceed down the starboard ladder to the lower deck."

CNN's news director held that scene until he could find out what was happening. The scene turned ominous as the ship's loudspeakers came over loud and clear. Klaxons sounded. Speakers blared. "General quarters, general quarters. All hands to battle stations. All hands to battle stations. Stand by to launch planes. Stand by to launch planes." Similar activity was seen on the other ships of the fleet now moving to encircle the carrier in case of an attack.

Geoff watched, reliving each well-known general quarter's procedure of the ship's crew, as trepidation wracked his senses. Aircraft moved to the launchers. Bomb cradles wheeled up to the planes. Pilots clambered out of the passageways running to their aircraft. The world was shuddering at the news of invasion fleets. It was well known that both Taiwan and China had nuclear armament and this could portend the Suicide of China.

Hu Banyi returned and pulled Fan away from the table to talk to him without Geoff hearing. Fan turned back and beckoned Geoff over to hear the news. "Please repeat what you have told me, Hu."

Stuttering, shaking, Hu fumbled out the news. "China is paralyzed. Our reports are simply telephone calls from eyewitness observers and a very few still-loyal MSS agents. Confirmation is only if we get the same information from different areas. Tragically, we know that Chinese Air Force marked aircraft were sighted heading toward the Zhongnanhai. Massive explosions and huge fires in the total area probably have killed everyone within the complex."

Geoff couldn't restrain himself from urging more information quickly. He would have to get to a communication facility to report what he could from here. "Hu, have they definitely identified the invasion force and what reaction is your military taking?"

Hu looked for permission from Fan. "Go ahead, Hu. Put it all out. Martine, will you agree to hold your information for my clearance? I suspect your embassy and Washington know more than we do by this time."

"Of course, Fan, your control. I may be able to add some information for you after contact with my sources. It would appear to me that we are but little actors on a big stage."

"Shakespeare, Martine? I prefer Confucius, but do understand the great bard. Get on with it, Hu. What else do you have?"

"Invasion craft have been sighted all along the east coast from Dalien to Xiamen. Wu Xian's strike is nationwide. Early reports indicate the nation is paralyzed, asleep from border to border. All universities and lower-level schools are empty, including the teachers and administrators..."

Fan plied Hu anxiously. "What about buses, taxis, department and other stores? Surely the people must go out for food?"

"Our office in the park is empty. The information I got was from my sister who works at the Telephone center on Changan. She took my personal call at her home and said not to call again. Line-to-line phones are working, but there is no operator assistance or international service. The night crews removed and kept key parts from the equipment. The day crews never arrived. I could only get a brief report before she hung up. No buses, no taxis, no motorbikes or even bicycles are on the streets. Sister said all the schools, factories and stores are closed."

"Looks like you won't get to your contacts, Martine," Fan said. "Nothing open. I have heard there will be small phones in the future connected to satellites."

"Yes, Mr. Fan, the technology is there. We just have to implement it. In the meantime, am I to assume you're the Commissar of the MSS?"

The three men sat at the table. Hu Banyi poured fresh hot water from thermoses into their teacups. No one said a word, not wanting to interrupt each other's thoughts.

TWENTY-TWO
HONG KONG

0700 4 JUNE 1994

Geoff and the two policemen, isolated in Beidaihe, watched the events unfold with awe and amazement. CNN continued their broadcast, using anchor Ginny Chen in Hong Kong to describe the events. File material of London's Number 10 Downing Street, Bhutan's strange and eerie mountain territory, Taiwan, and Beidaihe backed up the lead stories. Wild street celebrations in Hong Kong and Kowloon provided fillers.

MANDARIN BALLROOM, HONG KONG

An hour later than scheduled, the delegates filed into the ballroom of the Mandarin Hotel and took their seats on the bandstand stage at one end of the room. A sea of people faced them. Seven hundred-and-eighty-two representatives of the world's press and broadcast news were restless and impatient.

Credential checking and body searching annoyed them. The hour-long delay and the refusal to allow them to leave had raised emotions higher. Now, they were almost riotous at the delay, guessing something was happening outside that room.

NEW YORK

It was 7 p.m. daylight saving time in New York as the lead from Hong Kong became live – almost an anti-climax to the day's events.

CNN's news director signaled to put on Hong Kong and Chen. There was a lead from Taiwan trying to break through, though they lacked representation there. Another strange signal hit the circuits. The technician said it looked like the old Beijing stringers, not heard from since '89.

LONDON

Number 10 Downing Street, London, 10 p.m. The Prime Minister and his wife watched from their couch, holding hands in anticipation of the news. The Prime Minister's advisors had just left to take various directed actions on the China happenings. The British Colony, three years less than a century old, was being reborn.

THIMPU BHUTAN

In Thimpu, Bhutan, the Royal Family of Dorji tuned in at 4 a.m. Thursday to watch their friend James Shan Leight achieve his goal of an independent Hong Kong. The other news from Taiwan and Beijing had riveted them to the television. Though high and away from the happenings in Beijing, the northern border of Bhutan locked with China along the Himalayas.

The young King departed to pray with his lamas for the fate of the world.

HONG KONG

"I'm James Shan Leight, Provisional President of a new nation, and the United Provinces of Cathay." Leight had taken the podium to face the disruptive audience, who were suddenly quieted by his calm, authoritative voice. "Would you please take your seats, ladies and gentlemen?"

"My intended long speech will be very brief. The Provinces of Hong Kong, Quandong, Shenzhen, Macau, Hainan, and Formosa have declared their independence from the People's Republic of China and agreed to join together in a new nation. The United Provinces of Cathay became official at 6 a.m. this morning on the signing of the charter. We thank the Prime Minister of England and the President of the United States for their recognition. The declarations hold and we will proceed with our intentions, despite frightening news from other places in the China Sea."

Leight looked at the others and they nodded. "That's all I have to say at this time. We'll hold an open news conference in two hours. You are free to leave the room."

Two sets of double doors opened and the media crowd rushed out to find out what was happening. Ginny Chen, in a suite in the Mandarin, gave a brief summary of the United Provinces of Cathay press release, the announcement now dwarfed by the other events. Ginny became the lead anchor of CNN, with an estimated audience of more than one billion people around the world.

PRESIDENTIAL SUITE OF THE SHANGRI LA, HONG KONG

Soong Aimei and Li Quohua met with a group of supporters after they left the meeting at the Mandarin. They agonized over the scattered reports from Taiwan. According to their sources, the entire military complex at Kaohsiung had disappeared in the cloud of a nuclear bomb. The timeline thus revealed was frighteningly brief and devastating in its consequences.

At 0555, the garrison at Taishong recorded on their air defense radar a single unidentified aircraft at 35000 feet.

At 0600, a spectacular mushroom-shaped cloud appeared, followed by a colossal explosion.

It would be several hours before an observation team, suitably protected from the fallout, could be flown in to assess the damage. The garrison commander, a naval officer, advised that General Feng, his entire staff, and the reserve military forces of the Republic of China had been at the base at the time and were presumed lost.

A nuclear scientist on their temporary staff considered the scope and size of the mushroom cloud. He opined that it was a new mini-type device developed by the Russians for pinpoint bombing and limited destruction to a five-mile radius. China was known to have such devices in their armament. There was no data at this time to confirm the source of the bomb.

The roads out of the Kaoshing area were blocked with vehicles fleeing the disaster. Emergency relief convoys were unable to get to the area.

Military invasion forces from the Kaoshing garrison had landed on the coast of China. Now headless, they waited for orders.

Soong Aimei and Li Quohua arranged to return to Taipei that afternoon. Friends in Taiwan advised that the coup was over. Civilians controlled the country. The Central Advisory Committee was ready to meet on their arrival.

A remote broadcast originating in the CNN suite of rooms at the Mandarin Hotel relayed to a portable dish on the roof of the hotel, pointed skyward slightly south to a line over the equator. The new satellite received the signals and repeated them down to Atlanta. A news director picked up the feed, programmed with files held ready on a bank of screens, and rebroadcast it to the world.

Ginny Chen, in the hot seat at CNN, Hong Kong, voiced the news clips as fast as they were received. She was careful to explain at each heading break that "This report is unconfirmed." She confessed, "Our sources are stringers sending unrelated data by fax and telephone. CNN camera crews are on their way into the troubled areas."

MAINLAND CHINA

A map of the southeast coast of China appeared on the screen. "Phone calls to relatives in Hong Kong, filtered out of Ningbo, Wenzhou, Fuzhou and Xiamen, and the southeast coast of the China mainland. Landing parties of the Republic of China arrived early in the morning. There was no gunfire. Local naval craft and troops apparently expected and welcomed them. The invading forces were seen milling around the target areas, waiting for orders, drinking, laughing and carousing with the PLA troops."

BEIJING

File photos of Changan Avenue, the Forbidden City, Tiananmen Square and the large red doors of the Zhongnanhai covered the screen while Ginny Chen spoke. She shuffled sheets of paper tossed to her, mentally shifting scenes in the chaos of news.

"Unverified early reports from Beijing describe a catastrophic explosion in the city's heart. The first account said the Forbidden

City was bombed. Harrison Salisbury, the noted author of China's modern history, was on the twenty-fifth floor of the new Beijing Tower Hotel with friends this morning. He called the South China Morning Post to relate the event. Following is a tape of Salisbury's report, courtesy of the Post:

"Sounds of aircraft directly overhead brought us to the windows of our room at 6 a.m. We could see military aircraft directly over the Zhongnanhai complex, next to the Forbidden City. The first bomber circled, then dove to five hundred feet, straddling the complex with three bombs. They appeared to drop in slow motion, on a diagonal, from one corner to the other. A minute later a second bomber came in and dropped three bombs on the reverse diagonal. At first we thought they were duds, as nothing happened. Two minutes later we saw three massive fire balls, followed by tremendous explosions. Someone in the room hollered to get away from the windows. We dropped to the floor just in time. All the windows in our room burst, throwing glass everywhere. While lying on the floor, we heard three more explosions followed by a whoosh of air through our open windows.

"We got up carefully and checked the scene. Flames were shooting hundreds of feet in the air, smoke billowing out in waves to the surrounding area. Debris flew into the Forbidden City and across the street into Tiananmen Square. Fortunately, the nationwide strike, starting this morning, had emptied the streets.

"Fires are still smoldering. The wind blew the smoke eastward, clearing our view. Buildings are reduced to rubble, as in Beirut rubble. The large carved red doors lie flat on the ground outside. Apparently the thick ancient walls of the Zhongnanhai contained the fires.

"We assume the whole Politburo except for those at the Beidaihe plenum was in the complex at the time, many of them accompanied by family, aides and staff that maintained the area. Other than the Standing Committee, at Beidaihe, there are no leadership survivors. Death was instantaneous. The bombs sucked the air out when they exploded.

"The plane markings were Chinese Air Force, the yellow crescent and stars on a red field clearly visible. A friend near the airbase reported seeing two planes land at the military airport, refuel and depart. Chinese Air Force planes have bombed their own leaders, virtually committing suicide."

HONG KONG

Hong Kong Harbor flashed on the screen. Live cameras traced boats criss-crossing the straits and panned the shoreline buildings of commerce. "The United States Consulate in Hong Kong released a news report from their Embassy in Beijing. Ambassador Lena Lao Duke advised she had received information from her attaché who happened to be on vacation in Beidaihe. Beidaihe is a seaside resort north of Beijing. The Standing Committee of the Politburo scheduled a plenum there before the National Congress meeting.

"The attaché reported that the General Secretary of the Chinese Communist Party, Liu Chinan, and the Minister of the Central Committee for Disciplinary Inspection, Cai Jixi, are dead at the hands of assassins. Apparently a hit team invaded the peaceful resort in the middle of the night, shot them and the guards around their villas."

Ginny stopped for a moment and picked up another sheet. "Supporting that news, we have a local bulletin. Two Hong Kong honeymoon couples called their parents on direct dialing lines this morning from Beidaihe. They partied on the beach late last night and heard a high-powered boat leave the harbor after the gunfire.

"Commander Martine, the attaché, also reported that General Tang Naiwa, head of the Chinese Military, was assassinated yesterday. State Security Ministry is investigating."

The screen went to grainy file shots of Wu Xian at a banquet, toasting visiting dignitaries, then to the coverage on the USS America. Ginny continued. "Vice Premier Wu Xian and Vice Premier Yang Yucie defected at Beidaihe last night in a daring boat voyage. Storms and a raging sea covered their escape. Their request for safe haven was seen internationally early this morning. A US submarine rescued them at sea and ferried them to the aircraft carrier. President Clinton personally granted them asylum in a television broadcast.

"According to my calculations, Wu Xian and Yang Yucie are the only survivors of the ruling Politburo of China. Commander Martine reported one other member apparently escaped the plot to erase the Politburo. Chou Shi, the Minister of State Security, was seen boarding a southbound train at midnight.

"The other fifteen members of the Politburo are presumed dead in the Zhongnanhai bombing."

Ginny put down the sheet she was reading. Grim reality sparked from the brooding dark eyes. Bright red lips, most often formed in the smile beloved by her worldwide audience, now firmed in a bright red line. "The Red Dragon, China, lies bleeding this morning, its head severed at the gates of the Zhongnanhai."

She paused and continued. "The world is not the same. The most populous nation in the world is decapitated. The devices of military power have unleashed a nuclear bomb, the first since Nagasaki. Before the pieces settled, the smoke cleared and Hong Kong gave birth to a new nation, the United Provinces of Cathay. History books of the next generation will relate the events of June fourth, 1994."

EDITORIAL – THE SOUTH CHINA POST
"THE SUICIDE OF CHINA"

6 JUNE 1996

"China is bleeding from a thousand wounds: dismemberment of limbs, gasping for economic life, production, communication, and education. Can Wu Xian, the only known surviving leader, breathe life back into the crippled nation? Centuries of Imperialism, Republicanism, and Communism have all failed the people. Releasing the fetters of more than one billion people will be chaotic at first. If Mao's flowers are indeed allowed to bloom... if those flowers seed and multiply... if modern thinking and technology fertilize the soil... immense treasures will replace the poverty of bureaucratic dogma. The last bastion of Communism will fall into the annals of history. Centuries of peace can be foretold. Quality of life will equalize. Confucian dreams will become a reality."

Epilogue

EPILOGUE
BEIJING

6 JUNE 1994

The apartment of Fan Riqi, Vice Commissar of the Ministry of State Security, was crowded but comfortable.

Commander Geoffrey Martine, Naval Attaché to the United States Embassy in Beijing, slouched in a well-worn lounge chair, poking around in his rice bowl with a pair of chopsticks. Hu Banyi, described by Martine as a Mensa, sat across from him in a similar chair. In him, Geoffrey had discovered a brilliant, humorous person, enjoying the world turned upside down the day before. The candle-light reflected on his bald head.

Fan prepared a simple dish of stir-fried rice, laced with pork, chicken and lightly steamed diced vegetables. The three men filled their bowls several times and emptied Fan's refrigerator of Tsingtao Pijou, the beer of popular choice.

"I'm embarrassed, my host," Geoff managed. The beer and rice bloated him, producing multiple belches and giving a rosy glow to the conversation. "We are eating all your food and it may be a while before you can replenish the larder."

"No problem, Martine. Our headquarters, I can tell you now, is behind and underneath a famous restaurant in Beihai Park, with enough food locked in to supply us for months if necessary."

"Well, I'll be damned," Geoff said. "You mean every time I went to the Fan Shan, you were hiding behind two-way mirrors and sliding panels."

Fan laughed. "No, Martine, not two-way mirrors – that's old fashioned. We're modern. We monitored you with the latest Sony miniature video cameras mounted inside light bulb canisters, with directional microphones built in. We don't use bugs planted in the sugar bowls anymore."

"Maybe I could get you and the brains here invited to Langley to bring our service up to date. Our gang can probably use a refresher course."

"No thanks, Commander. Congress has pulled the fangs from your tiger. The Company prefers the old fashioned way of spying, where results are important. By the way, thank you for piloting the helicopter yesterday. With my pilot suddenly absent, the trains not working, cars disabled, we would have been stuck on the beach for a long time."

"No problem, Mr. Fan. The controls were a little wobbly, and the engine could use some maintenance, but it got the three of us back here. At least you had a vehicle at the airport to get us into town. The Ambassador welcomed me with a hug and a kiss. The White House requests my presence at the earliest opportunity. I'm a busy man all of a sudden. The brass doesn't know yet, but I'm thinking about re-signing my commission and demitting from the Company."

"What will you do?" Hu asked, finally putting down his rice bowl. He had been shoving the food in, lip to bowl, chopsticks clicking for a long time, listening but not participating in the conversation.

"Oh, it suddenly occurred to me that the United Provinces of Cathay may need a secret service. There's a certain operative of the Royal Naval Intelligence Service that I may induce to come to bed with me, so to speak. Wouldn't care to join us, would you, Fan? And Hu too?"

"We have a few loose ends to clean up here. I would like to keep the option open, if I may. It does sound adventurous. What does it mean, come to bed with you? Like much of your language, there are double and triple meanings for many words and phrases."

"In this instance, it simply means a close association. In another, it could be literal." Geoff took a sip of his beer. "Did you figure out who killed the General? Tang had enough enemies. Any signs on the body when you dug it up?"

"Double garrote. Very unusual. Almost has to be an assigned sanction, executed by one of our own teams. Hu has taken over Yao Lin's records since he disappeared. We can track down which team it was in case they are still alive. It doesn't really make any difference now who killed him. The leaders in China and Taiwan did such a good job of wiping each other out, the net result is zero to zero."

"What else happened today, Commissar? You are the apparent head of the Ministry with as much authority as anyone in the country until Wu Xian returns."

"A few little odd jobs were expedient. I managed to open the gates of Qincheng number one, our political prison. The records somehow or another were destroyed, eh Hu?"

"Commissar, there was a virus that ran through all our records. If anyone entered the name of Zhao Ziyang backward, in any of the data banks, it signaled deletion of all names and supporting data. We lost the records of two hundred thousand dissidents in one fell swoop."

"Someone must have stayed up all night engineering that one," Geoff said. "To crash a program of that size took some fancy programming."

"Not if the one who invented the software program had foreseen a day of reckoning," Hu answered with a smug twinkle of the eye and a drum beat of his chopsticks on the table.

"Has the military done anything about the invasion? The report I heard was Taiwan assault troops were on the mainland, but not doing anything."

"Typical Chinese generalship. The high officers all like to direct things from operation centers and not risk their lives in the heat of battle. In this instance, the operation center was taken out, leaving a headless dragon."

"There are some junior officers that asked me to make a run of some records for them," Hu said. "It is their idea that if everyone over the rank of Major retires, they can form a new army of younger men without nepotism and territorial aims. My guess is that it's a good idea and may last for two or three generations until nature and greed regenerate the disease."

"The unions, will they have a chance now?"

"Under the previous regime, forming a union could bring a death sentence. There is a communication leader by the name of Liang Po that claims she has 94% of the Beijing communication workers signed up. With that kind of enrollment, there is no stopping the movement. The bus driver we almost picked up is organizing labor. The workers are already planning new routes, better equipment and a strange service called courtesy to the passengers. Lech Walesa from Poland has volunteered to come over and organize the shipyard workers."

Geoff patted his full stomach in satisfaction. "You're on the ball then."

"Yes, Commander Geoffrey Martine, a lot has happened already. How long will you be staying in Beijing?"

"If Cathay Pacific shows up at noon tomorrow, I'll be on the flight through the good graces of Emily Forbes. Emily is a providential kind of secretary who can do wonders with schedules. I would like to keep in touch, ex-comrade. Is it true that Fan Riqi and Hu Banyi resigned from the Communist Party today?"

Fan laughed, scratched his head, and started to unwrap the third cigar he had smoked this evening. "Not really, Commander. You see the Communist Party resigned. It is no more. We have decided to be non-partisan and unbiased policemen in the new Government. Hu suggests the new name of our organization be, Ministry of Sugar and Spice, the MSS."

HONG KONG, 7 JUNE 1994

Commander Geoffrey Martine cleared customs at Hong Kong and exited the Kai Tak arrival area, looking for the Shangri La Hotel limousine. Instead, a bright red Ferrari Dakota purred its motor, parked at the curb. The engine revved to get his attention. It got everybody's attention, as they waited to see who was going to get a ride in the roadster.

Geoff walked over, tossed his pack in the rear, slid in and leaned over to kiss the diminutive Chinese lady sitting in the driver's seat. "I can always tell the erotic sound of a bare foot heel-and-toeing car pedals. It just makes me jump in the car."

"Your place or mine, Commander?" Quan Quan said as she shifted into low gear and floored the pedal, spinning the wheels out from the curb. Taking the U-turn at the end of the driveway, she spun the car through the curve, into the straightaway along the fence, and out of the airport drive.

APPENDIX I

CURRENT ORGANIZATIONS AND POLITICAL GROUPS OF THE PEOPLE'S REPUBLIC OF CHINA

C.C.P.	CHINESE COMMUNIST PARTY, estimated at 47 million members, less than five percent of the total population.
C.C.	CENTRAL COMMITTEE of the C.C.P., normally 95 members, in 1990 estimated at 175 members.
POLITBURO	Ranking members of the C.C.P., 16 to 18 members.
STANDING COMMITTEE OF POLITBURO	5 to 6 members the top leaders of China.
C.A.C.	CENTRAL ADVISORY COMMITTEE, approximately 200 members, primarily Elders of C.C.P. who joined the Party prior to 1942.
C.M.C.	CENTRAL MILITARY COMMISSION, governing the P.L.A., headed by Deng Xiaoping in 1989, relinquished post in Spring of 1990
C.C.D.I.	CENTRAL COMMISSION FOR DISCIPLINARY INSPECTION. 69 members before Tienanman Massacre, doubled or tripled after.
M.S.S.	MINISTRY OF STATE SECURITY, equivalent of Russian K.G.B.

N.P.C.	NATIONAL PEOPLE'S CONGRESS, 2000 plus members.
S.C.N.P.C.	STANDING COMMITTEE OF THE N.P.C., 160 members.
G.S.	GENERAL SECRETARY of the C.C.P.
SECRETARIAT	4 members, aides to the G.S.
N.C.N.A.	NEW CHINA NEWS AGENCY, Hong Kong. Unofficial arm of the Chinese Government.
P.L.A.	PEOPLE'S LIBERATION ARMY. 35 Armies, supported by 13 armored, 17 artillery, several airborne units. Each Army has 4854 Officers, 40,223 enlisted persons. Total active military estimated at 3 to 3 and a half million, plus 17 million reserve main and regional ground forces, air force, navy and para-military units.

APPENDIX II
GENERAL TERMS AND PHRASES

WINTER OF REACTION Referring to hardliners taking over.

WENDINGPAI Faction of Stability, the hardliners.

TOUMINGDU Transparency. Chinese equivalent of Russian Glasnost.

ZHONGNANHAI Headquarters complex for the Politburo, an area next to and comparable in size to The Forbidden City.

GEIHU Private entrepreneur.

QUANSHANG Officials engaged in business.

MINSUDONG PAI Democratic Parties, non-Communists.

ZHUJIANG DELTA Quangzhou (Canton), Quandong Province, Zhongshan and Shenzhen.

SHENZHEN Autonomous economic zone, near Hong Kong.

NEW TERRITORIES Extension of Mainland, occupied by Hong Kong.

FOREIGN CORRES-PONDENTS CLUB OF BEIJING. Unrecognized Fraternity of the Press.

WHITE BROWED CLIQUE Gang of Elder Statesmen.

GUOJI GUANLI International norms or capitalistic entrepreneurs.

MODERNIZING	Avant-garde intellectuals.
MARXISM	Theories of Karl Marx, German Intellectual, on which Communism is based.
SUMMER ZHONGNANHAI	Meeting of the Politburo in Beidaihe in the hot summer months.
WENZHOU SHI SHI	Southern China Opportunists.
20 DECEMBER '86	SHANGHAI DEMONSTRATIONS. Thirty thousand students from Shanghai Universities and Medical College paraded down Nanjing Road.
PEOPLE'S PARK	Heart of Shanghai, similar to Tienanmen Square in Beijing.
TIANANMEN SQUARE	Largest people's square in the world, across from the Forbidden City, site of the 1989 Massacre.
TEMPT THE SNAKES	Give those who disagree a little string to expose themselves, and then we must cut off their heads.

ABOUT THE AUTHOR

Frederick Fisher first began writing when he was an apprentice seaman in the U.S. Navy. He has written numerous articles for various magazines and newspapers and has several published books including *China Adventures, Love and Marriage, Serendipity* and *Confucius Jade*. *Sinocide* is his latest novel.

A Certified Gemologist and Registered Jeweler with the American Gem Society for many years, Fred and his late wife, Eileen, shared a passion for travel and "treasure-hunting" fine jewelry, oriental art and antiques. Until a few years ago, Fred and Eileen spent six months each year in Southeast Asia.

Fred lives in Sonoita, Arizona and still travels whenever he can.

Meet Fred at www.FrederickFisher.com for more stories and to purchase his books.